THE INTERNET
Girls

THE INTERNET Girls

MISHA TRENT

authorHOUSE®

AuthorHouse™ UK Ltd.
1663 Liberty Drive
Bloomington, IN 47403 USA
www.authorhouse.co.uk
Phone: 0800.197.4150

© 2014 Misha Trent. All rights reserved.

No part of this book may be reproduced, stored in a retrieval system, or transmitted by any means without the written permission of the author.

Published by AuthorHouse   07/07/2014

ISBN: 978-1-4969-8176-9 (sc)
ISBN: 978-1-4969-8175-2 (hc)
ISBN: 978-1-4969-8177-6 (e)

Any people depicted in stock imagery provided by Thinkstock are models, and such images are being used for illustrative purposes only.
Certain stock imagery © Thinkstock.

This book is printed on acid-free paper.

Because of the dynamic nature of the Internet, any web addresses or links contained in this book may have changed since publication and may no longer be valid. The views expressed in this work are solely those of the author and do not necessarily reflect the views of the publisher, and the publisher hereby disclaims any responsibility for them.

Best regards Steven
Hope you enjoy the read

Larry Tierney

Chapter 1

London was experiencing a typical late November night with the wind swirling and gusting, driving the steady drizzle of rain so it drummed loudly against the windows of the shops and houses. The damp night air had turned misty, cold and miserable. It was definitely not the sort of night to be out walking, or even riding in a car. The darkness, swirling mist, and cold rain, gave the streets an air that was reminiscent of a scene from an old Victorian melodrama, complete with the lurking feeling of danger and fear. Most of the houses in the area were in darkness, suggesting that the residents were probably snuggled up in their nice warm beds, or maybe resting with their feet up in front of a glowing fire watching late night television behind drawn, heavy drapes. All very normal. However for some very brutal and unpleasant men who at that moment were enjoying a good meal in a Turkish restaurant, with plenty of wine to help wash it down, the night was about to erupt in an orgy of violence and pain. For these men the night would soon become worse than any nightmare they had ever experienced, or could imagine. Retribution for all the rapes, brutality, and horrendous crimes these men had committed against hundreds or maybe even thousands of females, was about to be demanded, and payment would be taken in full.

At five minutes to midnight, a nondescript, dark coloured car with partially darkened windows, and French number plates, turned slowly onto a quiet backstreet in one of the older parts of London. At the end of the street, the occupants of the car could just make out the fluorescent lights of the Turkish restaurant they had been told about. For the three men in the car, Dmitri, Mikhail, and Jimmy, this was another step along the violent blood soaked trail of a woman who had been kidnapped during an evening out in Russia, then sold as a slave into the European sex market. The three men were hot on the trail of this woman, and they were determined to find her and return her to her parents. With only its side lights showing, the car rolled quietly down the street. Not a word was spoken by the three men as their car drifted to a halt in a parking space next to the restaurant. Only the sound of the windscreen wipers, and the distinctive click clack noises of metal on metal, could be heard as they checked their weapons before finally pulling on thin black leather gloves. The three men were ex-military and all highly trained special forces. Dmitri, and Mikhail, from the Russian Spetznas, and Jimmy from the British Combined Operations, so they knew exactly what was required of each other. Dressed in black combat gear the three men got out of the car and immediately blended with the shadows as they moved to the entrance of the restaurant. A glance through the large window told them the information they had forcefully obtained from some petty crooks, was accurate. Even though the lighting within the restaurant had been set low the cream walls with polished dark wood panels and paintings of Turkish life could be clearly seen. It was also obvious that the restaurant staff had all been sent home after they served the meals and wine, and the place was now empty, except for the twelve Albanian gangsters they were looking for. The unsuspecting Albanians were sitting around a large oblong table talking and laughing, enjoying themselves without the least suspicion of what was about to happen to them.

Almost silently the three men entered the restaurant, Dmitri carrying an old AK47 assault rifle he had taken a fancy to when they bought their weapons, while Mikhail and Jimmy both carried Heckler and Koch automatic weapons in their gloved hands. The weapons and ammunition had been acquired from an address given to them by Jimmy's friends,

Danny and Lenny. They had been expensive, but were all in excellent condition. Quickly the three men spread out until everyone sitting at the table was covered by their guns. The speed with which the three men entered the restaurant and moved into position surprised the Albanians, and the atmosphere around the table changed from relaxed pleasure, to fear, anger and uncertainty. A heavily built man with a large stomach, and a broad peasant face that had been badly scarred by a knife at sometime, sat at the head of the table. It was obvious he was the gang leader, and he looked at the gunmen with a belligerent expression on his face, but there was a momentary and nearly unnoticeable flicker of fear in his eyes.

"Who the fucking hell are you?" He shouted, banging his fist on the table. "This is a private meeting, so what the fuckin' hell do you mean by bursting in here like this? Do you stupid bastards know who we are, and what will happen to you when our men get here?"

His double chins quivered with apparent rage and indignation, but his voice wasn't quite steady, and it was the slight quiver in his tone that belied his aggressive attitude. Even with the gangster's heavy accent, the three gunmen knew he was a worried or frightened man, so they ignored him. Dmitri, who was acting as the leader of the trio, knew the gang leader would never tell them in front of his men where the girl they were searching for was being held. So he looked around the rest of the gangsters with eyes that were slate grey and emotionless, like the eyes of a shark just before its teeth sink into its prey. Then he leaned forward, and with a sweep of his arm, sent plates and glasses crashing to the floor, clearing a space on the table. The crashing sounds made everyone round the table jump and look at each other in bewilderment, wondering what was going to happen next. Into the space he'd cleared, Dmitri threw down some photographs of a pretty blonde woman, and after giving the gangsters time to look at the photographs, he quietly said.

"I know at least one of you sitting around this table knows of this woman, and where she is, so please don't insult my intelligence by trying to tell me that you know nothing about her. You should also be aware that if any of you do try this tactic, I will cause you more agony than you ever thought possible, and I sincerely doubt that my two colleagues will be in a hurry to take you to hospital."

There was complete silence as the men around the table looked first at the photographs and then at each other. Then one of the younger gangsters sitting at the table cleared his throat, and after glancing briefly at the photographs, he looked up at Dmitri, the hurt macho pride, hatred and anger that boiled inside him, was obvious in his eyes as he spoke.

"I don't know who the hell you think you are, or what you want, but I want you bastards to know that you are all fuckin' dead men walking. Even if you kill me, my men will hunt you down, and when they find you you'll scream for mercy, until you eventually beg them to kill you. For what you are doing today, you will go to hell screaming in agony. For myself, I know nothing about this bloody woman, and you certainly don't frighten me enough to make me talk. So why don't you take yourselves, and your guns, and bugger off while you can still walk."

Dmitri, with a knowing smile on his face turned away from the table and casually sauntered over to the large window where he checked to make sure the blinds were tightly closed and no casual passer-by would be able to see what was about to happen. As Dmitri turned away from the table and moved towards the window one gangster had fixed his eyes on Dmitri's back, and slowly moved his right hand towards the pistol he carried in a shoulder holster. But he stopped the move as soon as he realised Jimmy was watching him like a hawk over the sights of his gun, just waiting for an excuse to pull the trigger.

After closing the blinds Dmitri made his way, in the same casual fashion, back around the table until he was standing next to the gangster's shoulder. The gangster looked up, and saw Dmitri's face change, his eyes suddenly blazed with hatred and his face hardened like stone. This was the moment the gangster knew there would be no mercy shown by this man. The gangster looked away quickly knowing he was between a rock and a hard place, and his life expectancy had now plummeted to zero. The only way he could change things would be to tell the gunman what he wanted to know, but if he gave the gunman this information one of the other gang members would certainly kill him. So either way he was a dead man. Dmitri's voice brought the gangster back to reality.

"You're a bloody gang of gutless bastards whose only claim to fame is that you have forced more innocent women into a life of prostitution and drug addiction, than any other gang in London. Well now you're going to get a lesson in what happens to greedy useless parasites like you, who prey on the backs of the weaker people, who cannot defend themselves."

As he was speaking Dmitri let the AK47 hang from its strap around his neck then he took a 9mm semi-automatic handgun from one of his overall pockets, and a silencer from another. Slowly he fitted the silencer onto the weapon, then with the pistol in his left hand, he aimed it downwards and slowly fired two shots. The shots blasted into the gangster's knees and turned them into a mess of smashed bones and shredded, pulped flesh. The pistol had been loaded with hollow point or dumdum type bullets so when they hit anything they split open and tore huge holes through whatever they hit. To stifle the man's screams Dmitri wrapped his gloved right hand around the man's mouth as he fired the first shot. The gangster still managed to scream, but it was a muffled high pitched sound, full of unimaginable pain. The screaming abruptly stopped as Dmitri fired his pistol for the third time. The bullet ripping down through the man's stomach before shattering his genitals and smashing the pelvic bone causing him to die in absolute agony. Casually Dmitri released his grip on the man's mouth and turned his back on the dead man to gaze around the table searching for his next victim. As Dmitri released the dead gangster, Jimmy stepped in and duct taped the gangsters mouth shut in case the bullets had not done their job.

The faces of the men sitting around the table showed shock, but not horror. They were no strangers to handing out similar punishment to their enemies. Jimmy had just picked up the large roll of duct tape after taping the dead gangsters mouth when he caught a movement out of the corner of his eye, it was the gangster with the shoulder holster. Jimmy reacted instantly, his arm swung, and with great power and accuracy he hurled the heavy roll across the table at the gangster. The roll of duct tape smacked into the gangsters face a fraction of a second before he could aim his pistol at Dmitri's back. Instinctively the gangster had raised his arms to try and ward off the roll of duct tape, but the gun still fired and the bullet embedded itself into the ceiling. After throwing the duct tape, Jimmy had dived across the table causing plates of food and glasses of wine to go crashing to the floor. Then the barrel of Jimmy's gun slammed into the gangster's nose, with the sickening sound of breaking cartilage and bone. Blood geysered out of the gaping wound in the gangster's face, and he screamed out in shocked agony. Dropping his pistol he clutched a table napkin to his wrecked face as Jimmy smoothly rolled off the table, picked up the gangster's pistol and dropped it into one of his pockets. At the same time bringing his gun up so he once again covered the gangsters opposite him. Fortunately for Jimmy, and his two friends, everything had happened so quickly the gangsters hadn't had enough time to react to the situation. Dmitri walked over to the whimpering, half conscious gangster, and asked if he was going to tell him where the woman was, but the man, grimacing in pain, slowly shook his head. Dmitri's pistol pointed down and three shots later the gangster died in even greater agony. With a deaths head smile on his face Dmitri gazed around at the gangsters sitting around the table, and once again he spoke.

"Now, who amongst you is going to speak to me? If no one volunteers I will choose one of you and if that person doesn't speak to me he will get the same treatment as these two, and I don't mind increasing the pain."

No one sitting around the table spoke, but there was now stark fear showing on some of their faces, and Dmitri, Mikhail, and Jimmy, knew that one of the Albanians would crack before long and then they would hopefully learn everything they wanted to know.

Dmitri walked slowly around the table and stopped next to another man. He tapped the gangster on the shoulder.

"It's your turn. Tell me what I want to know or suffer the same fate as your friends over there."

"I know nothing," the man croaked, his face twisted in terror, "I'm just a guest here. I'm not one of these people."

The pistol swivelled down and fired twice. There was no response from the man, he had already fainted, and collapsed face down amongst the remains of his dinner, one of the few plates still left on the table. Dmitri looked around at the gangsters faces again, deliberately making eye contact, before pulling the man's head back and firing the final shot into the man's groin. Silence seemed to echo around the room as once more Dmitri slowly started to move around the table.

"I will continue shooting you evil bastards until one of you tells me what we want to know. So who is next?"

The big fat man at the head of the table glared at Dmitri with a mixture of hatred and fear in his eyes.

"You bastards might kill us all, but we'll have our revenge on you. One of my men will find you, and use a fuckin' chainsaw on each of you."

Dmitri laughed, a harsh cynical sound, his face showing no emotion, except contempt.

"We've already killed most of your gang, and your contacts, and you would be surprised at how many of them told us everything we wanted to know, plus a lot more. How do you think we found out about this meeting? By the time we've finished with you, there will be very few of your people left to come looking for revenge, even if they had the stomach for it. So forget it, there will be no cavalry charging in to save you this time, you're all on your own. Now unless you tell us what we want to know, you will all die here, crushed like the vermin you are."

During the next ten minutes, four more of the men sitting at the table were shot and left to die in agony from their wounds and loss of blood. But then one of the five remaining gangsters held his hand up.

"I will tell you whatever you want to know, so don't shoot anyone else."

The fat man at the end of the table screamed.

"Don't you say a fuckin' word, you little shite. Tell these bastards nothing!"

As soon as the fat gangster uttered the words, Dmitri, raised his arm and his gun coughed. The fat gangster's head cracked back against the wall behind him, driven back by the force of the bullet that had opened up a large, grotesquely gaping hole between his eyes. In the shocked silence that followed the shooting, everyone could hear the steady drip, drip, drip, of the fat man's blood and brains as they landed on the floor. Dmitri, completely unmoved by the deaths, moved towards the gangster who still had his hand up. The man had totally ignored the outburst and the shooting, instead he was watching Dmitri, and trying to gauge if he was about to be shot like the rest before he finally asked.

"What do you want to know?"

Dmitri, pushed forward the pictures of the blonde girl.

"Where is this girl? I want the exact address, and I want to know how many men are guarding her? I also want to know how many more girls are at this address, plus the addresses of all the other girls you control. The sooner we have this information the sooner we will leave you to continue your meal."

The gangster started talking and it wasn't long before Dmitri, Mikhail, and Jimmy, had all the information they needed, assuming the information was correct. They now knew that The German had sold the girl to a man known as Nino, which confirmed what they had already been told. But now they knew the address of the house where the girl was living, as well as how many men were guarding the house. The gangsters also told them that if the girl was not in the house she may have been taken to Nino's house to entertain him and his friends, or she may have been sent back to The German's house to entertain his guests. The gangsters maintained they had very few dealings with the men called Nino, or The German. They were only concerned with bringing the girls into the UK, and they had no idea where either of the gang bosses lived. The only person who would have known where The German or Nino lived was the fat man who Dmitri had just shot. Or The German's bodyguards who could usually be found in a drinking den that catered specially for people like them. Dmitri was handed the address of the drinking den written clearly on a napkin, and the gangsters pleaded with him not to reveal where he had got the address from. Once the gangster had started talking, the remaining members of the gang also began to talk, and soon it was difficult to keep them quiet, but most of what they had to say was irrelevant to the three friends. When Dmitri felt the information they'd been given appeared to be reasonably truthful, he nodded to Mikhail, who slipped a rucksack off his back and took out a twelve inch square cardboard box, and a roll of lightweight 2 core cable. The box contained one pound of plastic explosive at its centre with ten pounds of nails and various other bits of metal packed around the explosive. Enough metal to shred every person in the room into small pieces when it went off.

Placing the cardboard box in the centre of the table Mikhail worked swiftly and confidently. First he bared the wires at one end of the cable and fixed them to connections that were inside the box. Then, after uncoiling all the lightweight cable he started to tie it tightly around the wrists of each gangster who was still alive, in one continuous line, leaving about six feet of cable between each of them. With the cable around the gangsters wrists secured, Mikhail fastened the loose ends of the wire to more connectors inside the box. As he finished he gave the okay signal of a thumb and first finger in a circle, and grinned. Dmitri nodded and turned to the surviving gangsters.

"This box is full of Semtex, and the detonator is connected to a very sensitive trembler switch, so any movement of the box will result in a very big bang. The cable that's tied around your wrists is to ensure that none of you decide to leave before we want you to. Any attempt to cut it, or break it, will also result in a big bang, so I strongly suggest that you all sit very still and quietly wait until we get back and release you, after we find the girl."

While Dmitri had been talking, Jimmy had searched every gangster around the table, dead or alive, and removed all their mobile phones and weapons, and dumped them in his rucksack. While Jimmy was busy, Mikhail had moved around the table watching the remaining gangsters to make sure they did not try any rash moves. When he had finished searching everyone Jimmy went round the table again and using the duct tape he taped all the live gangsters to their seats. When it was done he nodded and gave the circled thumb and first finger signal. Dmitri, spoke to the gangsters again.

"We'll be back as soon as we have found the girl, to release you. But remember this. If we find that you have told us lies, we will come back, and you will all die in agony. Does anyone want to change the information you've given us?"

The gangsters sullenly shook their heads, and watched as the three gunmen made sure the curtains and blinds were taped completely closed over the windows so no one could possibly see into the restaurant, and then left, locking the door behind them.

As the three men climbed into their car, Mikhail, the tall Russian, chuckled and made a comment in Russian. The other Russian, Dmitri, grinned and said in English,

"Mikhail wonders why you didn't just shoot that idiot who was going to shoot me, and also how long do you think it will be before they blow themselves up?"

The Englishman, Jimmy, laughed as he started the engine and put the car into gear.

"I thought I'd better keep him alive in case you wanted to question him, and I bet we don't get past the end of the road before one of those thick bastards sets the bomb off."

The car moved off and had just turned the corner back onto the main road when they heard a tremendous explosion followed by the crackling sounds of flames. One of the gangsters, obviously unable to curb his impatience, had done something to trigger the bomb, and the traders in human misery had now paid the ultimate price for their crimes.

"Okay," said Jimmy, "at least we wont have to come back here to release that lot, so let's go and deal with the scum who may be holding Anna prisoner. However, first let's go and give Danny and Lenny a call otherwise they will be very unhappy if they miss out on our next rumble."

Chapter 2

Four months before the search for Anna the Russian girl and all the associated killing had started, James Roberts, better known to his friends as Jimmy, arrived home from work tired and hungry. It was the end of another long and hectic day, but he still managed to sprint up the flight of stairs that led to his front door, and after unlocking the heavy door pushed his way into his second floor apartment. Without conscious thought, he back-heeled the front door shut, and made his way down the hallway where, following his usual routine, he dropped his briefcase on the floor beside the lounge door then draped his jacket casually over the back of a dining chair. The lounge was a comfortable and conventional layout with television and audio system at one end, and a dining area at the other. Stopping for a moment as he made his way through the lounge, he stared around at the numerous paintings, and photographs hanging on the walls. Each scene bringing back pleasurable memories of his travels, and some of the people he had met on those travels. The memories caused a happy smile to flit across his face until his need for a coffee overcame his memories, then with a sigh he shook himself and walked into the kitchen to make a cup of instant decaffeinated coffee. A few minutes later, with his mind on numerous other things, mainly technical problems at work, he lifted the mug to his lips and cursed when the hot liquid scalded him. Dabbing his lips with a cold damp cloth he cursed again and yawned whilst carefully carrying the coffee through to his personal computer system, wondering who, if anyone, he might have received an email from. But it was an urgent rumble from his stomach that grabbed his immediate attention, and as he made his way back to the kitchen he started to think about what he should throw together for his dinner.

Jimmy was divorced, but he still hankered after the close companionship and love of a special woman. Stockport was not his home town, but after leaving home when he was fifteen to join the military, he had gone on to live and work in a number of different countries, and it seemed to him that Stockport was as good a place to live as anywhere else. And better than a lot of other places he could think of! In some ways his life style reminded him of his time in the military, looking after himself and doing his own washing, ironing, and cleaning, but he wasn't too sure about his cooking ability. Although he did manage to surprise himself from time to time by making a meal that was both edible, and tasty. However, he had to admit, even to himself, that without a recipe he wasn't safe on his own when it came to making a meal.

At 5 feet 10 inches and 160 pounds, Jimmy worked hard to keep himself in good physical shape. He tried to call into the swimming pool every morning before work and spend forty-five minutes swimming lengths to help maintain his endurance and lung power. He also found the swimming relaxed him, and put him in a good frame of mind for the rest of the day. However, the activity that gave him most pleasure were his twice weekly meetings with the T'ai Chi Chuan style Grand Master. During these sessions he and the Grand Master often explored the unarmed combat and silent killing techniques that Jimmy had been taught during his time in the military with Combined Operations. Sometimes the two men even incorporated some of the techniques into their routines. To the purist, some of their martial bouts were often very strange looking affairs, with each man trying to deceive, and strike faster, than the other. Jimmy found the sessions, and in particular the calming, meditation exercises and teachings, allowed him to view the world positively and objectively. He also found himself more able to closely observe everything that was happening around him, instantly understanding, or accurately interpreting, exactly what his eyes were seeing. But perhaps the biggest change he had noticed in himself came as a complete surprise. The aggressive, hard nosed attitude to life that had served him so well through his youth and his time in the military, had now softened considerably. Maybe it was due to the confidence he had in his own physical abilities, or maybe it was due to him maturing as a man, but whatever it was that had caused him to change meant that he now found that some classical music, and the words of certain popular songs could bring tears to his eyes. When he talked to the Grand Master about this he had been told that he was now approaching the highest level of awareness. This was because his growing sensitivity allowed him to see and appreciate the beauty and wonder of everything around him. This growth of his sensitivity was quite normal and had occurred because his fighting skills had given him the confidence to be totally comfortable with himself.

Jimmy still hoped that one day he would find the woman of his dreams. But so far he had not had much success, and was beginning to think that no matter how positive he was, it might never happen for him. He had tried to find his dream woman in all the usual places like bars, nightclubs, and singles clubs, but although it had all been an interesting experience, nothing had come of it. He'd even tried talking to a few ladies in the supermarket using his favourite chat up lines, 'can you tell me what this tastes like? Or, can you tell me how to cook this?' His questions had produced some remarkable comments and conversations. One lady had even suggested that he come and stay with her for a few days and she would teach him everything he wanted to know. But if Jimmy ever found his hormones were running riot and in need of a woman's touch, he wasn't short of one or two unattached girlfriends who were happy to spend a weekend with him. It was the quest for the woman of his dreams, not just sex, that kept him single, and it was this quest that had started him searching the Internet to see if his special lady might be out there somewhere in cyberspace.

After finishing his evening meal and cleaning up the kitchen, Jimmy wandered through to the small bedroom and sat down in front of his computer. A few minutes later he had logged onto the first of the many dating sites he usually surfed. He'd been looking at endless photographs of women for about half an hour when one of the photographs caught his eye. He quickly enlarged the picture, and smiled appreciatively. It showed a full length photograph of a woman dressed in a dark maroon polo neck sweater and tight, faded blue jeans tucked into knee length boots. Although her body appeared very shapely, it was her face that caught his attention. Her long dark brown, copper tinted hair framed an attractive oval face, with high cheek bones, and beautiful almond shaped green eyes above a neat nose and a wide sensuous mouth. Bloody hell, he thought, this one is a really stunning woman, and her lips look so kissable. But I wonder why she's putting her picture on the web, she should be able to get any man she wants. Then quickly before he could change his mind, he sent her a message saying he thought she was very attractive and would like to write to her. He didn't really expect to get an answer from such a good looking woman, but felt it was worth a try. Maybe if he had known what the fates had in store for him, he might have hesitated for a moment before hitting the send button. However after sending the message he carried on reading through her personal details and noticed she was only 24 years old and his expectations of receiving a reply to his message receded even further. However, when he saw she was Russian, he began to understand why she had put her picture on the dating site. A few years before the Berlin Wall had been brought down he had spent quite a lot of time in Poland and Russia, and been told by some Russian people, that many Russian women preferred to meet older men, especially foreign men. They said it was because Russian women believed that older men would be more settled, have a better income, and a more secure lifestyle than younger men. A couple of hours later, after sending messages to a further four or five ladies who looked interesting, he sat back and wondered what the future would bring.

Getting up from the computer, he walked back into the lounge and poured himself a nightcap of dark rum and coke, and after savouring the first mouthful let his mind drift back to the Russian woman. She certainly looks great, he thought, assuming it's actually a current photo of her. This cynical thought was prompted by an incident that occurred about eight weeks previously when he had contacted a lovely looking blonde, supposedly in her late twenties. At least that's what her details and photo had claimed. However when they met in a town centre bar of her choice, she turned out to be in her forties, and only interested in watching soap operas on television. Certainly she may have been a good looking woman in her late twenties, but she was now quite a bit over weight, and gave the impression that she didn't care too much about her appearance any more. Needless to say neither of them made any attempt to suggest a further meeting, but at least they parted on friendly terms. Although he was certain that the ladies who used the internet dating could also tell similar stories about the men they met. Returning with the drink to his computer, he looked again at the picture of the Russian woman on the screen, and gave a whimsical sigh as he wondered what she might be like in real life. Then with a final glance at the picture on the screen, he closed the equipment down and headed for a shower before climbing into bed.

The next day passed by quickly enough for Jimmy. There were a number of minor breakdowns amongst the machines in the factory where he was employed as an electronics engineer, and the work kept his mind fully occupied resolving the various problems. But by late afternoon the problems had been resolved and he noticed that it was almost five o'clock, and time for him to finish off the work he was doing and tidy up. On his way out of the printing works, his two long time friends Lenny and Danny caught up with him. Danny, a tall, well built, muscular black man with hands like shovels, and a big perpetual smile on his face, called out.

"Hi, you crabby old bugger, why are you trying to sneak out without speaking to us?"

Jimmy laughed as he turned, and looked at the two men.

"There is absolutely no way anyone can get out of this building without you two layabouts seeing them, because you are always standing around this door drinking tea. But, as you're about to ask if I'm going to the pub, the answer is yes, so you can take me there and buy me a couple of pints at the George."

Lenny and Danny stopped in their tracks when they heard Jimmy's response, and looked at each other, before shrugging their shoulders. Lenny, had recently started shaving his head and the skin was still pale pink which looked strange against his tanned face, was a few inches shorter than Danny, shrugged his wide powerful shoulders, and looked at Danny.

"Damn me Danny, the old bugger's about as sharp as the elastic in my girlfriend's knickers. Maybe we should just put him in a taxi and send him home, because I'm not sure he is safe to be out on his own tonight. What do you think mate?"

Before Danny could reply, Jimmy held up his hands in surrender.

"Okay, Okay, I get the message, you two are penniless again, and you want me to buy the pints, and not the other way round, right?"

His two friends grinned happily and positioned themselves on each side of him before wrapping their arms around his shoulders and picking him up easily before propelling him in the direction of the bar. The three men liked this bar and in particular they enjoyed chatting with the barmaid, a lady in her late forties with a wicked sense of humour, so they often stopped and shared a few beers together at the end of the working day.

It was nearly ten pm before Jimmy eventually arrived home, after enjoying a couple of pints of beer with his friends. Jimmy had no illusions about his two friends, and had no doubt they where very capable of holding their own in any sort of a rough house. He also knew that both men spent time on the shooting range so they knew how to handle a variety of guns. Jimmy was also quite certain that if he ever needed serious back up for any reason his two friends would be there for him. Wearily he dumped his briefcase, and coat in their usual places, before slowly making his way to the kitchen for a much needed cup of coffee. While waiting for the water to boil, images of the Russian woman suddenly flared in his imagination, and he wondered hopefully if there might be a message from her. With this thought in his mind he finished making the coffee and carried it through to his computer and switched the equipment on.

Chapter 3

Ekaterinburg, the capital city of the Urals in central Russia, had for many years been known as Sverdlovsk, until 1991, when it reverted back to its original name. It's a lively bustling city whose citizens are friendly and well educated. On a world wide basis the city is possibly most famous because it was where the last Tsar and his family were murdered, the site of which is now overlooked by the imposing Cathedral of the blood. However, it's also well known in Russia amongst the people under 30, as the home of Russian rock music, similar in a way to Liverpool and the Mersey sound. As the crossroads between the East and West of Russia it benefits from the rich cultures of both sides.

In an area of the city where the properties are obviously home to some of the wealthier business and political families a woman deep in thought, wandered lethargically around a well tended garden. It was late Friday afternoon, and Katrina Novikova, a tall, good looking 24 year old, was trying to decide what to do with herself, although there were not too many options for her to choose from. She could log onto the Internet and spend a few hours trying to find an interesting man to chat to, or she could get ready and go to visit her best friend Anna Fedorova. It was possible that she might be able to talk Anna into accompanying her on a walk around Plotinka (The Dam) which is the historical centre of the city. Or they could maybe even take a stroll around the huge Central Park area. It was a nice sunny day which was quite rare once winter had started to set in, so there would be lots of people out walking and taking advantage of the sunshine. Of course there would also be lots of men either on their own or in groups, for her and Anna to look at and admire, or otherwise.

She and Anna were as physically as different as they could be. Anna, blond, and petite at five feet two inches tall, and a year younger than Katrina, who was dark haired, curvy, and five foot nine inches in height. But mentally they were very close, often knowing what each other was about to say before it was said, so there were no secrets between the two women. They had been the best of friends since they were small children and still spent a lot of time together. But these days their discussions had changed from dolls and kittens, to men and sex, and what it would be like to be married, as well as all the other things that normal women discuss. Both women came from wealthy families, and had strong dominant fathers, which is maybe why neither of them had any, or very little, experience of men, and in fact both were still virgins. It wasn't that they were saving themselves for marriage, it was just that they hadn't managed to find the opportunity to be alone with a man they wanted to have sex with. From their biology classes they were well aware of what happened between men and women, but neither of them had experienced anything more than the clumsy groping of hormone driven students in the back row of the cinema.

In the end Katrina, who preferred to be called by her nickname Katya, decided to spend some time on the Internet because she felt sure her friend would already have people at her house. Unfortunately most of the single males at Anna's house would be in their early twenties, and Katya was looking for an older and more sophisticated man. She wanted to meet men like those who she thought worked for her father. Not that she knew much about what her father did. But most of the men who came to the house to see him, seemed to her inexperienced eyes, to be under 40, well dressed, and worldly wise. Therefore to her they were very interesting. Strangely though she could never remember any particular details of these men like their hair colour or height, or even if they were clean shaven or not, and this puzzled her. Her friend Anna, maintained that it was her hormones causing the feelings of lust, and that she was just naturally randy, but to Katya, it seemed as though she fell madly love with each man she saw. Not only did she fall in love, but the feelings came complete with all the heartache she had read about in her books and magazines. This was one of the reasons why she wished she had the freedom of the women in the west, because judging by the stories in some of the magazines she had read, western women of her age were allowed to go out on their own and meet men whenever they wanted to. It also seemed to her that western girls had already had two or three lovers by the time they got to her age, so they were quite used to being with men and talking to them. What a huge difference to her lifestyle.

Having decided to spend some time on the Internet, she headed back to the house, and the privacy of her bedroom. As she walked she wondered, not for the first time, why her father had become so strict with her, and whether she would ever have an opportunity to live her own life. Katya's mother had died from breast cancer when Katya was four years old, and since that time she had grown up idolising her father. From childhood, and through most of her teenage years, she had felt safe and happy, always seeing her father as a tall well built man, with a handsome smiling face, and thick wavy black hair. Her wonderful father had been someone she had always been ready and willing to talk to about any subject, and not once had she ever questioned his decisions or his instructions. He gave her a very generous allowance so she didn't have to ask him for money to buy the things that she wanted, she had even managed to save most of this money and now had a sizeable bank account. This happy state of affairs had lasted until about twelve months ago when it all started to change. She had discussed the situation with Anna and they had come to the conclusion that her father was changing due to the demands that his businesses were putting on him. Her father had slowly become more and more withdrawn from her. He had stopped giving her a hug when he arrived home from work, and ruffling her hair as he walked past her. Nor was he interested in going out for walks with her any more, or in taking her to the cinema to see the latest film from the West. But most importantly they had stopped talking about the things that she considered to be of mutual interest or importance. Now she could only see his face as hard and unsmiling, almost the face of a stranger, a stranger she could no longer bring herself to talk to. She felt sure her father realised they had grown apart, but unfortunately it seemed that neither of them knew how to bridge the gap that had grown between them. Sure her father was very strict, but he had never raised his hand to her, or shown any signs of having a violent nature. In fact the only time she had witnessed real anger in her father was after she had gone to a hairdresser in the city centre and had her long hair trimmed, and copper coloured highlights added. She had also treated herself by having her nails done by a professional nail care woman, and painted pink. When her father saw her new hair style and the nails, he had become very angry with her. He shouted and raged at her, pushing his face close to hers, telling her that she was making herself look cheap and no better than the girls who earned their living on the streets, or in the bars. She had been frightened by the intensity of his rage, and for the first time in her life she thought he might actually raise his hand to her, but he didn't. She was so upset by his reaction that she had not spoken to him since.

Switching on her computer, she settled into her chair and waited impatiently for the screen to light up so she could log on to one of her favourite dating websites. Browsing through these sites was something she enjoyed. She could look at the pictures of men and fantasize about meeting one of them and falling in love, and going to live in another country, away from the restrictions placed upon her by her father. Imagining herself married to a handsome man and having two or three lovely children, and cooking wonderful meals for her hard working husband to come home to, was one of her favourite daydreams. The screen came to life and she quickly logged on to her favourite dating page, and found there were two new messages waiting for her in response to her photographs. One of the messages was from a man called James Roberts who lived in England. She read through the Englishman's message thinking that at long last her English language studies were proving useful. The short message said he thought she looked very attractive in her photograph, and it would give him great pleasure if she would write to him. Katya was thrilled, all the love stories she'd read seemed to indicate that Englishmen always acted like gentlemen in the presence of a lady, plus they always treated their ladies with respect, love, and consideration. Excitedly she searched for his photograph and personal details. When she found his photo she was not disappointed, he looked quite nice with curly brown hair, and athletically built. His personal details said he was in his 30s, single, and widely travelled. His age didn't bother her, she wanted an older man, a man with some experience of life because she had often heard her father say the best way for a man to gain experience of life was to travel. She quickly composed a short message saying that she would be very happy to write to him.

The second message had come from an Albanian man called Enver Ceka, who said he'd been born on a farm in the mountains, but now lived in the city of Tirana. He was in his middle twenties, and in his picture he appeared to be thickset with long dark hair that had been dyed blonde. His eyes were deep set under black eyebrows that seemed to go across his face without a break, a large hooked nose, and thin lips gave his face a hard cruel appearance. Like some of the men who worked for my father, she thought. His message was also written in English, saying how pretty he thought she looked, he also said he was planning to travel to Russia in the near future, so he hoped it would be possible for them to meet. Katya was intrigued, and although she didn't find the man attractive, she wrote back saying that it might be possible for them to meet, but only if he happened to be visiting Ekaterinburg. After all, she thought, it would be interesting to hear about Albania, and Tirana in particular, from someone who lives there. As soon as the message to the Albanian had been sent, she went back to browsing through the photographs. But no matter how hard she tried to concentrate on whatever photo appeared on her screen, she kept thinking about the Englishman. In the end she went back to look at his photograph and read through his details again. Then she settled back in her chair and allowed her imagination to take her to the beautiful places she felt sure the Englishman could take her.

During the weeks that followed she carried on occasionally emailing with Ceka, the Albanian, but always in a rather formal manner. She didn't want him to think there could ever be anything more than a pen pal friendship between them. This was because she had decided the Englishman, James Roberts, had won her heart, and she wasn't in the least bit interested in any other man. At first the emails between Katya and Jimmy were quite formal, but slowly as the weeks went by, Katya came to look forward more and more to his mail. She started spending a lot more time in her bedroom with her computer, writing long letters about life in Ekaterinburg, and how much she longed to travel to other countries. They exchanged lots of photographs of their friends and family, and told each other about their lives, and the way they lived. Then one day Jimmy mentioned that he would love to come over to Russia to meet her, and her family. Katya was thrilled, she had visions of Jimmy holding her in his arms and kissing her, it was all so exciting, until thoughts of what her father would say stopped her in her tracks. For a minute her mind was in a whirl, but then she smiled to herself, she would worry about her father in a day or two, and in the meantime she would enjoy her dreams.

Her father had noticed the change in her, and made a point of commenting about it on a number of occasions until she felt obliged to tell him about the Englishman she was corresponding with. After listening to the story of how she had met Jimmy on the internet, her father had tried to look very stern, but then he'd laughed and told her to enjoy herself. Katya was overjoyed, and could hardly wait to write to Jimmy and tell him that her father was happy that she was corresponding with him. Dmitri Novikov, was truly very happy with the situation, not only did it make his daughter feel good, but if she was spending her time with men in cyberspace then she would not be getting involved with some of the less desirable males in Ekaterinburg.

For Katya this was a wonderful time, all her girl friends wanted to know how she had managed to make contact with the Englishman, and soon there were a lot more Russian women on the dating sites. In particular, her best friend Anna had become quite attracted to the photograph of Enver Ceka, the Albanian man. She kept trying to persuade Katya to send him one of her photographs, until eventually Katya agreed. She sent Anna's photograph, with a covering email explaining that she had now found a regular boyfriend and no longer had time to exchange emails with him, but her friend Anna would like to write to him. Ceka replied that he was happy for Katya, and that he would enjoy writing to such a pretty lady. He also hoped that he would be able to meet both of them when he arrived in Ekaterinburg, possibly sometime in the coming weeks, and perhaps they could all go out to somewhere nice for dinner together. In the first email that Anna sent to Ceka she told him that she would be very happy to meet him for dinner when he arrived, but unfortunately Katya would probably not be able to join them. Three weeks later Ceka telephoned Anna to say he would soon arrive in Ekaterinburg, and he would like to meet her and if possible Katya, if she would like to join them. Anna rushed around to Katya's house to tell her all the news and ask her if she would like to come to dinner. Katya immediately said no, so they discussed what Anna should wear and how she should act for this first date, to make sure that Enver Ceka did not get the wrong idea about her. Anna was excited about the idea of going out with Ceka for dinner, but she was also worried about what would happen afterwards. Would he expect her to go back to his hotel with him, and what would he think of her if she said no. What would she do if he got angry with her and dragged her into his car? There had been a large number of stories in the newspapers about women who had been kidnapped and never seen again, even after the parents had paid the ransom demanded. Her mind reeled under the implications. But slowly as she and Katya discussed all of the possible problems they decided that if everything was okay, Anna would telephone Katya at 10 p.m. However if Katya did not receive the telephone call by 10 pm, she would phone Anna's father and explain the situation to him and let him decide what to do.

Back in her own house, Anna was feeling good as she tried to decide what clothes to wear for her dinner date. Whatever she chose had to be something that was mildly attractive to men, but not so much that he would think she was easy. Initially she wanted to try and give the Albanian the impression that she was interested in him as a pen friend, but unsure about anything more than this. Selecting the outfit took her a long time but in the end she selected a simple white dress with roses embroidered on it. This was the only dress she had which reached below her knees, and was high necked with long sleeves. The thought that it was probably the only dress that her father would approve of, made her smile, and she sat down to write a brief note to her father telling him who she had gone to meet.

Chapter 4

A well dressed middle-aged man with a strong aquiline face and wavy black hair sat behind a large walnut veneered desk in a well appointed office within a printing works. The colour scheme for the office were mute autumn tones which had been blended tastefully together to give a calm relaxing atmosphere. An oasis of quiet where even the thunder of the printing presses did not intrude. The printing works were situated on a prime site on the outskirts of Ekaterinberg, near the River Iset and produced high quality magazines and books. This is where Dmitri Novikov liked to spend as much time as he could, he liked to watch the printers skilfully performing their magic. Dmitri's hands were well shaped with long fingers, similar to those of a classical pianist, and were holding a report he had been reading. However the report now lay in his hands, forgotten, as his eyes gazed out of the large windows in front of him admiring the beauty of the scene. Outside the air was full of huge snowflakes swirling around the corners of the buildings allowing his imagination to create wonderful images of castles and dragons. A smile softened the hard lines of his face as he hoped that children everywhere were enjoying themselves making snowmen and having snowball fights. As his slate grey eyes switched back to his desk they locked on to the two large photographs in elegant silver frames. Each frame containing the photograph of a very attractive woman, and from the similarity of their features it was obvious they were Mother and Daughter. This was the true image of Dmitri Novikov. A widower, and a man who tried hard to be good father, and an honest business man.

Since leaving the Russian military, Dmitri had set up a number of new retail, and manufacturing businesses, creating a lot of new jobs for the local people most of whom thought him to be a good man to work for. When his wife had died, the neighbours all felt great sympathy for him, in particular the Fedorov family who lived next door. The two families had been good friends for a number of years, and Dmitri's daughter Katya spent a lot of time at the Fedorov home with their daughter, Anna. Physically Dmitri, and Anna's father Boris, were very different, Boris being a short rotund man with a ready smile, happy disposition and a razor sharp business brain. Dmitri enjoyed the company of Boris Fedorov, but their business activities didn't allow them a lot of time to spend socialising on the occasions when they met. Boris with his contacts and head for business, had introduced Dmitri to many of the cities top business and political people which had helped Dmitri to set up his various businesses. The two men, although unable to spend much time together, became good friends, and often passed business gossip and tips to each other. However, there was another side to Dmitri Novikov, that Boris and the general public did not see, or know about. This was the side of his life that he referred to as his Other Businesses.

It was maybe ten years since Dmitri had set up his first nightclub for adult entertainment. That business had quickly prospered and over the years he had opened up another dozen clubs spread all over the city. Each of these clubs quickly became profitable so he introduced some gambling into the most luxurious of them. The money rolled in, but slowly the staff running his clubs allowed the seamier side of life to creep into the activities of the clubs. Unfortunately as these Other Businesses become more profitable, they demanded a lot more of his time which meant that he spent less and less time with Katya. These pressures were the reason he and Katya had drawn slowly further and further apart. However, the situation between he and Katya, had reached a crises point when one evening he had arrived home to find his little girl had coloured her hair and changed into a beautiful, sexually alluring, woman. The sight had been such a shock to his system that it had stopped him in his tracks, and because he didn't know how to handle the situation he had lost his temper and shouted at her. He had instinctively reverted to the only form of discipline that he knew, military discipline, and he had treated his daughter as though she were a soldier under his command. He had given her a terrible tongue lashing and afterwards realised that he'd badly overreacted to the situation. Overcome with feelings of guilt because he knew she did not deserve it he had tried to compensate, but the shock of his outburst on Katya meant that her feelings for her father changed. Unfortunately neither father or daughter knew how to overcome the breakdown in their communications, and consequently they had not really spoken since. It was the bust up with Katya that started Dmitri thinking about how he could spend less time on his Other Businesses, and more time being a father.

The problem for Dmitri, was simple. Katya had suddenly changed from his lovely little girl into a beautiful, intelligent and headstrong woman who reminded him of his dead wife. But he had no idea how to communicate with her as a father, or a friend. In the end he had resorted to taking a hard line with her to try and prevent her falling into the easy life, like the girls who now worked in his clubs. Dmitri was at a loss to know what to do with his daughter. He had thought about sending her away to a suitable school, but felt sure that if he did she would run away and get into trouble. It was not for the first time that he wished he could talk to someone who had a daughter or daughters of Katya's age. Maybe then he would get some answers. Of course he could always have a chat with Boris Fedorov and his wife, but Dmitri couldn't stand Boris's wife. It was the sound of her coarse, high pitched voice, which to him was similar to the sound made when fingernails were dragged down a blackboard, that put Dmitri off and it really upset him. So he avoided her company as much as possible, and as much as he liked Boris, he suspected that Boris, like himself, knew little about strong minded women.

Dmitri Novikov was a well educated man. His parents had been well placed at the end of the second world war, and made sure he had received the best education that Moscow could provide. He was a naturally very quick witted man who during his military career had quickly learned how to make the best of the harsh realities of life in Russia during the 60s, 70s, and 80s. It was during the time that Dmitri and his friend Mikhail Bukolov had been serving with the Spetznas that Dmitri had placed his life on the line to save the life of Mikhail. In return Mikhail Bukolov, a six feet five inches tall, thin, cadaverous looking man who shaved his head every day, would have been happy to lay down his life for Dmitri, at any time and for any reason. Dmitri who had been quite badly wounded during the incident, slowly recovered in hospital where he was told he would always walk with a slight limp. As a result of the injury he could no longer serve in Spetznas but if he wanted to, he could stay in the military and sit behind a desk. It was a terrible blow for such a physically active man, because the Spetznas had become his life and family. However after careful thought, and much soul searching, Dmitri decided that under the circumstances he would accept this new challenge and he left the military to start a new life. As the various businesses he set up prospered he started to become more involved with the bars and nightclubs, and after the angry scene with Katya he realised that it was vital for him not to become too personally involved with the adult clubs aspect of his business. Having more time to spend at home might improve the situation with Katya, and it might also help if future clients associated with his manufacturing and retailing businesses did not know he was associated with adult leisure enterprises. If these people did find out about his 'other businesses' they might be tempted to go elsewhere for whatever they wanted. A lot of Ekaterinberg people who were involved in commerce were highly moral people and thoughts of dealing with someone involved with the adult leisure business would send them into a self righteous rage. So in order to distance himself, but still retain some control over his 'Other Businesses' he contacted his old friend and comrade in arms, Mikhail Bukolov, and offered him a partnership. The two men met for a long discussion about the situation, and what was on offer. At the end of the meeting, they shook hands and Mikhail Bukolov became the head of Dmitri's 'Other Businesses'. Although he didn't look it, Mikhail was a weapons expert, as well as a very good operational analyst, and like all Spetznas, a fearsome opponent in a fight so he was ideally suited to control this side of the business. The two men quickly developed their business relationship, and within a short period of time Mikhail had surrounded himself with tough, hard, ex-Spetznas men from his old unit. These men were the backbone of the operation, making sure there was never any trouble in the clubs, casinos, or brothels, and they all earned more money in a week than a top military officer earned in a month. They were totally loyal to Mikhail, and quite prepared to carry out any orders that he gave them. Including the killing of anyone who wouldn't or couldn't pay what was owed.

All Dmitri's 'Other Businesses' were now running smoothly and efficiently, although at first there had been some trouble getting the adult entertainment side established. The three or four major gangs who were operating in Ekaterinburg at that time thought they could easily scare off Mikhail with a bit of rough stuff. But he and his men, very quickly, and brutally, put an end to this opposition. Dmitri then arranged for his friend Mikhail, to buy up the best parts of the other gang's now defunct operations, and after refurbishment, reopen them in Mikhail's own name. Everyone who worked for Mikhail was treated with respect and paid a good wage. This meant that everyone wanted to work for him. Consequently he could pick the very best people to be employed in the organisation, people he knew would be totally loyal to him. The fact that the major gangs were quickly put out of business did not go unnoticed by the police, and Mikhail took advantage of the situation to cultivate their friendship. Of course it didn't take long for the police and the politicos to realise that Mikhail could keep the criminal elements under control. So they told him that as long as there was never any trouble in his clubs, they would leave him alone. After that everyone assumed it was Mikhail, who owned and ran the clubs, and it quickly became known amongst the criminal fraternity that anyone who caused problems for the Bukolov organisation would soon be found and dealt with. The troublemaker might even find himself floating face down in the river. So the gangsters kept well away from Mikhail and his operations, and the ordinary people of Ekaterinburg lived normal, peaceful lives, and were rarely bothered by any criminal activity, so everyone was happy, except for the displaced gangsters.

Chapter 5

Sitting in his favourite bar Enver Ceka, smiled to himself, he had come a long way since he had left the small village in the mountains of Northern Albania, where he'd been born. Life in the village had been very hard. None of the families had any money and lived on what they could grow or steal. His father had ruled with a wooden stick and his fists, often beating his wife, and children just because he felt it was necessary. It was from his father that Enva Ceka had learned his values and moral standards, or lack of them, which included the treatment of all women as nothing more than chattels. As a child this treatment of women had seemed normal because none of the women in his village had any traditional standing, and were all treated as slaves to do the bidding of the men in their family. Even now, living in Tirana the capital city, the women he met seemed docile and accepting of his harsh treatment. If any women didn't do what he wanted, quickly and with a smile, he would think nothing of hitting the girl in the face with a clenched fist, or beating her with a heavy stick. Once or twice he had even broken a girls arm because she would not submit willingly to his lust. It didn't occur to him that the women were not interested in him as a man, only in how much money he would either give them, or spend on them.

When he had first arrived in Tirana, Ceka, had nothing but the patched and ragged clothes he stood up in. At first he begged and stole to survive, sleeping on the streets, and generally living like a wild animal. But then one day he tried to steal some fruit from a market stall, and the owner, a man nicknamed Turkish Ali, had caught him. Turkish Ali had given Ceka a severe beating but then made him bathe and shave before sitting him down and feeding him. After the food, Turkish Ali, had put a proposition to the Ceka, who immediately accepted the deal. He had lived with his new boss for three months learning exactly what his new duties were, and how he had to carry them out. What Turkish Ali, or boss, as Ceka called him, wanted him to do was to meet women, and seduce them with promises of jobs in the West. Then tell the parents, that he could arrange for their daughter to get a good job in either France, Germany, Italy or the United Kingdom, with good wages. The only thing he needed the parents to do was to sign the necessary paperwork so that their daughter could travel to a different country, and then he would arrange everything else. He had to promise the parents that their daughter would be well cared for, and he would drive her to Tirana and pay for her to buy new clothes for her flight to her new life. As a gesture of good faith, he even gave the parents $50 as an advance from the girl's first wage packet. Of course the parents were overjoyed, this was more money than they might see in twelve months, and it was an opportunity for their daughter to make something of her life in a way they could only dream about. As soon as the papers were signed Ceka had to bring the daughter back to his house, get her drunk and into bed so he could have sex with her. If she didn't want to drink or have sex, Ceka would beat her until she agreed. After a day or two when he had tired of her, he would take her to his boss's house in Tirana, for dinner. The sight of the house usually made the women feel inferior because to them the large white painted building seemed like the house of a king, by comparison to the places they had grown up in. This, plus the drugs, and the use of harsh violence, if required, made them easy to control.

During the time Ceka lived in Turkish Ali's, house he met a number of men who also brought women to the house. Occasionally Ceka would join the men for a night out drinking and eating and it was from them that he learned what happened to the women after they left their homes and were brought to Turkish Ali. It was whispered that most of them were taken to a secret, and very remote barn in a mountain forest, where they were kept prisoner. Speculation said that while the women were prisoners, they were beaten, repeatedly raped, and forced into drug addiction. To Ceka this easy to believe. It didn't take a lot of thought for a man such as himself to realise that as soon as they could be easily controlled through drugs their minds were hardly their own any more and they would do anything they were told. In this state these women could easily be sold onto the middle men who would transport them into a European country and sell them on. The criminals to whom the girls were sold made them work as sex slaves, or forced them onto the streets of cities across Europe to work as prostitutes. Any of these women who proved particularly difficult to handle where killed, often by being given a drug overdose and left in a dark alley to be found by the police. However a lot of these difficult girls met their end through extreme violence and ended up minus their heads, arms and legs making identification almost impossible. But some of the women who were brought to Turkish Ali's house were lucky because he did not consider them as suitable for selling. The reasons for his decision were usually their appearance, or maybe their family connections, but whatever it was, he allowed them to leave his house, and go home. It was unlikely that any of these girls would ever realise how lucky they had been. During the period he lived with Turkish Ali, Ceka brought around forty girls to the house, where they were raped and abused by various men. This was how he made his money and he enjoyed his work.

Soon after moving out of Turkish Ali's, house, Ceka found himself a nice place to live, not far from Scanderbeg Square in Tirana, and was soon surrounded by lots of new friends who seemed to enjoy his company. He had even acquired a nearly new Mercedes car, thanks to his criminal contacts. This certainly helped to impress the women from the small villages, but he didn't use the car very often around the city because the Tirana roads were generally full of potholes, some of which were very deep.

At first, Ceka had plenty of time to enjoy his new found wealth, but as time went by the word had started to spread around the small mountain villages that he was a liar and a very bad man. This meant he was spending less time at home due to the extra travelling time he had to do searching further afield to find gullible women and their parents. The extra travel meant he was having difficulty finding the number of women his boss wanted, and his income started to fall. After discussing the situation with Turkish Ali it was arranged that he should get a computer and have lessons on how to use it, then Turkish Ali would show him how to contact hundreds of women via the internet. Like people all over the world, this was a major turning point for Ceka. Access to the Internet became an essential tool for what he laughingly called his most enjoyable hobby. This hobby meant that for three or four hours during the day he surfed through all the European dating sites he could find, attempting to contact and date as many women as he could. If he met and passed on around twenty or more a month to his boss, he could continue to live well. The difference with these Internet Girls was they were generally better educated and not so easily impressed which meant they had to be drugged to get them away from their homes and into the hands of his boss. Ceka didn't like this situation very much because he could only have sex with the girls while they were drugged, and he preferred them to be alive and kicking rather than laying immobile and submissive. But he liked the money more than the lively sex. Then came the day he received the message from Katya, the Russian, and was surprised that such a good looking women had agreed to meet him if he went to Ekaterinburg. He immediately started making plans to travel into Russia, knowing it could take weeks to acquire the necessary travel documents. But looking at her picture, he knew if he could get Katya back to Turkish Ali, he could expect to earn at least twice his usual fee.

After printing off Katya's details, and a copy of her picture, he visited his boss to ask him to arrange the necessary travel documents. Turkish Ali looked carefully at the Russian woman's details and picture, before squinting at Ceka.

"You must be very careful with this one," he said, "there are some very wealthy families in Ekaterinburg, and it's possible this woman is part of one of these families. If she is, and you are caught messing about with her they will kill you very slowly, and painfully."

Ceka gave a disdainful shrug of his shoulders, as if he wasn't bothered by his boss' words.

"They don't frighten me, I learned how to look after myself in a very hard school."

Turkish Ali gave a knowing grin, and nodded.

"Okay I'll see what I can do for you. When the documents are ready for you I'll let you know. In the meantime I'll speak to some friends of mine and ask them to make enquiries about this woman. It maybe that she will be worth a lot of ransom money, but we will see. If everything checks out okay, I'll make the necessary arrangements for dealing with her. Now go and stay out of trouble, if you can."

Ceka grinned and nodded.

"Okay boss, I'll see you soon."

Then he received the email from Katya to say she couldn't write to him any more. He ranted and raged for 20 minutes, screaming obscenities and threats about what he would like to do to her. He punched holes in doors and smashed anything that came to hand, imagining it was Katya he was hitting. After calming down he started to worry about what Turkish Ali, would say after spending so much time and money getting all the paperwork sorted out. But when Ceka, eventually read all of Katya's email and looked at the picture of Anna, he instantly knew this women with her long blonde hair and air of innocence would command a very high price. Katya no longer seemed like such a loss, and he realised he should have read the whole email right through, if he had he might have saved more than half of his ornament collection. Ceka immediately jumped in his car and drove round to see Turkish Ali, knowing the sooner he faced his boss and told him what had happened the better it would be for him. At first Ali was enraged, blaming Ceka for the failure to get Katya into the net. He even threatened to have him tortured and killed. But as soon as Ceka gave him the photograph, and personal details of the new girl, Turkish Ali's manner immediately changed. He smiled and patted Ceka on the cheek in a friendly manner, and again gave him a beaming smile. After looking carefully at the picture of Anna and all her details Turkish Ali, agreed this new girl seemed to be too good to be true. Then he smiled and told Ceka that the information he had received from his contacts in Ekaterinberg indicated that Katya, was part of a very wealthy and well connected family so it was a good thing that he wasn't going to kidnap her. He also told Ceka the paperwork needed to get him, and the new women, out of Russia, would be ready in a few days. A couple of days later Turkish Ali contacted Ceka and told him it was time to pack a suitcase, and pick up the blonde from Ekaterinburg. He also told Ceka, that he'd not heard from his Russian contacts about her but because she was a friend of the first woman he had to assume that she was also the daughter of a wealthy and influential businessman. If this was the case Ceka would be very wise to get her into the car, and out of Russia, as quickly as possible. The next day Ceka, went to to collect the paperwork. He was also given very specific instructions about the route he was to travel for his return journey, if he wanted safe places to stay overnight. Finally Turkish Ali told Ceka that it was possible the woman might be a virgin, and therefore worth a lot more money, so Ceka must not, under any circumstances, spoil her. Ceka wasn't happy with this instruction, because he enjoyed seeing the fear and pain in the eyes of the women who were virgins, as he raped and abused them. He enjoyed the power he had over them, finding it to be almost orgasmic as he ordered them to do things that they thought were obscene. But he knew better than to argue with his boss, so he loaded up his car with all the stuff he needed, and set off on the long haul to Ekaterinburg.

On a damp overcast afternoon, after many long hours of hard driving, Ceka arrived in Ekaterinburg and checked into a hotel where he paid cash for a three day stay. His room was large, clean and airy with a double bed in the middle. It was ideal for his plan, he thought with a smile, life was once again going to be very good to him. The roads had proved to be better than expected, making the journey a lot easier and quicker than he had anticipated. He was also very surprised at how easy it had been for him to get through the various border check points, and hoped it would be just as easy on the return journey. After checking into the hotel, Ceka dropped his case next to the wardrobe, but did not unpack it. Instead he climbed into bed slept deeply after his long drive. The next day he relaxed in his hotel room until it was time for him to meet Anna. Then shaved and showered he changed into his most fashionable clothes, and left his bags so that he could pick them up and walk straight out of the hotel when he wanted to. For the first time he felt nervous about this job, but he couldn't understand why. He had done similar jobs before but his nerves hadn't bothered him like this. Shrugging off the cold feeling in his belly, he picked up the phone and called Anna Fedorova. He asked Anna to bring Katya with her because he would like to meet her, but Anna told him that Katya could not come with her, she had other plans for the evening. He eventually had to agree to meet Anna at seven pm in the restaurant, even though he tried hard to persuade her that he should come and pick her up. He thought Anna's attitude was strange, and hoped it wouldn't affect his plans, but what he didn't know was that Anna had agreed with Katya, that as long as she didn't get in his car with him she couldn't come to much harm. So no matter what he said, Anna insisted that it would best for them meet at the restaurant.

The Albanian was ten minutes early when he arrived at the restaurant, he wanted to make sure he was there before Anna. He tipped the head waiter well to make sure that a fuss was made of Anna and she was brought to the correct table. This was all part of his plan to impress the woman, and make her more amenable to his advances. Anna was fifteen minutes late when she walked into the restaurant and Ceka almost drooled as he watched her walk with the casually confident air that caused most of the men, and some of the women, to cast admiring glances at her. As Anna walked towards him, Ceka couldn't help but lust after her as he watched and admired the swing of her hips and swell of her breasts under her dress. He stood up, greeting her with a big smile, and reached out to take her slim fingers, raising them to his lips. At first their conversation was a little hesitant, mainly because their common language was English, a language neither used very much, and their mistakes caused a lot of hilarity. However, an hour and a half after sitting down they appeared to be having a splendid time together. They had nearly finished their main course, and started telling each other some of their embarrassing moments which caused both of them to spend a lot of time laughing. This was the time that Anna decided she needed to go to the ladies rest room, and although she didn't know it, this was perhaps the biggest mistake of her life. As soon as she had disappeared from sight, Ceka took his chance to spike her drink with a strong anaesthetic drug. This should give him at least two or three hours before anyone would start to miss her. His planned return journey was different to his recent route which should ensure he was out of Russia and safe before the Russian police started a full scale search for her.

Anna returned to the table and after settling herself down, took a mouthful of the spiked drink. Two minutes after that mouthful her body started to feel strange and she became light headed and woozy. Ceka kept telling her to drink some more wine as it would help to make her feel better so she drank what was left in the glass. Soon her eyes started closing and she couldn't focus on anything. She kept trying to speak, but her mouth refused to work properly, and she couldn't stop herself slipping down her seat. Ceka left a pile of money next to his plate to pay the bill, and walked casually around the table to help her to her feet. Then with his arm around her waist to support her, he led her out of the restaurant to his car. As he made the girl comfortable on the back seat and covered her with a warm rug, she slowly gave up the struggle and lapsed in to the pleasurable blackness. Ceka with an evil smirk on his face slid behind the wheel and started the long journey back to Tirana.

Chapter 6

Ceka had been driving hard for a couple of hours when he crossed the river at Zelenodolsk, trying to put as much distance as possible between himself and Ekaterinburg. During this time Anna, had slept quietly under the influence of the drug he had put in her drink, and he hoped she would stay this way until he arrived back home. Half an hour after leaving the river behind, he spotted a quiet place where he could pull off the road, and eased the Mercedes to a halt. He listened to the girl's breathing for a few minutes, it was even and steady, so he pulled the seat belts over the sleeping girl and wedged them to make sure she couldn't do anything foolish while he was driving.

About a hundred kilometres from the Ukrainian border, the Mercedes pulled over to the side of the road, and Ceka climbed stiffly out of the car to stretch his muscles, and relieve himself. As the car slowed down, Anna's eyes flickered open, and for a moment she couldn't understand where she was or what had happened. She was just about to call out when she realised she was in a car, and for some unknown reason she stopped herself. Maybe it was the fact that she couldn't move because the seat belts held her firmly, or maybe it was just the age old survival instinct, but whatever it was, she remained quiet, and tried to figure out what had happened. Slowly, as Anna calmed herself and tried to think straight, memories of the previous night in the restaurant came back to her. She remembered having an enjoyable time with Ceka, before having to go to the ladies rest room, and afterwards sitting back down at the table and drinking her glass of wine. Oh God, she thought, it was the wine. He must have drugged it. This is very very bad. With this realisation came a cold horrible feeling in the pit of her stomach, her limbs started to shake, and she was almost physically sick with fear. With tears in her eyes, and without hope in her heart, Anna prayed in a way she had never prayed before, for forgiveness, and to be saved from whatever terrible things Ceka was going to do to her. She wanted to cry out to him that her father would pay whatever ransom demand he made, as long as she was returned unharmed to her family. She also considered telling him that he could do whatever he wanted to her as long as he didn't hurt her or kill her. But as soon as the car door opened and Ceka stepped into the car, Anna closed her eyes and tried to control her breathing in an attempt to make him think she was still asleep. She was trying to convince herself that as long as she was alive, there could be a chance for her to escape. Ceka didn't even bother to glance at her before putting the car into gear and pulling smoothly out onto the main highway once more, not noticing the new raggedness of Anna's breathing or the rapid beating of her pulse. She felt sure he could at least hear her pulse pounding because it sounded so loud in her in her ears. Making small movements every time the car went over a rough patch of road, so she would not be noticed, Anna manoeuvred herself until she could just see her watch. At first she thought it must have stopped because it showed seven o'clock, but a glance through the windows at the pale grey sky told her it was correct, but seven o'clock in the morning not seven o'clock at night. Oh God, she thought, I wonder if Katya has been in touch with my father. If she has, would he have called the police to have all the border crossing police alerted, and will the police be looking for me now? Anna would have given anything to know the answers to these questions, but knew she had to assume the worst, maybe her friend Katya had fallen asleep, and hadn't informed her father yet. Half an hour later, Anna's bladder started to ache making her realise it had been a long time since that fateful last visit to the toilet in the restaurant and she had to relieve herself as a matter of urgency. She lifted her head and called out to Ceka.

"Why am I strapped here? Please stop the car and let me up, I desperately need to urinate."

Ceka was surprised to hear her voice. Glancing over his shoulder at her, he snarled.

"Shut up bitch and keep quiet or I'll tape your mouth shut."

But he realised that if he didn't pull over and let her relieve herself, she could end up urinating all over the back seat, and that would soon cause his car to stink. A few minutes later he saw a suitable site and pulled the car over to the side of the road. He got out and went to the boot and took out a twenty yard length of tough cord, then he opened the rear door and tied one end of the cord around her neck before unfastening the seat belts.

"Okay," he said. "You can get out now, but remember if you make the slightest attempt to escape, this cord will tell me. Then I will beat you and tie your ankles together and make you sit in the back of the car naked. Now go behind those bushes over there and do whatever you need to do."

Tears of frustration rolled down Anna's face. She had hoped she might have a chance to run away and hide from Ceka, but he was obviously used to kidnapping women, and had anticipated her plan. She made her way around the bushes, squatting down to relieve herself, trying to be as quiet as possible because Ceka was standing fairly close to the bush, and she didn't want to embarrass herself despite the fact she knew this should be the least of her worries. As soon as she was finished, Ceka used the string to drag her back to the car. He forced her to lay down on the back seat of the car while he covered her with the blanket and fastened the seat belts over her so she was trapped again. The last thing he did was offer her a drink of lemonade. Visually Anna examined the bottle as best as she could but it looked as if it had not been opened before, so she took a drink. A few seconds later, as she drifted towards unconsciousness, she realised the lemonade had been tampered with, and felt a fool for being caught out for the second time by this man. Ceka smiled, it would be easy for him to get her through the border controls. He would just tell the guards she was on medication for a sever stomach complaint, and show them the medical certificate that Turkish Ali, had given him. Ceka was sure the guards wouldn't want to wake up a sick woman. From this point until he arrived back in Tirana, he would make sure that Anna stayed drugged and unconscious, this should make his journey a lot easier, and quicker.

The journey went quicker and easier than he could have hoped for, apart from a small act of rebellion on the part of Anna. It happened when she awoke from her drugged sleep and demanded to be allowed to urinate. Ceka stopped the car and this time tied the string around Anna's ankle so she couldn't run away. But while she was squatting behind a bush Anna carefully untied the string and retied it to the base of the bush, and crept away as quietly as she could. Had Ceka, not been so exhausted he would have been suspicious of the length of time Anna had been behind the bush and investigated sooner. But he was very tired and as he relaxed his eyes closed and it was some time before he realised that he hadn't felt the string move. He jumped to his feet and ran around to the far side of the bush. There was no sign of Anna. In desperation he looked around frantically for some indication of which way she had gone, but there was nothing. His mind went blank with fear, the fear of what Turkish Ali would do to him when he found out that the girl had been lost. At that moment Ceka heard a branch break, and immediately he turned and ran towards the sound. Anna heard him start to run towards her, but no matter how hard she tried to make her legs work, she couldn't run properly. Ceka could now hear her as she stumbled and fell in the dark,. She was trying to run, but the drugs he'd been giving her had made her legs weak. Within five minutes he'd caught her, and was dragging her, weeping, back to the car. As soon as Anna saw the car, she made another desperate attempt to break free, but this time he was ready for it. He grabbed her by the hair and threw her to the ground, but as he drew back his foot to kick her in the stomach, he remembered his boss saying he had to deliver the girl undamaged in any way. So instead of kicking her, he waited until she had got back on her feet, and then hit her with a heavy open handed slap across the face that knocked her off her feet. Then he grabbed her by the hair and threw her onto the back seat of the car and secured her with the seat belts. Before setting off, he lifted the semi-conscious girl's head and carefully dribbled some of the drugged lemonade into her mouth, hoping that she wouldn't wake up again until he arrived back in Tirana.

Chapter 7

During the time that Jimmy and Katya, had been writing to each other their relationship had developed, growing stronger, and becoming quite intimate. Their emails became more and more frequent until they were writing to each other at the end of every day. The content of their mail also became more personal and affectionate, to the point where Jimmy began making plans to telephone Katya, and if possible to visit her. Although he knew it was foolish to let himself believe that he might have found that special woman through a few emails, he couldn't stop himself from logging onto his computer and typing a new email to her. Then he eagerly awaited a reply after pressing the 'send' button even though he knew it might be hours before she read his email. No matter how cautious he tried to be he couldn't help letting his imagination create interesting fantasies about what the future might hold for the two of them. The first indication that something was wrong came when the emails from Katya ceased. At first Jimmy carried on writing every night, thinking that maybe she had gone away for a few days with her friends. But after a week had passed without a word from her, he began to wonder what could have happened that would cause her to stop writing. Had she met someone who had taken her fancy? After all she's a gorgeous woman and there must be thousands of suitable Russian men that she could pick from. But in his heart he knew it wasn't as simple as Katya finding a new man, because she would have emailed him and explained why she wouldn't be contacting him any more. Sadly, he sent the last email to Katya saying how much he missed their daily exchange of emails, and hoped that she was enjoying her life. At the same time he wondered if he would ever know what had happened.

Slowly as the days went by Jimmy tried to put Katya to the back of his mind. He couldn't forget her, so he just tried to stop thinking about her so much in an effort to get on with his life. His two friends, Lenny and Danny realised he was having a hard time, and did their best to lift his spirits. The two men were always great fun to be with, and they insisted that he join them on their nights out. They were a lively pair with wide ranging interests, particularly when it came to women and making money. Often spending long weekends away in various parts of the country doing things they never talked about. Jimmy had once asked about their activities outside of their normal work, and was politely told that it was better he didn't ask because friends didn't tell lies to each other, and what he didn't know could never be a problem for him. After that Jimmy never asked again, preferring their friendship, and honesty with each other, to anything else. Although he had a suspicion, gained from snippets of overheard conversations, that they were involved in the sort of work that often came under the heading of 'security work' that frequently involved them with some heavy members of the criminal underworld. Then one day, out of the blue, as Jimmy was leaving work, Danny and Lenny stopped him and asked if he would like to take a trip to London with them for a weekend.

"You've been looking fairly miserable for the past week or two so we figured that a weekend with lots of girls, booze, and hangovers, would put a smile on your face."
said Lenny with a smile. Jimmy shook his head doubtfully.
"I don't know. I'm not sure I'd be much fun to drag around London. But on the other hand it sounds like it could be a bloody good idea. When are you planning on going down?"
His friends laughed, and Danny replied.

"That's what we like to hear. A man who is keen to get drunk out of his skull, and if he can remember how it's done, to get his leg over. We'll be going down on the train this Friday lunch time and staying in a three bedroom apartment that a friend of mine is letting us use. So pack your best hot tottie hunting kit, and meet us at the railway station ready to catch the lunchtime train."

Jimmy nodded.

"Okay, that sounds great, and now I suppose I'd better take you two down to the George and fill you full of beer to get you ready for the weekend."

The three men strolled down the road laughing and joking about the things they hoped to do over the coming weekend.

At the appointed time that Friday the three friends met on the station platform, and as soon as the train doors opened they found themselves three seats around a table and settled down. When the train had left the station, Danny pulled a bottle of whisky, and a bottle of ginger ale out of his bag, while Lenny produced three plastic cups. With the drinks poured Jimmy raised his cup to his friends.

"Thanks for the invite guys, and here's to a great weekend. I'm really looking forward to the next couple of days."

The journey passed quickly and pleasantly, and they were soon walking through London's Euston Station to find a taxi to take them to the apartment that would be their home for the weekend. The apartment surprised Jimmy. It was large with highly polished wooden floors and lots of beautiful wood panelling in the lounge and dinning room. The bedrooms all had en-suite bathrooms, and walk in wardrobes. Obviously it was the property of a very wealthy person, and certainly well outside Jimmy's price bracket. When he asked Lenny who owned the property, Lenny grinned and told him to never look a gift horse in the mouth. After unpacking their bags and showering, the three friends casually strolled a short distance to an Italian restaurant that Lenny and Danny seemed to know well. They were all hungry and ready for a good meal, and Lenny insisted the food would be memorable, and a good starting point for a night out. The meal and the wine was every bit as good as Lenny had promised, but between leaving the Italian and the clocks striking midnight, Jimmy lost count of how many bars they'd been drinking in. He was beginning to feel a bit light headed and was worried in case he became a burden on his two friends. But just after midnight they rolled out of yet another pub together with a group of people who had joined them and fell into three taxis for a five minute ride to a popular nightclub. On the way, Jimmy was surprised to see one of the other taxis overtaking them and the cheeky sight of a bare white backside 'mooning' out of a side window at them. It was Lenny, clowning around and Jimmy couldn't help but laugh at his antics.

Outside the main entrance to the nightclub the three friends got out of the taxis and walked straight to the head of a large queue of revellers who were waiting to get into the club. Jimmy quickly realised that this must be a regular occurrence because the rest of the people who had been in the taxis with them had made their way to the end of the queue. Lenny and Danny were recognized by the security men on the door, and the three of them were waved through. This experience of walking to the front of a queue was something new to Jimmy, and he glanced at the nearby people to see if there was any hostility, but there was none. The crowd seemed to be more interested in trying to figure out who the newcomers were, and what made them so important they could just jump the queue and walk straight in. The manager, who obviously knew Lenny and Danny well, met them as they walked into the large bar and dance floor area, and was introduced to Jimmy as 'Swampy'. Jimmy was immediately curious to know how Swampy got his nickname, but unfortunately Swampy was so busy he couldn't stay to chat with them. After shaking hands, Swampy left them and they where shown to one of the private horseshoe shaped areas with a table surrounded on three sides by comfortable seating. When they were settled in their seats a very pretty waitress dressed in an almost see through blouse, minuscule black skirt, fishnet stockings and high heels, appeared and took their drinks order. Jimmy was impressed with the club, he'd heard about it many times before, and had even read some of the gossip in the national newspapers about the celebrities who cavorted in the place. It was bigger than he expected, and crowded with mostly people, all dancing, and talking animatedly, or just sitting around drinking. Before long Danny and Lenny were surrounded by a group of people who were all introduced to Jimmy so it wasn't long before he was chatting with everyone. In his rather intoxicated state Jimmy was soon chatting to and then dancing with a petite blonde who was gyrating in a very sexy way to the pounding rhythm. For Jimmy the sight of so many nubile women showing what they could do on the dance floor was both very enjoyable, and highly erotic. But after enjoying the view and the dancing for twenty minutes Jimmy made his way back to their table for a large glass of water. He realised he had to cool down or he could end up making a fool of himself, so he sat at the table quietly drinking water for a while before deciding it was time for a glass of red wine. Danny and Lenny where still absorbed with the conversations they were having with the various people who had gathered round them, so Jimmy took the opportunity to casually gaze around at the people sitting at the nearby tables. Suddenly, as his gaze swept across one of the tables his eyes focused, and he frowned, he was looking at a blond woman whom he felt sure he knew but for the life of him he couldn't remember where he knew her from. She was sitting with another woman and two men at a table perhaps three or four yards away. The two men looked like successful businessmen on expense accounts, the sort of men who were happy to spend a lot of their company's money to entertain the two women sitting opposite them. Unfortunately the alcohol had fogged Jimmy's brain, and before he could recall why he felt he knew the blonde women, the four people got up and disappeared into the crowd. Jimmy didn't see them again, and soon forgot about the incident.

It was at work a few days later when Jimmy was busy setting up one of the computerised typesetting machines that he suddenly remembered who the woman he'd seen at the nightclub was. The more he thought about it, the more convinced he was that it had been Katya's best friend Anna. He couldn't be absolutely certain about it, but he would certainly check it out when he got home.

That night Jimmy switched on his PC and checked his picture file to see if the girl he had seen in the nightclub was really Katya's friend. The instant he saw the picture of Anna and Katya together, he knew for certain it was the same girl. Slowly he sat back in his chair and tried to make sense of this situation, assuming that there was some sense to be made of it. But no matter which way he looked at it, he remained confused. Surely, he thought, if Anna had come over to the UK for a holiday, Katya would have said something to him about it. Then the thought jumped into his mind, if Anna was here on holiday, was Katya with her? The thoughts kept messing with his mind and he found it impossible to sleep. In the end he had to use the breathing and muscle tensioning and relaxing technique that he had been taught by a Buddhist monk during the time he'd been fighting the Communist terrorists in the Malay jungle, but it still took him fifteen minutes to drop off.

Chapter 8

Ceka had been driving for nearly sixteen hours, stopping only for occasional toilet breaks, and to pour a measure of the drugged drink down Anna's throat. So when he eventually pulled up outside Turkish Ali's house he was exhausted, and hungry. Struggling out of the car he made his way to the heavy wooden front door and rang the bell. After a few minutes Turkish Ali opened the door, and quickly looked up and down the street to see if anyone was showing an interest in Ceka, or himself. There was no one. His face turned ugly when he didn't see the girl, and he growled.

"Have you been followed, and where is the girl?"
Ceka shook his head.
"No I wasn't followed, and yes I've got the girl. She is drugged, wrapped in a blanket and safely strapped onto the back seat. Do you want me to carry her inside?"
As soon as he heard the news that the girl was in the car, Ali's demeanour changed, he smiled and patted Ceka on the head.
"Good, very good. Bring her inside, and be careful not to damage her, I want to see this beautiful virgin."
Ceka went back to his car and unstrapped Anna, then keeping the blanket wrapped around her he lifted her out of the car and took her inside the house. Ali led him to a small bedroom at the back of the house and smiling happily said.

"Put her on the bed, then go home and get drunk or sleep, or whatever you want to do. I will look after her now, and make arrangements for her future."

"Thanks Boss, I think I'll go and get myself a meal and a good bottle of wine, or maybe three."

As soon as Ceka, had left, Turkish Ali shouted for the two women he kept in the house as his servants. When they appeared he instructed them to bathe the blonde women when she woke up, and then get her dressed in clean clothes. The women immediately went into the bedroom and started to strip Anna's clothes off her, taking everything off until she was naked. As soon as Ali could see that the girl was a natural blonde he left the two women to complete their work and walked off to phone some of his contacts. He wanted to find out who was prepared to pay the most for the pleasure of owning a very pretty, natural blond virgin. After several phone calls, he had sold the Anna to his German contact, a man who he knew for certain always carried at least $100,000 US Dollars in cash with him. The German told him that he would be at the barn in the hills later the same day to collect the blonde virgin and pay the $25,500 asking price. As soon as the deal was struck Ali phoned one of his men to come to the house, pick Anna and take her up to the barn in the hills. The man was told to wait for The German to arrive and as soon as the money was in his hands he had to bring it straight back to Ali's house. Then Ali put the phone down and looked over at Anna's clothes and shoes, and it was obvious to him that she came from a wealthy family. Therefore it was essential that the girl be hidden as quickly as possible in case some of her Russian family came looking for her. The Russians could be bastards, and likely to be extremely violent and brutal if they found her or any of her things in his house. If they did find something they would certainly torture him to find out what had happened to her. Once they had extracted the information they would kill him and everyone else in the house, and then burn the place down. It would be the end of his very lucrative life style, and he cursed his contacts who hadn't told him the girl's family were wealthy, because in his own mind he was certain that all wealthy Russians had major political and criminal contacts. If he had known she was from a wealthy family, he wouldn't have allowed Ceka to go into Russia. But it was too late now, and he hoped the Russians didn't know, or somehow find out, about his part in kidnapping the girl.

Some time later Anna woke from her drug induced sleep, in a pitch black, chilly, airless room. and for some time she couldn't orientate herself. She knew she was chained to a bed because every time she moved she could hear the clinking sound of the chain, and feel metal rubbing around her wrists and ankles. As far as she could tell she was still fully dressed. The clothes felt different to the type she was used to and she knew they weren't her own, but at least her body didn't feel as though it had been raped or violated in any way. She hoped the knowledge would make her feel better, but her body continued to shiver and shake violently from fear and shock. Her head felt as if it was full of cotton wool, and a headache was starting to pound behind her eyes. She struggled hard to get some control of her body to stop the shaking, but try as she might she couldn't concentrate. Her mind kept flitting from idea to speculation and she couldn't focus on anything long enough to calm herself down. Her breathing had become fast and shallow and her teeth were chattering. She had been unconscious for hours but her body was exhausted and eventually she fell back into a deep sleep. Even being carried from the airless room to the back of a four wheel drive vehicle did not wake her up. Her exhaustion and the drugs, made sure she slept right through the journey from Turkish Ali's house to the barn in the mountain forest. She was still asleep when they reached the barn, and two men carried her inside and dumped onto another bed.

Hours later Anna was woken by someone shaking her shoulder, and she slowly realised her arms were no longer shackled to the bed. When she opened her eyes, the room was still dark, but her eyes soon got used to the dark, and she could make out a figure standing next to the bed. The voice, when the figure spoke to her in Russian, sounded female and rough. Anna, guessed from the accent that the woman probably came from somewhere on the border between Russia and the Ukraine, and was uneducated.

"Get up and get washed. There is some food ready for you." The woman snapped, as she unfastened the last shackle holding Anna, to the bed.

"Where am I? What time is it?" Anna mumbled, her voice still sleepy.

"Don't ask stupid questions, just do as your told. There is a shower and toilet in the next room that you can use. But be quick."

As she stood back from the bed, she tossed a threadbare towel and a comb onto the bed, and told her.

"Tidy yourself up, and remember there is no escape from this place, so don't get any funny ideas. I will be outside in the corridor waiting for you. You are very lucky, The German and his men will collect you soon. If it was the Albanians you'd be in real trouble, so get your arse moving."

After showering quickly and combing her hair Anna, was led to a large room lit only by candles. The room seemed to contain about eighteen or maybe twenty small tables scattered around, each with a single chair next to it. Anna was shocked to see that on each chair sat a women who was handcuffed to the chair leaving one hand free so she could eat. The female guard led Anna to a table then handcuffed her left wrist securely to the chair, which Anna realised was bolted to the floor. A bowl of some sort of soup or stew was placed on the table in front of her with some hard black bread, a spoon and a glass of water. Although the food didn't look appetizing, the smell made Anna realise it had been a long time since she had eaten, and she picked up a piece of the black bread. As she ate, Anna glanced around at the other girls, and was surprised that they all looked strangely cowed, and their eyes were blank as though there was nothing going on within their minds. Then it came to her that they were all probably under the influence of drugs, and eyeing the soup, she wondered when they would start to drug her again. The thick soup didn't taste very nice, but with the bread she managed to eat it all. She knew it was essential she try to keep her strength up, and starving herself would not do her any good at all. Two of the female guards approached Anna. One of them grabbed her right arm, and held it in a grip of iron, while the other woman quickly found a vein and injected her. The needle stung as it went into her skin and Anna cried out, but the two women just laughed at her. When the women completed the injection they unfastened the handcuff that secured her to the chair, and left her. Anna sat there without moving a muscle for what seemed like five minutes, wondering what the drug was going to do to her, and was surprised when nothing seemed to be happening. It seemed to Anna, that she had been sitting motionless for a long time but a glance at her watch told her it had only been ten minutes. She lifted her arms and moved her head around without noticing anything different. Then she stood up and started walking around her table, trying to gauge what effect the drug was having on her, but her arms and legs and everything seemed to be working as normal. Sitting down again she relaxed, and her mind drifted back to the meal with Ceka. She had been enjoying the attention that Ceka had been showing her, like the way he stroked her hand when he reached across the table to emphasis something in the conversation, or the way he tried to look down her cleavage when he thought she wasn't looking. A few minutes after she started thinking about Ceka, Anna could feel that she was beginning to feel extremely aroused. It was then the realisation hit her, the people who were holding her prisoner had deliberately injected her with a drug that was probably the cause of her becoming aroused. Suddenly she began to panic as the truth of the situation dawned on her. Why would they want her to feel like this, unless they were planning on doing things to her that no one, except perhaps herself, had ever done before.

Once again Anna looked around the room, and now noticed that somehow all the other girls had left, without her being aware of it, and she was now on her own in the room. A door across to her right opened, and she saw a large overweight man enter. He seemed well dressed, with close cropped fair hair, and a for a moment she thought he might have come to save her, and her spirits soared. But then she looked again at his florid face with its heavy jowls around a thin cruel mouth, and her heart sank as she instinctively knew he was not there to help her. Her shoulders drooped and she felt frightened by his threatening and dominant aura. The man stopped for a moment to look around before he walked over to Anna and sat his large backside on the edge of a table and snapped..

"Do you speak English?"

Anna dumbly nodded her head. For a moment he was silent while he looked at her, then he barked.

"Stand up girl, and let me look at what I've bought."

Without thinking, Anna obeyed the authoritarian voice, and stood in front of the fat blonde man, her mind whirling, what did he mean, how could he have bought her? Then once again the voice commanded her.

"Turn around very slowly."

Anna was so frightened that she could no longer think, her mind was totally blank, and she automatically started to slowly turn in a circle. When she had completed the circle and faced the blonde man once more, she found she could not bring herself to look at him and kept her eyes on the floor. But then the strident domineering voice commanded her attention again.

"Take your clothes off. I want to see if your body is as good looking as your face."

Anna hesitated, all her instincts and upbringing were trying to force her not to comply with the man's demand. But before she could voice her objections the man's open hand slapped her very hard across the face, then he back handed her across the other side of her face and knocked her crashing to the floor. At first she was shocked, it was only the second time in her life she had been hit like that, and she had no idea why it had happened to her, but then the pain overcame the shock and she started to cry.

"Get up, you stupid bitch, get up now, and stop snivelling," the man snarled at her with his fists clenched and threatening. Anna struggled uncertainly to her feet once more.

"Now, get your clothes off, and unless you want to experience a lot more pain do it now! And remember this, if you do not immediately do as I tell you, I will have my men hold you down and I will whip you until you bleed. Do understand?"

Anna nodded her understanding and started unbuttoning the blouse someone had put on her. She felt so embarrassed, it was the first time a man had ever seen her naked, and because she could feel his eyes on her flesh it felt as if he was physically abusing her. But mostly she was embarrassed because even after he hit her, she still felt aroused. She felt ashamed that her body was betraying her in this way, but she didn't dare try and play for time because she was sure the man would hit her again, or whip her, or hurt her in ways she hadn't even thought of. Although her fingers felt clumsy and were shaking violently, she managed to take off the blouse and skirt, followed by her underwear so she was soon standing naked in a puddle of her clothes. Once again she was told to turn around slowly, and as she turned her back towards him, she felt his hands caressing and squeezing the cheeks of her bottom quite hard. The contact made her flesh creep with revulsion, and she longed to cringe away from him and cover herself, but fear along with the ache in her cheek kept her rooted to the spot. She forced herself to keep her eyes focused on the floor so her expression wouldn't give her away. If he knew what she was thinking she was sure he would start hitting her again.

The German's lust filled eyes devoured Anna, as she turned. He wanted to grab and squeeze her pale pink tipped breasts until the creamy white flesh turned an angry red and the girl screamed in pain. But he knew he didn't have the time to indulge his fantasies, then he got some control over himself and ordered her to keep turning around until she faced faced him again.

"Have you ever had sex with a man before?"
Anna shook her head and replied in a quiet frightened voice.
"No. I have never had any type of sex before."
The man laughed.
"Well I can see that you and I are going to have some fun together. Me the teacher and you the pupil, and your lessons might as well start now. Unzip my trousers."

Anna reached forward, but because her hands were shaking so much it took her a minute before she found the zip. She could sense the man was becoming impatient, and waited for another painful slap in the face. Steadfastly she kept her eyes focused on the floor so she couldn't see what was inside his trousers, and The German would not see the disgust in her eyes. Fortunately the problem was temporarily put on hold because the door opened and another man appeared. The man placed two heavy quilted topcoats on one of the tables and spoke to the blonde man in German, saying that the helicopter was ready to go. He also told The German that Enva Ceka had been brutally tortured, and Turkish Ali, and his bodyguards, had been killed by some Russians, who were thought to be on their way to the barn, and their ETA was within the next forty-five minutes. The German's face paled and he immediately got to his feet and zipped his trousers up before grabbing Anna by her hair and hauling her painfully to her feet. Anna, who was studying the German language at university, understood what had been said, and was suddenly filled with hope. The corners of her mouth nearly pulled up into a smile before the reality of her situation was once again thrust upon her with another tug of her hair. She now knew for sure that her friend Katya had told her father, and now there were people searching for her. But she she kept her eyes down, and remained staring at the floor giving no indication that she knew the language.

"Get dressed quickly, you stupid bitch," The German barked at her in English his accent thick with suppressed lust, "and put that big coat on or you'll freeze to death and I'm not ready to loose all the money I've paid for you. Come on, come on, hurry up."

Then he turned away from her, and walked quickly to the exit door where he stood tapping his foot impatiently while he waited for her. In a dream like state Anna did as she was told, wondering where they were going to take her, and if the men who were following her would ever catch up with the people who were now keeping her prisoner.

As soon as she followed The German through the door, two men grabbed her and quickly half carried and half dragged her out of the old barn building, to the waiting helicopter. The eight men who were with The German, all seemed very nervous, constantly checking their weapons, and looking around trying to see if there was anyone hiding in the nearby trees. Watching them, Anna, suddenly realised that the thought of the Russians arriving had terrified these men, including the big blonde German, and now they were rushing to get away from the site as quickly as they could. Slowly, as the rotors started to turn, the men started to relax, and as soon as the rotors reached flying speed and the machine took off, they all started to speak to each other with smiles on their faces. As she covertly watched the men, Anna carefully noted their descriptions, and any identifying marks, knowing that when the Russian men caught up with her, they would need all the information she could give them. She was determined that all the men involved in her kidnapping would either go to jail for life, or they would die. Her new found hardness surprised her, but logic told her that if she wanted to survive until she was rescued, she had to be as strong as she could be both mentally, and physically. From where she sat Anna could see out of one of the windows, and was surprised to see that the helicopter pilot was keeping his machine very close to the ground, only rising to clear the tops of the trees when necessary. Then she remembered a story she had once read about how Russian pilots during world war two would fly very low so the German radar was not able to pick them up, and she realised this is what the pilot was doing. Anna had no idea what direction they were flying in or how fast they were travelling so she was unable to even guess where they were going. Not that it really mattered to her, she was only interested in where she would end up, and what would happen to her when they got there. But she was under no illusions about her future, she would be expected to give her body to lots of different men every day, seven days a week, and if she objected she would be beaten, raped, abused, and drugged until she agreed. She may not have the experience of some other girls, but she wasn't oblivious to the darker aspects of the world.

The German held his hand out to one of his men who handed him a long narrow chromed box. From the padding inside the box The German removed a loaded hypodermic syringe, and looked over Anna, with a gloating look in his eye, and chuckled as he said in a sadistic gloating way.

"Don't look so frightened you stupid little bitch, this is good stuff, it cost a lot of money and it will make you feel wonderful."

Then he shoved up the sleeve of the big coat to bare her arm, and held her steady while he injected her with whatever was in the syringe. Anna screamed with fear as she felt the needle enter her skin, and cried out.

"What is it you are putting into me, and why are you doing this to me?"

The blonde man stopped and leered at her.

"I'm injecting you with heroin, so in a few days, you will do whatever I want you to do without question or hesitation. Soon you'll be begging me for a shot, or crying for another dose of whatever you can get. Then I will enjoy your virgin body in any way I choose, until you bore me. When that happens I'll sell you to another man who will make sure that you'll make him lots of money by having sex with every man who is prepared to pay for your company. Now shut your mouth bitch, and in future you will speak only when I tell you to."

Anna closed her eyes to try and stop the tears of fear and frustration. Fear because of the stories she had read and heard about drugs like heroin, and what it could do to any person taking it. The frustration was because she couldn't do anything to stop it.

After a while Anna, felt the drug starting to take hold of her. It was a feeling she had never experienced before in her life. She began to feel so powerful and mentally strong that nothing could affect her, and yet at the same time she felt so wonderfully relaxed. While all these different feelings were rushing through her body, her mind seemed to be capable of resolving every problem known to the modern world. She stopped worrying about anything and everything, and with a lazy smile, just enjoyed the wonderful high that swept over her. Watching her, the blonde man smiled as he saw that she was under the influence of the drug, and laughed as he said to the other men in the helicopter.

"That's the way I like to see these girls. Quiet, submissive, and willing to do anything I ask of them."

Then, with a laugh, he pushed his hand under her skirt and forced her legs apart. If he expected a response from her he was out of luck, she was so far gone with the drug that she never even noticed he was doing something to her that no man had ever been allowed to do before. There were one or two titters and giggles from the other men, but most of them just kept quiet, they didn't share their boss's perversions. They preferred their women to be normal, or maybe under the influence of alcohol, but certainly in a state where the women could react with pleasure to their advances.

Chapter 9

The discordant sound of the front door bell clashed with the sound of the television and brought Jimmy out of his reverie. He glanced up at the clock, it was late and he wondered who the hell wanted to speak to him at this time of the night. Quietly cursing to himself, he walked to the front door wondering if it was his friends Danny and Lenny looking for a late night drink on their way home. But on opening the door he was surprised to find two well dressed men standing there, each holding a suitcase. One man, tall, bald, and thin, the other a few inches shorter, but powerfully built, with a full head of wavy dark hair streaked with grey. Both men wore serious expressions.

"Good evening gentlemen, how can I help you?" Jimmy asked politely. As soon as Jimmy opened the door he recognised Katya's father from the pictures she'd sent him, but not the tall bald man with him. Katya's father stepped forward and replied in accented English.

"Are you Jimmy Roberts, the man who has been emailing with a woman called Katya?"

Jimmy nodded and smiled.

"Yes, I was emailing with a lady called Katya, but unfortunately she stopped writing to me a few weeks ago. Why do you ask?"

The man nodded and his face softened, losing some of its hard lines.

"We are sorry to bother you, but we have a problem that you may be able to help us with. Is it possible that we can discuss this inside?"

Jimmy stepped back and waved the two men inside. As he closed the front door he said.

"Please go through to the lounge, on the left. If Katya has a problem, I'll be happy to help you in any way I can."

Katya's father nodded.

"Thank you, I appreciate that. First though, I must apologise to you. It was my fault that Katya stopped writing to you, because I was afraid that she might be writing to one of these guys who kidnap women and sell them into the sex slave business. I'm sure you will understand why, when I tell you what has happened."

Jimmy raised an eyebrow as he looked at both men.

"This must be very serious for you to travel all this way to speak to me, but before we start talking let me get us all a drink of something?"

The Russians nodded and Jimmy poured them a large measure of whisky each, and put a jug of water on the table.

"Please take your coats off, and make yourselves comfortable."

As the two men settled into armchairs Dmitri Novikov introduced himself and his friend Mikhail Bukolov. Jimmy raised his glass towards the two men.

"Yes, I know you are Katya's father, I recognised you from the photos she sent to me. She told me that you and she had been very close, but had argued and fallen out sometime ago, and hardly spoken to each other since. She also told me you are a very good man, and she respects you. But I'm afraid she never mentioned your friend. Anyway I'm interrupting you, please continue."

Dmitri leaned forward.

"Thank you for your comments I appreciate them, but this story is not so pleasant. A couple of weeks ago Katya's girl friend Anna, went out to dinner with an Albanian man who she had been emailing with. This man, whose name is Enver Ceka, arrived in Ekaterinburg and invited the two girls out to dinner. Katya did not want to go, and the two girls arranged that if Anna did not telephone Katya by ten pm that night, Katya would contact Anna's father and tell him about

The Internet Girls

the arrangement. Anna did not contact Katya, so Katya telephoned Anna's father as promised, and then he phoned me. I contacted my friend Mikhail and told him what had happened, and asked him to meet us at the restaurant. Anna's father Boris, Mikhail, and I went to the restaurant and showed them pictures of Ceka, and Anna. The staff recognised them, but told us they had left an hour or two before we got there. The head waiter remembered them leaving early because the lady seemed to have drunk too much wine which he thought was strange because the only bottle of wine they had ordered was still half full. The three of us left the restaurant and went straight to the hotel where Ceka was supposed to be staying, but he had already checked out and left. The receptionist had not seen him with a woman, but she remembered that he was driving a dark coloured Mercedes car. It was obvious to me that Ceka had come to Ekaterinburg to kidnap one or both girls, and the whole operation had been planned very carefully. I suggested to my friend Boris that we go to see his friends in the police and get them mobilised, although we didn't expect too much help from the local police. At the same time Mikhail, and three of his men, set off in two cars along the road that would be the most likely route for Ceka to take to the border. Unfortunately they were unable to catch up with the Mercedes before they reached the Romanian border, or maybe the Mercedes had taken a different route."

Dmitri paused and took a mouthful of his drink before continuing.

"Mikhail phoned me to tell me the bad news, and I told him that Ceka would be heading back to Tirana. In Tirana Mikhail showed Ceka's picture around a few bars in the City centre and soon found out where he lived. Mikhail and his men knocked on his front door but there was no answer, so one of the men picked the lock and they let themselves into Ceka's house. They searched the place and found enough information to suggest that Ceka was working for an Albanian man known to us as Turkish Ali. This was the worst possible news because this man is well known as a major supplier of women to the European sex trade. Mikhail decided they would wait for Ceka to arrive home, and then question him to find out who the girl had been sold to. Mikhail and his men had been waiting for a while, and were wondering if they should split up and try searching for Ceka in the bars. But just as they were about to leave, they heard the front door open, and someone stagger along the passage way towards the room they were in. Mikhail and his men took up positions around the room. Suddenly the door burst open and Enva Ceka, the man they were looking for collapsed on the floor in a drunken stupor. Mikhail and his men stripped him and tied him to a chair before pouring cold water over him until he started to wake up. Ceka thought he was a tough, hard man, but after his fingers, hands, and wrists, followed by his feet and ankles had been broken beyond repair he was happy to tell Mikhail everything he needed to know. In fact they found it difficult to stop him talking."

Jimmy leaned forward, refilled their glasses, and looked across at Mikhail.

"I'm sorry to interrupt Dmitri, but your friend Mikhail and his men seem to be able to look after themselves quite well."

Mikhail looked at Dmitri, and muttered something in Russian. Dmitri smiled briefly.

"About four years ago Mikhail learned to speak English, so he understands the language although his speech is a little rusty at the moment, but he says that all Spetznas can look after themselves."

Jimmy raised an eyebrow and smiled.

"Ah, Spetznas! That tells me everything, so I don't need to ask any more questions."

"You have heard of our Spetznas forces?" Dmitri asked.

Jimmy nodded.

"Yes. When I was younger I was in the military for nine years, during which time I spent a couple of years operating with British Special Forces, and learned enough to know what the Spetznas could do."

Dmitri translated for Mikhail, and the two Russians looked at Jimmy with something approaching respect in their eyes.

"It is good to know that you also know how to handle yourself. But now I will continue the story as we know it."

Dmitri put down his glass and looked across at Jimmy.

"Ceka, told Mikhail that he had handed Anna to a man called Turkish Ali and gave him the address where the man lived. When Mikhail asked Ceka where Anna was now, he said that all the kidnapped girls were kept in an isolated barn in a mountain forest until they were sold. However the best bit of information they acquired was that Anna was unlikely to be hurt in anyway because she is a virgin. When they had finished questioning Ceka, Mikhail who had recorded everything on audio tape, packed up the equipment and untied the now unconscious man. They didn't bother to kill Ceka because it was impossible for him to walk or use his hands ever again, so he wouldn't be kidnapping any more women."

Dimitri took a long drink of his whiskey, and then smiled at Jimmy, and said.

"Sorry to be a bit long winded Jimmy, but there isn't much more to go. The next stop for Mikhail and his men was the home of Turkish Ali, where it took them a relatively short time to capture his bodyguards before making Ali a prisoner. Then they softened him up a bit by making him watch while his bodyguards were slowly killed. When the killing was over, they told Ali to strip naked and sit on a wooden stool, and he very quickly did exactly as he had been told. Once again Mikhail set up the recording equipment and started to question the gang boss. After a few minutes Mikhail realised the man was bluffing and trying to feed them incorrect information, so one of Mikhail's men cut off the small finger of the man's left hand. This was the last time he tried to tell them lies. Unfortunately it turned out that Mikhail and his men were just too late. Anna had been sold to a German gang master who ran a gang involved in the sex trade that operated in London. The German had agreed to pay twentyfive and a half thousand US dollars for the blonde woman. When Ali told him that the girl had already left the barn in the mountains Mikhail realised that Anna was probably already on her way to the UK. After that Mikhail obtained a reasonable description of The German, but Ali couldn't tell them how Anna would be transported from the barn in the hills to the UK. Mikhail's men searched the house to see if they could find out how to get to the barn, but found nothing that gave them an indication of its location. What they did find though was $75,000 in mixed denomination bills which they packed in a shopping bag and put in their car before shooting Turkish Ali and setting fire to his house. The money will help to pay for the expenses involved in finding Anna."

"How ironic," Jimmy noted quietly and Dmitri looked at him questioningly.

"I thought it was quite ironic that Turkish Ali's money should pay for you to find Anna after his men abducted her."

Dmitri nodded.

"Yes, but that is part of the ups and downs of life. Now back to our story. When Mikhail, phoned me and told me what had happened I told him to come home and I would make the arrangements for the two of us to travel to London. Actually it was Anna's father Boris, who organised all the travel documents through his political contacts, and here we are. Boris wanted to come with us, but I managed to convince him that he was more use to us in Russia doing the things he is very good at, like handling all the political problems as well as the police."

Jimmy looked at his two visitors and shook his head slowly.

"This is very strange," he said thoughtfully. "Last weekend I was in London with two very good friends of mine and we visited one of the well known clubs for a few drinks. While I was looking around to see if I knew anyone, I noticed a blonde woman sitting with two men and another woman. I felt sure I knew the blonde woman, but the beer had fogged my brain, and it was only recently that I remembered who it was. It was Anna. I confirmed this by checking the photos that Katya sent to me. It was definitely Katya's friend. So at least we now have a starting point for our search."

Dmitri translated what Jimmy had said to Mikhail, and they both laughed.

"Jimmy I was hoping for your help, but I certainly didn't expect you to offer it so willingly. Can you take some time off work to come down to London with Mikhail and me?"

Jimmy smiled at the two men.

"Any friend of Katya is a friend of mine. Even if you were not here, I would still make it my business to find Anna, and yes, I'm sure my boss will give me a couple of weeks off. So, Dmitri, what's our next move?"

"Well, Mikhail and I have to find a place to stay for tonight, and then possibly tomorrow afternoon we could go down to London, and start asking questions."

Jimmy stood up to refresh their drinks, and told the Russians.

"I insist that you stay here. I know it's a bit cramped for three of us, but I'm sure we can all muck in for one night."

The two Russians nodded gratefully.

"Thank you Jimmy, that's a very kind offer, and we appreciate it. This arrangement will give us time to get to know each other, and discuss our plans, but first of all I have a great favour to ask you. Will you please send an email to Katya and tell her that we are here with you, and tomorrow the three of us will go to London to start our search for Anna. You could also tell her that you have seen Anna recently and she looked okay, but unfortunately you didn't recognise her straight away."

Jimmy's face broke into a big smile.

"Now that is a favour I will be very happy to do for you, but first let me show you the main bedroom, I hope you and Mikhail don't mind sharing a bed, and I'll use the single bedroom."

The three men soon sorted their sleeping arrangements out. Then Jimmy sat down at his computer, and with Dmitri and Mikhail leaning over his shoulder he sent the email to Katya. Thirty minutes later an email came back from Katya saying hello to the three men from herself and Boris. Boris was so desperate for any information that he had been waiting in Dmitri's house hoping to hear some good news. When Katya showed Boris the email, he was overwhelmed to hear that his daughter had been seen recently, and appeared to be in reasonable physical shape. Katya's message said that Boris had tears in his eyes, but he wished them all good fortune in their search for Anna. Dmitri then asked Jimmy if he could send an email to Katya, so Jimmy moved over and went to the kitchen to make some coffee, leaving Dmitri to chat to his daughter and Boris in Russian.

Later, Jimmy and Mikhail were standing in the kitchen, trying to chat using Mikhail's growing grasp of English, and Jimmy's almost long forgotten Russian, when Dmitri came in and put his hand on Jimmy's shoulder.

"Jimmy, I will be very happy if you and Katya start to email to each other again, and when all this business is over, it would give me great pleasure if you would come over to Russia and stay at my house. Boris will make all the necessary arrangements for your visa and I think he will be happy to pay for your flights as well. I'm sure Katya, would be very happy with this idea, and overjoyed to look after you and show you around our fair city. It will also give Mikhail a chance to show you around our clubs and casinos, and pick your brains for any new ideas you may have. Afterwards you can tell us how our clubs compare with similar places in the UK."

Jimmy laughed.

"Dmitri that's the best bit of news I have had for a very long time, and the thought of coming over to Russia to meet you both, and more importantly to meet Katya, fills me with happy thoughts. Thank you for your offer. Now I think we should all get some sleep, it could be a long day tomorrow."

Chapter 10

By 9.30 the next morning the three men had finished their breakfast, and their packing. Then while Mikhail washed the breakfast crockery, and Dmitri did his share by drying the dishes, Jimmy telephoned his boss to arrange for a couple of weeks off. His boss was a bit grumpy about it because of the short notice, but accepted Jimmy's assurance that his assistant could handle anything that was likely to happen, and he, Jimmy, would check in with his assistant regularly on the phone. Jimmy also spoke to Danny and Lenny to find out the name of the club they had been in when he had seen Anna. Lenny told him the name of the club and said he would phone the chief of security and tell him that Jimmy and two friends would be visiting and to ensure that they were well looked after. This help, thought Jimmy, could prove invaluable if Anna appeared in the club fairly regularly. Then Lenny handed over the telephone to Danny who gave Jimmy the address of a small hotel in Knightsbridge which he thought would make a good base for their search, and promised he would phone the hotel and arrange a good rate for them. In response to their questions Jimmy had told them that he and a couple of Russian friends were going to London to search for a Russian lady who was missing. Danny and Lenny didn't ask any further questions, instead they gave Jimmy the name of a place where weapons and ammunition could be bought with no questions asked. Then Lenny insisted they all meet up in London as soon as possible so they could help with the search. Jimmy thanked his two friends, and then called the railway station to check the times of the trains to London, and book them seats on the next train.

It was the first time that Mikhail had travelled on a train outside Russia and he was astounded at the way the station was laid out, and the size of the trains. The trains in Russia were larger than British trains, and the English stations were so neat, tidy, and well organised. He was full of questions about almost everything he saw, so Jimmy bought him a book full of coloured photographs of all the places of tourist interest in the UK, and a book about the history of British railways. Mikhail was so surprised that anyone would buy him such wonderful presents, that he stood with his mouth open when Jimmy gave him the books. He was absolutely lost for words, and Dmitri had to explain to him that people in the UK often gave books as presents to their friends. Mikhail grabbed Jimmy and gave him a huge kiss on each cheek to show how much he appreciated the gifts.

The two and a half hour journey passed quickly and easily as the three men talked over their plans, and Jimmy explained about the hotel that Danny was arranging for them. Then he told the Russians about the availability of the weapons, and about Lenny making arrangements for them to visit the club where Anna had been seen, and how he would make sure they would get help from the staff, if they knew anything. As he heard this, Dmitri looked up to the sky.

"If I was a Christian I think this is the point that I would lift up my arms and say thank you God. But like a lot of people in Russia I'm not a religious man, so I will instead say thank you to your friends Lenny and Danny, they are good men, and I look forward to meeting them soon."

Mikhail spoke to Dmitri for a couple of minutes, and then Dmitri looked over at Jimmy.

"Mikhail is in a bit of a blood thirsty mood, and would like to know what type of hand to hand fighting you where taught while you were with the military?"

Jimmy shook his head slowly.

"Your friend is certainly curious about the strangest things, from trains to killing, but I was originally trained in the same, or at least a similar way, to the Spetznas. But in recent years I have concentrated on Tai Chi, with a Grand Master who lives near me in Stockport. And for the past couple of years we have been concentrating on combining my military training into the Tai Chi with some remarkable results."

Dmitri translated everything Jimmy said, to Mikhail, who had been watching Jimmy carefully. Mikhail nodded and quietly made a comment in Russian.

Dmitri turned back to Jimmy.

"Mikhail says that he would be very interested to see this fighting style of yours in action because if it is any good he would like to find out more about it. He is always interested in new styles of combat, because it could help to keep his men from getting hurt at work."

After this, the conversation slowly petered out as the noise of the wheels and the gentle rocking of the train sent the men off to sleep. Except for Mikhail who prowled up and down the train looking at everything, and taking photographs of anything that looked remotely interesting.

The train arrived on time and the three friends made their way out of the station to a car rental office where they hired a small car suitable for driving around London streets. They quickly climbed into the car and with Jimmy driving, made their way firstly to the address where they could buy the arms, ammunition and plastic explosive that they would need. Plus detonators, highly sensitive trembler switches and fifty yards of lightweight twin cable that Mikhail wanted. With the hardware hidden in the boot of the car they made their way to the hotel in Knightsbridge that Danny had suggested. At the reception, the lady smiled at them and told them that Danny had been in touch and their rooms were now ready for them, and in response to Jimmy's request for a city centre map, she handed him a detailed map of central London. A porter showed the three men to their rooms on the first floor, and was happy with the tip that Dmitri gave him. Jimmy cast his eye around his room after the porter had left, not bad, he thought, certainly better than I expected. The large room was decorated in pastel shades of green and pink with pale green curtains over the large windows. The king-size bed looked comfortable and there was plenty of storage space for clothing and his suitcase, and behind a rather ornate door the bathroom looked impressive. Although he had to laugh to himself when he saw the size of the shower head, it looked big enough to put down a spread of water that could drown an unsuspecting guest. Just as Jimmy finished unpacking his suitcase he heard a knock at the door, and in response to his call, the two Russians walked in.

"Sorry to bother you Jimmy," said Dmitri, "but we thought it wise to have a discussion about how we should approach our visit to this club tonight. Do you have any ideas on this subject?"

Jimmy's eyes sparkled as he grinned at his friends.

"Well I think we will learn more useful information if we go in quietly and ask a few discrete questions rather than if we go in and shoot the place up. Frightened crowds tend to allow the bad guys to escape quite easily, and we don't want that to happen, do we? Besides I'm sure we'll have plenty of occasions later when we can play at being soldiers, and shoot people."

Mikhail laughed and made a comment in Russian to Dmitri, who smiled and said.

"Mikhail is sure that you served in the Russian Spetznas, and he is happy to be here with you and me. But all joking aside, I agree with you. We need to find out who knows where these women are being kept prisoner and then make sure that no one reveals who we are, and what we are doing here. So Jimmy, I suggest that you go into the club on your own to scout around and see what you can find out. Mikhail and I will go in together and make out that we are just a couple of drunken Russian business men looking for some female company for the night. After an hour or two we can meet up and check out what progress, if any, is being made. But there is one very important factor that we must remember. If we find a few of these girls and release them, they will all probably refuse to go home because they think they have disgraced their family name. So we have to find a place where they can stay here in London while they sort themselves out. If you know of anyone who could be helpful to these girls, it could be a great help because it will take the responsibility from us. Please try to remember if you have a suitable contact Jimmy, and maybe we can talk about this later."

Jimmy looked thoughtful for a minute before he answered.

"Yes that shouldn't be too much of a problem, there are a number of places that cater for women in trouble. These places offer them a secure refuge and any legal help they may need, plus they also have people who speak many languages so the girls can talk to them. But there is one other thing that could be a problem after we free Anna from the clutches of these bastards. How do you propose to get her back to Russia? She will need her passport, or else the airlines will refuse to let her get on board the plane."

Dmitri chuckled, and said

"That's not a problem Jimmy, but thanks for considering all the different aspects to this problem. I have two passports hidden in my case, ready for her to use after we find her, and Boris has made sure that all the correct stamps are in both. One of the passports is Anna's own official one, but just in case something goes wrong and the authorities are looking for us, the three of us have a second passport made out in a different name. Hopefully this will be enough to get us back into Russia. So what we need now is information."

Jimmy and Mikhail nodded their agreement and the three men got themselves ready for their night out. When they were dressed and ready Jimmy suggested they take a taxi to the club instead of the hire car which would probably take time to park, and the taxi would make them more mobile. He also reminded them that the police were always on the look out for drivers who had consumed alcohol or drugs, and they couldn't afford to have any problems with the police, especially with all the guns and ammunition in the boot of the hire car. The two Russians agreed, and Jimmy asked the hotel receptionist to order a taxi for them.

Chapter 11

Slowly Anna came down from the heroin high until she hit the emotional and physical low, and felt as though she might be dying. She felt so depressed and ill she was convinced she should be in hospital because almost every part of her body, but mostly her insides, felt as though they were in sickening pain. All her organs felt as though some terrible disease was slowly eating its way through them. Reluctantly she tried to concentrate and focus her mind elsewhere, pushing the pain to the back of her mind. Her memories of being injected, and the consequent high came back to her and she found it hard to believe she had actually experienced all those unusual and incredibly wonderful feelings and emotions. Thoughts of the high she had been through made her feel a little better and started her thinking about the high in more detail. It had been so wonderfully fantastic that she couldn't think of any words that would begin to describe the sensations, and she wondered if, or how, she might experience it again. Maybe another injection would bring the high and make her feel wonderful again, and take away all the pain and suffering she was presently experiencing. Suddenly she pinched herself so hard she cried out in pain, and shook her head angrily. How could she think like this. This was surely the way an addict must think, and she had read many articles about what happened to them. Anna knew she had to avoid these thoughts at all cost if she wanted to survive and avoid becoming an addict.

The noise of the helicopter's rotor blades changed and the machine roughly touched down and bounced a couple of times before settling on the ground. It had landed on a small makeshift runway and a short distance away stood a squat turboprop aeroplane painted in a strange blue and white swirling design. Glancing out of the window of the helicopter towards the setting sun, Anna could see they had landed in what appeared to be a large, remote, grassy field. Down the centre of field a flattened area a few yards wide ran the full length of the field to form a rough runway. She could also see that the field was surrounded by trees on three sides which would make it difficult to find this place unless you knew where to look. It was a clever idea because within a week or two the flattened grass of the runway area would have grown back, so no one would ever know what it was used for. During the flight none of the men had said anything that might have given her a clue to their final destination, and she wondered how the Russian men who were trying to find and rescue her, would ever be able to find her. As soon as the helicopter was down, the blue and white painted plane started its engines, and even though it was designed to take off and land on very short runways, the pilot obviously wanted to make sure he would get full power out of the engines as soon as the plane started to roll. The side door of the helicopter was thrown open, and the men leapt out with their guns at the ready, to form a protective perimeter around them. With the door open the freezing cold air blasted in causing Anna to shiver and soon her legs soon starting to turn blue and she hoped she wouldn't have to sit there for long. The men had not expected any trouble, but with the Russians searching for them they were not about to take any chances, and were being very cautious. The German got out, stretched and yawned, then ordered the two men who were acting as his bodyguard to get Anna out, and bring her over to the plane. Quickly the men gathered around the blue and white plane, patiently waiting their turn to get on board, and talking to each other quietly. As Anna was carried onto the plane she heard one of the men say in English.

"Not long now, Fred, and we'll be back in London."
The other man grunted.

"The sooner the bloody better for me mate."
Anna lost track of the conversation as she was carried to a seat at the front of the plane and pushed into it. But at least it seemed that at last she knew where they were going, assuming she had heard the men correctly. As soon as everyone was seated, and Anna still wrapped up in the big coat and a blanket, had been strapped in so she couldn't easily move, The German ordered the pilot to take off. Immediately the noise from the engines increased to a deafening roar and the plane started to bump down the runway rapidly picking up speed.

In what seemed like an impossibly short time the pilot lifted the nose of the plane and they were airborne. Looking around, Anna couldn't see much of the interior of the plane because in front of her was the bulkhead separating the seats from the pilots cabin. Fortunately for her she had been put next to a window so at least she had something to look at. Looking out of the window also helped to take her mind of what was probably going to happen to her when they eventually reached their destination. She desperately hoped that her first real experience of sex wouldn't be as painful, and messy, as some of the girls at University had said it was. But, the big German had already told her he'd paid a lot of money for her, so she was sure this revolting man would be the first to ravage her body. The thought made her feel physically sick, but as there didn't seem to be any alternatives, she knew she'd better get used to the idea and keep her feelings to herself. If she refused to give in to The German in any way, she knew he would take considerable pleasure from inflicting great pain on her. Then, when she could no longer refuse to cooperate, he would take his pleasure, and she would have received a severe beating for nothing. He might smash her face, break her arms, and legs, or use a knife on her body. She couldn't allow this to happen if she ever wanted to physically escape from him. Escape! The thought of escaping from The German's clutches immediately filled her mind and became the focal point for her rebellious thoughts. No matter what The German did to her she was determined to escape from him and contact her father and the Russians, who were trying to find her. In her imagination she could see herself helping them to find The German, and watching while the Russians did terrible things to him. Then just before he died she was going to spit in his face. At first her callousness appalled her, but slowly she realised that if she wanted to survive until she was saved, she would have to change her attitude to life and become a very different woman. She also knew that she had to try and stay away from the heroin, because as long as she stayed away from the drugs The German might have control of her body, but he would never have control of her mind. Her father, mother, and friends would forgive her for anything that happened to her, except perhaps for the drugs. They would find it difficult to understand how she could allow herself to become addicted, and the only way she could avoid the drugs was to make The German think that she didn't need them. Carefully she envisaged, in all its gory detail, The German doing the things to her that she had discussed with her friends at University, trying to get herself mentally prepared for what was going to happen, trying to repress the sick feelings that the mere image brought upon her. Hearing the noise of the engines change and feeling the plane start to descend made Anna glance at her watch then look out of the window. She immediately started to worry, it was still early in the evening yet it was dark, but if they were landing in the U.K. it shouldn't be dark, so where were they taking her? Then she relaxed as she remembered that in Britain, during the winter, there was a time change so it got dark early. Staring out, she noticed there were very few lights to be seen, nothing to indicate where in the U.K. the plane was about to land, but it was obviously somewhere remote. So she stopped looking, and wondered what would happen next.

The plane touched down and slowly came to a halt next to a squat single story building with a small tower at one end, and a car park at the other. When the plane stopped the two men seated next to the door stood up. One of them opened the main door while the other operated the automatic steps, then the rest of the men picked up their bags and followed each other off the plane. Close to where the plane had stopped stood four Range Rover vehicles with their drivers, standing waiting for them. The men from the plane tossed their equipment into the back of three of the vehicles then climbed in and made themselves comfortable. The leading Range Rover was clearly left for The German and Anna to travel in. Anna noticed that everyone moved in a swift and coordinated way that suggested they had done this many times before, and within a few minutes the Range Rovers moved off in convoy.

During the next couple of hours they passed the odd farm house, but mostly they were driving through fields and trees, until they suddenly turned onto a wide dual carriageway, and Anna saw an overhead sign pointing towards London. Once they were on the motorway, The German told Anna to take the blanket off her shoulders and throw it in the space behind the seats, and then undo the overcoat she had on, and open it. When everything was to his satisfaction he put his arm around her shoulders, and shifted his backside forward to the edge of the seat. Then he pointed to his crotch and ordered Anna to unzip his trousers, and continue with what she had started just before they left the old barn building in Albania. Anna's heart sank, but she mentally kicked herself and remembered how she had promised herself to be strong, no matter what she was forced to do. The pain or the drugs, or the sex act! None were options that she really wanted to consider, but she knew what she had to do and reached for The German's zip. Quickly she pulled it down, hoping that it might catch his flesh in the teeth of the zip. The thought made her smile, that would certainly take The German's mind off sex for a while. Unfortunately it didn't happen, so Anna tried to remember what her girlfriends had said the girl was supposed to do during oral sex. She forced herself to put her hand inside his trousers, expecting to easily find his penis. But then she started to panic because she couldn't find it, and he was starting to get impatient. Then she realised that it must be caught in his underwear and shirt, so she started to try and work her way through the layers of material. A few minutes passed before her searching fingers found a small gap and touched the bare flesh of his stomach. But this was all far too slow for The German, and in frustration he pushed her hand out of the way so he could reach in and pull his penis out. Anna was surprised with her first view of this supposedly wonderful piece of male flesh. After all the stories she had heard about how it could make a woman feel incredibly excited, she expected it to be a bit bigger and more interesting somehow. But looking down on the pitiful flaccid little thing she felt the fear of her first encounter with it begin to disappear, to be replaced with a feeling of disdain and disgust. Reaching over she held the flaccid penis between her thumb and first finger. As she did this, The German put his hand at the back of her head and forced her face into his lap, and growled.

"Make sure I don't feel your teeth on my skin."
Oh God she thought, as her lips came into contact with The German's penis, please help me not to be sick all over this revolting man. God or fate, or something else must have been listening to her plea because before The German could become more aroused, Anna heard the driver announce that they were approaching The German's house. The German swore and stamped his feet in frustration, and grabbing Anna by the hair he roughly hauled her head up and pushed her away from him before zipping his trousers up. Anna's first thought was oh thank you God, but she knew that very soon The German would have his opportunity and then there would be nothing to stop him raping and abusing her in any way he wanted.

Chapter 12

The taxi ordered by the hotel arrived and Dmitri, Mikhail and Jimmy climbed in for the short drive to the nightclub. When it pulled up outside the club, Jimmy climbed out, leaving Dmitri and Mikhail to be driven to the end of the queue. One of the security men at the entrance recognised Jimmy, and took him through to the bar area and suggested he make himself known to the manager. Swampy, the manager, arrived from somewhere near the dance floor and greeted Jimmy warmly.

"Hello and good evening Jimmy, it's good to see you again. Of course we're always happy to see friends of Danny and Lenny, and I remember you from your last visit and I've reserved a table for you in a corner and set back from the dance floor. From this table you can see almost everything that is going on but because of the shadows no one will be able to see you very well. This is what Lenny thought you would like. Is it okay for you?"

Jimmy shook hands with Swampy, and showed him a photograph of Anna.

"Thanks Swampy, those two scallywags read too many spy novels, but yes that table will be great. Actually I'm looking for this pretty blonde who I saw the last time I was here with Danny and Lenny. She was with another girl and two guys who looked like business men on expense accounts. I don't suppose you can remember seeing her around can you?"

Swampy looked at the photograph for a minute his face screwed up in concentration, and slowly shaking his head, but then he smiled and handed back the picture.

"Yes, now I remember her. She's been in here a couple of times with different boyfriends but I haven't seen her for the past week or two. So I'm afraid I can't be of much help to you, and I can't help if you want to meet her because I don't have an address or phone number for her. But I'll have a word with the staff, and if anyone knows anything I'll send them over to speak with you."

Jimmy put his arm around Swampy's shoulder.

"You're a grand fella', and I'd much appreciate any information that might help me find this lady."

At that moment, one of Swampy's assistants came over and brought his attention to something that was happening on the other side of the dance floor.

"Sorry about this Jimmy, something has come up that I need to sort out. But I'll try and catch up with you later in the evening."

"No problem Swampy, and thanks for your help, I really appreciate it. See you later."

With a quick wave, Swampy rushed off in response to some urgent signalling from one of the waitresses.

Jimmy made his way to the table that had been reserved for him and his two Russian friends, and settled into a comfortable seat. As he sat down the music started again, it was a pounding rhythm that made it difficult to think, never mind talk. Jeez he thought to himself I'll never be able to understand how the people who come here three or four times every week never seem to suffer from damaged hearing. A couple of minutes later a waitress came to take his order, and after a few shouted words about the type of wine available, he asked her for a large carafe of cold water and a bottle of Australian Shiraz wine. The water was for drinking, and the wine more for show. As much as he liked red wine he didn't want to take the chance of drinking too much alcohol in case it slowed his reactions down.

When the waitress returned and put the wine and water on the table, Jimmy, showed her the picture of Anna, and by putting his mouth next to her ear, asked if she recognised the blonde in the photo. She looked at the photograph carefully for a minute then looked at Jimmy, before putting her mouth next to his ear and telling him.

"Yes, I think I've seen her in here before. I'm not one hundred percent certain about this, but I think she usually comes in with a dark haired girl, and with different men who always seem happy to spend lots of money on them. I haven't seen this girl lately, but the dark haired girl who is usually with her, is sat with a man on the other side of the dance floor. She is wearing a green dress with a black shawl over her shoulders, but she doesn't look very well, and I'm surprised she is out drinking."

Jimmy slipped the girl a five pound note, and was rewarded with a big smile.

"Thanks very much," he said, "you've been very helpful."

Jimmy relaxed and sipped his glass of water, as he tried to see who was sat on the opposite side of the dance floor, but because of the pulsing lights over the dance floor he couldn't see very much so he just watched the women dancing. After five minutes of glamour watching he decided it was time for him to take a walk around the club to see if he could spot Anna's dark haired friend. His first thought was she would be able to tell them where Anna was being kept, but then he remembered that she might be a drug addict, so anything she said could be very unreliable. In view of this he decided that talking to her would not be a good idea because she might go and tell her pimp that some people were looking for Anna, hoping he would reward her with an extra drug fix. Instead Jimmy took a walk around the club to check out who was hanging around and not joining the fun, because amongst these people would almost certainly be the pimp. The quickest way of obtaining the information that he and the two Russians needed would be to take the pimp to a quiet place, and make him talk. Jimmy was certain that he could make the man, whoever he was, give them the information that would lead them to Anna. But from experience

The Internet Girls

Jimmy knew that information gained in this way could often be untrue because some people were more afraid of what would happen if they gave information away than the pain being inflicted upon them, and this could easily be the case with the pimp.

During his casual stroll around the club, Jimmy spotted the women who the waitress thought she'd seen with Anna. He carefully checked her out and was fairly sure she was the woman he'd seen with Anna. She was sitting with a plump well dressed middle-aged man, and neither of them looked very happy. The waitress was right, the women looked quite ill, her nose was red and she sneezed and coughed occasionally into the handkerchief she held to her nose. She looked forlorn sitting slumped in her chair staring with glazed eyes at the drink in front of her, obviously wishing she could be in bed, instead of the nightclub. The man with her didn't look as though he was enjoying himself either, and spent most of the time watching the people on the dance floor, Jimmy felt sorry for both of them. After carefully looking around, Jimmy felt sure he had pinpointed the pimp. He was a big well muscled man dressed in a dark suit that appeared expensive even though it didn't seem to fit him properly, and a black T shirt, but he looked as though he knew how to take care of himself. His ensemble was finished off with a heavy gold necklace round his throat, and matching chunky gold bracelet on his wrist. The necklace and bracelet seemed out of place against the man's hard looking, pock-marked face, and his ill fitting suit. I hope he's the pimp, thought Jimmy, as he headed back to his table. He looks like he might be a tough nut to crack, but I bet if we put our minds to the job, Mikhail, and I, will have him broken in a very short space of time. Walking casually back to his table, Jimmy noticed the man he thought was the pimp talking seriously to a male face that he hadn't noticed before. The new face belonged to a very thin looking man, dressed in what appeared to be a very expensive shirt and casual trousers, and Jimmy thought, I'd like to know what those two are talking about. Then a face he immediately recognised joined the two men and started talking to them. It was Dmitri, with a big smile on his face, and he was chatting away with the pimp and the thin faced man as though he didn't have a care in the world. The conversation between the three men continued for a few minutes, and then Dmitri patted both men on the shoulder and walked away.

Back at the table Jimmy relaxed and poured himself a small glass of wine while he waited for his Russian friends to join him. There was still no sign of Mikhail, when Dmitri sat down next to Jimmy, but a waitress appeared as if by magic and handed Dmitri, a large glass of clear liquid that Jimmy doubted was water. After taking a mouthful of his drink, Dmitri chuckled.

"You look as if you have lost a five pound note and found a kopeck!" Jimmy laughed.

"You're right, but it's because I'm waiting for you to tell me what you were talking about with that hard faced pimp, and his insipid looking friend, and more importantly where the hell is Mikhail?"

Dmitri, tried to look surprised and hurt, but his big smile made it impossible.

"Jimmy, you are full of curiosity, like the cat. I only hope you have the same number of lives as our feline friends are supposed to have, and I will be happy to tell you what Mikhail, and I have been doing as soon as he arrives back here. Then I will not have to explain everything twice. Afterwards we can discuss our next move. It takes Mikhail a bit longer to talk to people because his English is not fluent, so I find it quicker if I explain things to him in Russian. That way it means we have no misunderstandings."

Jimmy nodded and shrugged his shoulders, and the two men sat back and sipped their drinks in companionable silence while they waited for Mikhail.

It seemed a long time before they saw Mikhail making his way towards the table, but it was probably only five minutes. Of course he was easy to spot standing head and shoulders above everyone else on or around the dance floor. When he saw them watching him, his sombre look brightened up, so that when he sat down he actually had a smile on his face, and spoke in

Russian to Dmitri, after asking Jimmy, in broken English to excuse him for speaking Russian.

"Dmitri, the first thing is, I like this club and all these gorgeous, half dressed, women who are obviously enjoying themselves. When we get home I have a few ideas that I think could go very well in one or two of our better quality clubs, but for the moment I will forget about these things and concentrate on finding Anna. When I spoke to a couple of the security men, they told me there are only four or five big time pimps who use this club because it is too upmarket for the rest of them. But the one with the biggest reputation is the man I saw you talking to earlier, the one with the gold necklace. No one knows how many women he and his friends control but it could be as many as a hundred, all under the age of 25. Everyone I've spoken to thinks they have been brought in from the old Russian states, mainly by the Albanians. They force all the women onto drugs until they are addicted so they can be controlled easily, and because the women are all good looking, they are forced to service as many as ten men a day. In return the girls are fed, given good clothes to wear, a bed to sleep in, and supplied with free drugs. So as you can tell, there is a huge amount of money in this trade, and the Albanians will not give it up easily. The pimp over there keeps the girls housed in a number of cheap, run down houses, and I think it's possible that Anna is under his control. When I asked the security men what would be the best way to get the pimp out of here without causing any trouble, they laughed and said it would be best to knock him out when he goes to the lavatory then carry him out saying he had drunk himself unconscious. If we wait until he goes outside at the end of the night, there will be so many people hanging around it will be impossible for us to do anything to him without someone seeing what is going on. So what do we think about this?"

Dmitri had translated everything that Mikhail had said, and Jimmy responded.

"That's very interesting, because I showed the photograph of Anna to the waitress, and she recognised her. She also described the woman who is normally with Anna when she comes in here, and told me she is sitting at a table on the other side of the dance floor. So I went over to have a look, and I am fairly sure it is the same person that was with Anna on the night that I saw her. Then I had a good look at everyone standing around, and came to the conclusion that the guy with the gold necklace is her pimp. If he is the pimp, then if we can get him to a nice quiet place, I'm sure we can encourage him to tell us where Anna is being held, as well as everything else he knows. So I agree. We should wait until he goes to the lavatory, and make him go to sleep, then, as the security man suggested, we carry him outside like a drunk. Do we agree on this?"

Dmitri, nodded his head as he finished translating what Jimmy had said, and added.

"You two are such a bloodthirsty pair. All you want to do is grab this fellow who might be quite innocent and beat the crap out of him. However, I agree we have to knock him out and carry him outside, but I think the threat of using an electric drill to put holes in his knee caps will be all it'll take to make him talk. Anyway, the thing we have to do now is watch him until he goes to the toilet, and follow him in. But now let me tell you what I was doing while you two were planning world war three. I spoke to one of the security men and asked him if there were any prostitutes in the club. He said that they were not allowed in the club to do business. The only single ladies allowed into the club are the high class escort girls and they can only come into the club if they were already fixed up with a customer. However, he told me that if a lady came into the club with a client, the pimp would also be in the club to keep an eye on her. Then the security man pointed to the fellow with the gold necklace, and said he was a pimp and might be able to fix me up with a girl, if the price was right. To make sure I got the right guy, the security man took me over to where the pimp was standing. I introduced myself to him, and asked if he had any girls available. He told me there were no girls available tonight because a lot of them had caught flu and had to stay at home in bed for a few days, but next week everything should be back to normal. The pimp also told the same story to the little thin guy who came over and asked the same question. So I agree with you both, he could be Anna's pimp and even if he isn't, he will surely know where she is, so we should follow him into the toilet and put him to sleep."

The three men raised their glasses in a toast to each other, then turned so they could watch the toilet area and the pimp.

They had to wait a frustrating thirty minutes before the pimp headed off to the toilet. As soon as he started to move, Jimmy, who was much closer to the toilets was off like a shot to get there before him. Dmitri and Mikhail then timed their move to arrive immediately after the pimp. The trap was set. Fortunately there was nobody using the toilet at that moment, so Jimmy stood at the end of the row of urinals waiting for the pimp to come through the door. Then making as though he had just finished, Jimmy walked towards the man and smiled, then raising his left hand to stroke the top of his head. As soon as the man's eyes followed the movement, the knuckles of Jimmy's right fist slammed into the side of the pimp's jaw, just under his left ear. The blow was not hard enough to kill the man, but it was certainly hard enough to knock him out for at least fifteen minutes. As the blow landed, Dmitri and Mikhail came through the door and caught the pimp before he could collapse on the floor. Mikhail, quickly searched him, removing a 9mm semi-automatic pistol, a large vicious looking knife, a heavy brass knuckle duster, and the man's wallet before smiling and giving the circled thumb and first finger sign, meaning everything was okay. Jimmy and Dmitri, who were a similar height, took an arm each around their shoulders and carried the unconscious pimp towards the main entrance, while Mikhail walked in front to clear a way through the crowds. As they approached the main door, Swampy appeared as if by magic, with a big smile on his face.

"Hi, guys, it's very kind of you to help our security team by taking this drunken bum outside. If he wasn't associated with a bunch of nasty gangsters, I wouldn't allow him in the place, but it's a case of either allowing him in, or have them tear my club to pieces. So I take the easy option. But if you find yourselves on top of a very tall building with this bastard, I'd be very happy if he accidentally slipped off the roof." Jimmy and the two Russians were still laughing at Swampy's remark as they went out through the main door onto the main road to look for a taxi. They hadn't been standing for more than a minute when a black cab stopped to pick them up. Jimmy asked the driver to take them somewhere quiet, and not over looked, so their drunken friend could sleep it off without frightening anyone. The driver laughed, and a short while later dropped them off near an allotment full of flower and vegetable patches surrounded by a thick hedge. The nearest houses were maybe sixty yards away and the place seemed ideal for what they had in mind. Jimmy and Dmitri, carried the unconscious man through a gate in the hedge until they were well out of sight of the road and dumped him on the ground near a cold water standpipe that had a hosepipe attached. Jimmy uncoiled the hosepipe, tucked the end inside the pimps black T shirt, then switched on the water. The two Russians watched Jimmy, and grinned when they saw the cold water gushing all over the man.

"I bet it wont take very long for him to wake up now," said Dmitri,

"either that or he'll end up with bloody pneumonia, and die on us."
The laughter of the three men was cut short when they heard the pimp groan. Jimmy turned off the water, then Dmitri lifted him into a sitting position and slapped his face a few times causing the man to groan and start coughing up some of the water that had got into his mouth. Slowly he looked up at the three men standing around him, and mumbled.

"What the fuck's the meaning of this? Who are you, and why are you doing this to me?"
His accent made it difficult to understand what he was saying, but it was the violent shivering from the cold water that made him almost incomprehensible. Dmitri looked at Jimmy and Mikhail, then nodded. The two men lifted the pimp to his feet, and held him till he could stand. Mikhail towered over him in a threatening manner, watching him like a hawk while he stood shivering and shaking. The slightest wrong move by

the pimp would have resulted in Mikhail's huge fist slamming into some vulnerable part of his body. At the same time Jimmy moved slightly to the side and turned towards the pimp, slowly sizing the man up, like an undertaker working out what size coffin was required. Suddenly Jimmy's mind was filled with the scene of a jungle clearing, with a man tethered by his wrists to an overhead branch. The man was looking at Jimmy with pure hatred in his eyes, challenging him to do his worst, because he felt sure there was no way Jimmy would be able to make him talk. On that occasion it had taken Jimmy fifteen minutes to inflict sufficient pain on the man's body to make him talk. The pain was developed through striking, or grinding his knuckles into the various nerve centres and pressure points and was meant to incapacitate rather than kill. Jimmy shook his head slightly and the gruesome scene faded from his mind. His arm shot out and he drove his pointed knuckles into the first nerve centre. The pimp gasped as his arm became numb and almost completely paralysed, but then he gritted his teeth and looked at Jimmy with a smile on his lips. But Jimmy had already seen the tears momentarily flood the pimps eyes. Once again his arm shot out and his knuckles crashed into another nerve centre. This time the pimp cried out in agony before forcing himself to stand upright, but he was finding it difficult to remain standing because his body was starting to shake. With Jimmy's next strike the pimp's knees folded and he collapsed, panting and gulping like a fish out of water, onto the wet grass moaning.

"What the fuckin' hell d'yu bastards want with me?"
He gasped, his face etched in pain, as he struggled to try and get to his knees. Dmitri stepped forward and crouched down in front of the pimp so they were almost face to face. Then pulling out a photograph of Anna, he held it in front of the pimp, and snarled.

"Tell me where you have this women hidden, and I will ask my friend to stop hurting you, but if you don't talk to me I'll ask my friend to increase the level of pain. Now where is this women?"

"I don't know this girl, I've never seen her before, so I can't help you." Jimmy's right hand shot out, and the pimp opened his mouth to scream, but Mikhail clamped his hand over the man's mouth, muffling the scream.

This time the pimp slumped to the ground and was unable to do anything but lie shaking, and moaning, face down on the grass. Dmitri waited for a full minute before nodding to Mikhail, who gripped the pimps hair and pulled his head up so Dmitri could push the picture of Anna back into the pimps face.

"Look at this woman's face and tell me where she is. This is the last chance I will give you. If you do not tell me what I want to know, my friend will continue to hurt you until you pass out. Then, when you wake up he will start creating pain all through your body. So it would be much more sensible for you to tell me what I want to know."

Shaking with pain the man looked up at Dmitri and nodded.

"Okay, okay, I'll tell you what you want to know, but tell him," he said pointing to Jimmy, "to stay away from me."

Then he struggled into a sitting position and gave Dmitri an address where he said all his working girls lived. He also told Dmitri that there was always at least four gang members living at this address, and they all had rooms on different floors so it was unlikely they could be taken by surprise. If the women they were looking for wasn't at the address, they would have to question the guards to find out where she had been sent. Dmitri, smiled briefly when he heard this, it might be another good step forward in their search for Anna. But Dmitri also suspected the pimp was lying because he knew the women the pimp controlled lived in more than one house, and was probably hoping to warn his friends so they could shoot Jimmy, Mikhail and himself. Then Dmitri asked Jimmy if he could find his way back to their hire car, and how long would it take to collect the car and come back to pick them up? Jimmy grinned and told Dmitri it would take him less than an hour, because he was in the mood for some fast walking. Then with a brief wave he left his friends to carry on questioning the pimp.

Less than an hour later Jimmy arrived back with the hire car to find the two Russians had tied the pimp's hands behind his back and shackled his legs together, leaving just enough slack between his ankles so he could walk, taking short paces. Dmitri and Mikhail, saw Jimmy approaching and waved. When Jimmy joined them, Dmitri led them away from the pimp, and quietly told Jimmy that he wasn't convinced the pimp, whose name was Tony, had told them the truth, so they should take him along with them. Then if they found he had lied they could give him a taste of real pain. Jimmy nodded his agreement, and the three men hoisted the pimp to his feet and forced him into the back of the car.

Chapter 13

The Range Rover carrying Anna and The German turned off the main road through a pair of tall black wrought iron gates and along a gravelled drive before stopping outside a large detached house. The house was surrounded by trees, large well kept gardens and a high wall which gave it almost total privacy from the nearest houses and the main road. The driver got out and opened the car door for The German, then went round to the back and lifted the luggage out, placing it next to the front door of the house. The German got out of the vehicle and then reached back, grabbed the collar of Anna's quilted overcoat and callously dragged her out of the vehicle. The force of being dragged out of the car caused Anna to stumble and fall taking the skin off her hands and knees, then before she could orientate herself and get back to her feet, The German kicked her painfully in the backside.

"Get up you stupid cow," he growled at her, "and stop making a fool of yourself in front of my neighbours. Get up and stand by that door there."

The driver started to help Anna get to her feet, but The German snarled at him.

"Get your hands off her! Just because you have only been on the payroll for a couple of days, is no excuse for interfering with my fun. What's your name?"

"Trevor, boss."

"Okay Trevor, take the car back to the garage and take the night off." Anna smiled gratefully at the driver as he closed the doors of the Range Rover, and drove away. It was the first time anyone had shown any sympathy or kindness towards her since Ceka had drugged her in Ekaterinburg, and it meant a lot to her.

The German opened the front door of his house, and gestured for Anna to go ahead of him, then he followed her in with his bag, and slammed the front door shut. To Anna, the noise sounded like the closing of a cell door, and she knew that until she was found and rescued, this disgusting German now owned her body, and ruled every aspect of her life. Her shoulders slumped, and her head dropped as she waited for what she was certain was going to happen, then he forced her forward with a punch in the kidneys.

"Go on, you stupid useless cow, get up the stairs until I tell you to stop."

Then as if to emphasize his words The German pushed her again. Anna stumbled over the first steps, and received a hard painful slap across the back of her head and she quickly ascended two flights of stairs before she was told to stop. The German opened a door and switched on the light then gestured for her to go into the room. Inside she looked around, and was surprised to find that the room was clean, and nicely decorated. The double bed in the middle of the room looked comfortable and clean. The floral patterned duvet cover had matching pillows and there were even matching curtains on the windows. In some ways it reminded Anna of her own bedroom, and before she could stop herself she sat on the edge of the bed and started crying. The German snorted in disgust and walked out of the room after telling her to get herself sorted out because he would be back later. As soon as she was alone, Anna slowly dried her tears and wandered across the room to look out of the window only to find that the glass was opaque so she couldn't see anything outside. She turned as she heard The German come back into the room. He was carrying a tray, and she looked at him questioningly, but he ignored her, and instead handed her a bubble pack of pills.

"Follow the instructions on the packet, and take one of these tablets at the same time every day," he told her, "if you stop taking them you could become pregnant, and you will not like what happens to you if you do."

Then he handed her a box that had the word Durex Gossamer written across it and Anna wondered what was inside. But as soon as she heard his next words she knew.

"Every time a man wants to have sex with you, you must make him wear one of these. If you follow this simple rule it will help to keep you alive, and safe from sexual diseases. Do you understand? There is also something for you to eat and drink, I'll be back when you're finished."

Anna nodded her understanding as The German stood watching her, but her mind was in a whirl as once again it was driven home to her exactly what her future was to be. She shivered briefly, then thought about Enva Ceka, the man who was the cause of all her problems, and fervently hoped the Russians who were searching for her had caught him then tortured him very slowly and painfully. If the Russians hadn't already killed him, she promised herself that one day she would find him and take a knife to his body. The thoughts of what she would do to him made her feel better, then once again she focused on The German. He was pointing to a door, and telling her to get showered and cleaned up and then to put on one of the dressing gowns, and select some of the clean clothes that fitted her which were in the wardrobes and chest of drawers. Then he put his hand under her chin and looked into her eyes, and she heard the words that she had been dreading.

"I have a phone call to make but I'll be back later and then I'll teach you all the things you'll need to know about sex, especially about how to please a man."

With that he patted her bottom and walked out of the room. When the door closed Anna lifted the cover off the plate on the tray and saw bacon, eggs, mushrooms and beans, and her stomach growled as she realised how hungry she was. There was also a plate of toast with butter and marmalade on the side, and her hunger took charge, she picked up a slice of bacon in her fingers and started eating.

After clearing every item of food on the tray she sat back on the bed and belched. The belch surprised her and she suddenly giggled as she thought of what her mother would have said if she had been in the room. Feeling a lot better after the food, she walked into the bathroom and decided to shower away the travel fatigue and grime under the hot water. The shower made her feel better, but what made it feel really good was the realization that this was the first time she had been left on her own without being chained or tied up, and that small freedom made her feel wonderful. Standing in the steam and covered with soap bubbles Anna relaxed and tried to forget about what had happened to her, and the changes forced upon her by that swine Enva Ceka. With a surge of anger she hoped he would die screaming in agony and rot in hell for what he had done. Half an hour later Anna's ordeal began. The German walked into her bedroom dressed only in a black bathrobe and carrying a bottle of lubrication and a black vibrator shaped like a penis which he placed next to the bed before ordering her to strip naked. As soon as her dressing gown lay in a heap on the floor The German threw off his bathrobe and laid himself on the bed, beckoning her to join him. At long last, he thought, I am going to experience oral sex with her, and for once there will not be any interruptions. This time it was obvious to Anna that even though his penis was not very big it was erect and The German was now very aroused.

"Come on, come on," he shouted impatiently at her, "you know what I want you to do, so get yourself on this bed and start earning your keep. If you don't hurry up I'll tie you down and inject you with heroin. That'll soon get you started, and then you will enjoy it as much as me." Anna heard the dreaded word heroin, and climbed onto the bed and reached out to wrap two fingers around his penis. Her mind seemed to have crept away into a small space somewhere at the back of her brain, a space where the sun was shining down on green grass and flowers, with a small stream that tinkled and burbled over little white stones. In this special place no one could reach her or hurt her, and no matter what her body did, it didn't register in that special place.

Nearly three excruciating hours passed before The German rolled his fat, sweat soaked body off the bed and pulled on his bathrobe. He was exhausted, but very disappointed with the sex because Anna had not been active, and she hadn't given any indication that she'd enjoyed any part of it. In fact, apart from screaming in pain, she had just laid on the bed totally submissive and unmoving no matter what he did to her. Even when he had forced the vibrator into her anus for the first time, Anna had just desperately tried to relax her muscles even though she was in agony. Even the oral sex had been a disaster, he'd had to masturbate himself so he could ejaculate into her mouth. Because of this The German had already started to wonder who would pay the best price for Anna. Then he shouted at her.

"Get under the shower you dirty bitch and clean yourself up, then change the sheets, there is some clean bedding on the top shelf of the wardrobe, and don't forget to open the window and let some fresh clean air in. I might be back for some more fun in a few hours, and this time use the enema pack that's hanging in the shower cubicle so we wont end up getting covered in shit again."

Anna lay unmoving on the bed with pain ripping through her belly. She was totally past any feelings of embarrassment from his words. Her vagina felt as though it had been ripped apart, and the terrible burning pain in her anus felt as though a large piece of red hot metal had been inserted into her. Her breasts had been bitten, slapped and roughly squeezed, and now showed bright red finger marks and the bruises could be clearly seen. Her mouth felt as though her jaws had been forced apart, and tasted and smelt as though something horrible had died in there. She wanted to scream with the pain that seemed, to emanate from every fibre of her abused body. But somehow she managed to choke back her cries of pain, determined that The German wouldn't know how much he'd hurt her. Finally, after he'd left the room, the tears of pain and self pity rolled down her face as she lay on the bed and sobbed, but the tears were short lived as the realisation that she was on her own washed over her. Slowly Anna relaxed and started to enjoy the wonderful feeling of relief that flowed through her as she realised her ordeal was over for the time being.

After The German had left, Anna roused herself and climbed slowly and gingerly off the bed trying to avoid causing herself more pain. The feelings of self pity and fear of the unknown had left her, and once again her fighting spirit started to surface as she realised there really wasn't much more The German could do to her that he hadn't already done. Then she saw the mess covering a large area in the middle of the bed and was both shocked and embarrassed. In a large wet patch in the middle of the sheet was a mix of blood, semen, faeces, urine and used condoms all mixed together. With a shudder she thought Oh God, has all that come from me? Then she turned and opened the window to help clear the smell from the room, but found it would only open about six inches at the top, just enough for her to see the metal bars that ran from the top to the bottom of the window. Well, she thought, that's one way of escape I wont be able to use. Then she pulled the soiled sheets off the bed and rolled them into a ball and without thinking walked to the door intending to put the soiled sheets outside the room. She turned the handle and the door was fully open before the realisation hit her that she hadn't been locked in. Was this the opportunity to escape, she wondered as she looked out through the doorway. Do I have time to get myself cleaned up and dressed before The German reappears, and if there is time will I be able to get down the stairs and out of the front door? She didn't need to answer that question because she knew she had to try. But she also knew the price of failure if she was caught, The German would certainly cause her terrible physical pain, and he would also make sure she became heavily addicted to heroin or some other drug so he could control her. But even knowing this she dropped the dirty sheets in the hallway and crept across to the top of the stairs. Quickly she poked her head round the corner of the stairs to see if there was anyone around, but that brief glance told her she couldn't escape that way. Standing near the bottom of the stairs were two guards talking quietly.

Both guards were armed and although they appeared relaxed they seemed to be quite alert. This surprised her until she remembered The German and his criminals knew there were some Russian men searching for her.

Slowly and quietly she made her way back to her bedroom and closed the door. Although she was disappointed that she hadn't been able to take advantage of her first opportunity to escape, she found it had somehow strengthened her resolve. Maybe the mistake was caused by The Germans fear of retribution by the Russians who were on his trail. This was a thought that gave her great pleasure and she relished the idea of The German being badly beaten and slowly killed. She may not have been able to do anything about his mistake this time, but she was going to be ready for the next time. She was certain in her mind there would be a next time, and perhaps the possibility of another chance to escape. With this thought in her mind she walked into the bathroom and switched on the shower. Standing under the hot water she let it wash away the stains on her skin left by the rape and abuse, soothing her torn, scratched and bruised skin. As Anna stood with her head bowed under the flow of water, she decided that one day she would have her revenge on The German. She could feel the rage and anger building up inside as she thought about her revenge, and decided the first thing would be for her to find a knife and slowly castrate him. The second thing would be for her to force something large into his rectum, preferably something that she could heat until it was very hot, and leave him to bleed to death in agony. It was, she decided, an excellent form of punishment for the man she now hated with every fibre of her being. With these thoughts in her mind she slowly prepared herself for what was going to happen in a couple of hours time by using the enema pack and putting lots of lubricant around, and inside, the painful areas.

Then Anna lay on the bed waiting and worrying, but instead of The German it was one of the guards who knocked on her door and walked into the room.

"Hi, I'm Trevor, please get yourself packed and ready to leave in about half an hour, I've been told to take you to your new home. You will live with some of the other girls and meet the man who will be responsible for you. No matter what he says to you, you must do exactly as he tells you. Now, take whatever clothes you need from the wardrobe, and if you need more clothes or any other stuff tell your new manager when you get to the new house and he will arrange it. Okay? I'll be back shortly."

Anna nodded and Trevor left the room. With a sigh she started to put the clothes in a plastic shopping bag she'd found in the wardrobe. Anything that looked as though it might fit her went into the bag plus some things that just looked warm. Then she sat on the bed and waited for whatever was going to happen next. The German obviously didn't want to have sex with her again and had decided to make her earn some money for him. What, she wondered, would this man who is now responsible for her going to be like. Would he be a sadistic bully like The German, or would he be more like a normal person. I guess I'll soon find out, she thought.

At that moment The German was talking to a Chinese man and trying to negotiate a lower price for the purchase of 20 or 30 Chinese women who would be brought into the country by sea in a large metal container. With the price agreed The German decided it was going to be more economical to deal with the Chinese gangsters in the future. The price of the orientals was around 25% cheaper than buying from the Albanians. It also meant that not only would they be delivered to him in good condition and ready to go to work they would also be delivered with a regular supply of good quality drugs. The German, like a lot of western men, often fantasised about having sex with petite nubile and willing Orientals and was sure they would make a lot of money for him. So he phoned his friend Nino about doing a deal with the Chinese and the two men agreed to work together. Nino had an empty warehouse that he was willing to fit out so all the new women could be accommodated securely. To the German and Nino it seemed like a licence to print their own money, and both men agreed that bringing in the women in containers was much safer than bringing them into the country inside trucks. The thought of all the money they would make made both men happy and their conversation turned to the night they had tortured and killed four girls who had tried to escape. Nino said.

"Do you remember how that tall girl screamed when we stripped her and tied her so she was all spread out on that table? I thought she was the best of the four. But for me one of the best parts was how she screamed and fainted when I whipped her breasts and pussy until they started to bleed. It was almost as good as the noise she made when you forced that big butt plug up her arse. Although I still think the best part was when your cut her nipples off."

The German made a high pitched giggling sound that was supposed to be laughter.

"Oh yes I really enjoyed working her over, and I watched the video we made of it the other night. It was really good. The screams from the others were okay but the big one was definitely the best. It was a shame she died so quickly. I wonder who the next girls will be to enjoy our hospitality in the special room?"

At that moment one of the guards knocked on The German's office door. Quickly he put the phone down and asked the man if he was taking the girl to Nino's now. Trevor the guard nodded.

"Okay Trevor that's fine. I've also decided that you will work for Nino for the next four months training his men so they can do their jobs in a reasonable manner. None of his people know what the hell they are doing and need some discipline."

Again the guard nodded before turning and leaving the room.

Chapter 14

With Jimmy driving and Tony the pimp giving directions, the four men soon found themselves in a run-down area where some of the houses had signs on them saying they were dangerous and others had boards covering the doors and windows. Tony, thinking he might be able to warn the men in the house, directed Jimmy to one of the houses that looked more or less normal and suggested he stop, but Jimmy kept on going until he came to the next street where he turned off and then stopped. Mikhail patted Jimmy on the shoulder and smiled before grabbing Tony by the throat and snarling at him.

"If you ever try a trick like that again I will personally cut your balls off and throw them to the fishes. Now tell me, how many armed men are in that house, and how many women are in there?"

After being released Tony had to swallow hard a couple of times, to lubricate his throat enough for him to speak.

"There should be four armed men because the twelve women in that house are new, and they occupy the two bedrooms at the top of the stairs."

"If you knocked on the door," asked Dmitri, "would the men inside know you, and let you in?"

"Yes because a couple of the women in there are mine, so the men know me very well."

Dmitri nodded slowly.

"That's very good! You will knock on the door while we stand out of sight, then as soon as the door is open we will move in and either take them prisoner or kill them while the third man comes in from the back of the house. So now tell me how we get to the back of the house?"

"It's easy," Tony mumbled, as he continued to massage his throat, "over there is a walkway that leads down between all the houses, and the door you want is number fifteen."

Jimmy looked across at the passageway and decided he would take the back of the house and leave Dmitri and Mikhail to go in through the front. They were used to working as a team so were unlikely to make any elementary errors, and the first few seconds after going through the door was the time of most danger.

"That sounds okay," said Jimmy, "but I think it would be best if I take the back door while you two guys take the front. Less chance of us getting in each others way. But I think I'll need a two minute start so I can be ready when I hear the front door open."

Both Dmitri and Mikhail nodded their agreement, but then Jimmy asked what they were going to do with the pimp while they were rounding up the bad guys. Mikhail pulled a pair of handcuffs from his jacket pocket.

"I'll handcuff his right wrist to his left ankle. He wont be able to run far like that will he?"

"Now it sounds like we've got a real plan," said Jimmy, "so lets go and get these bad guys and see if Anna is in this house. If she isn't, the bad guys, or Tony the pimp, will tell us where she is."

Jimmy got out of the car and retrieved their weapons and ammunition from the boot, passing the weapons and other stuff to Mikhail and Dmitri, before holstering his own. When Tony the pimp saw all the weaponry they were carrying his eyes bulged.

"Fuckin' hell," he gasped, "where did you get all that bloody stuff from?"

"Never you mind," said Dmitri, quietly, "just remember when you're standing in front of that door one wrong word from your mouth and I will put a bullet through your spine so you'll spend the rest of your days in a wheel chair, if you're lucky. If you're not lucky you'll die very slowly and in great agony."

Tony gulped, now he knew for sure that he was dealing with very dangerous men who didn't just look like professional killers, but who obviously where. Suddenly his plan to warn the men in the house faded from his mind. He was more concerned with saving his own life than worrying about what would happen to the men in the house. He was also very worried what these men would do to him when they found out that this wasn't the house where Anna was being kept. More importantly what would they do to him when they found that Anna had been sold by The German to a new gang. Looking at the three men he decided that now was not a good time to change his story, or make them angry.

Mikhail looked at his two friends then nodded in the direction of the house where the women were supposed to be.

"Okay," he said, "if we're ready lets do it."

Jimmy retrieved his black overalls from the boot of the car and pulled them on, then with his guns comfortably positioned around his body he walked over to the passageway and disappeared from sight. Dmitri set his watch to give Jimmy the two minute start he wanted then he and Mikhail pulled on their black overalls and checked their weapons. As soon as the two minutes were up the two Russians and the pimp walked around the corner to the house. Dmitri stood on one side of the door and Mikhail on the other, then Dmitri prodded Tony the pimp with the barrel of his AK47. Tony knocked on the door and they waited for someone to answer. Suddenly with a rattle of chains the door opened three or four inches and a pair of eyes looked out. Tony rattled out a few words in Albanian, and the face in the gap suddenly broke into a smile, the door closed briefly while the chains were removed and then swung fully open, but the smile disappeared when the man behind the door saw the guns pointed at him. His hands shot up in the air and he backed away a couple of paces, and never uttered a sound. Dmitri and Mikhail stepped through the door, and while Dmitri closed and locked the door behind them Mikhail handcuffed

Tony and the other man together around the thick wooden bannister rail at the bottom of the stairs and taped their mouths shut with duct tape. When the two Russians were ready to move they looked around for Jimmy and were surprised to find him standing silently behind them. Mikhail grinned with pleasure when he saw Jimmy and patted him on the head to indicate everything was going well. Jimmy led the way up the stairs to the first landing where they found three closed doors, one of which had a light showing under it, and they could hear voices and laughter. The three men listened carefully to see how many men were in the room, then Jimmy held up three fingers, and the two Russians nodded their agreement. According to Tony the pimp, if he was to be believed, there could possibly be another one or two men around somewhere, so they had better find them first and silence them before tackling the three that were in the room. Some hand signals passed between the three men, and the two Russians moved to one of the doors and Jimmy moved to the other, as soon as they were in position they opened the doors quietly and moved into the rooms. The room Jimmy went into was empty so he silently closed the door and moved to back up the Russians. A quick glance into the room showed him that Dmitri had found a fifth gangster who had been asleep in bed, and who was now dead after Dmitri broke his neck.

Mikhail nodded towards the door where the three gangsters were relaxing, and the three men moved into position. Dmitri slowly and carefully cracked the door open a fraction of an inch and then waited a second until he felt the tap on the shoulder from Mikhail and Jimmy telling him they were ready. Dmitri pushed the door open and moved into the room, followed by Mikhail who moved to the left and Jimmy who went to the right. The three gangsters who were playing cards and gambling for quite large stakes, stared open mouthed in shock at the three gunmen. Suddenly one of the men suddenly banged his hand on the table sending the chips and cards all over the floor, and screamed.

"How the fuck did you lot get into this house? Don't you realise the new guards will be arriving in a few minutes and when they see you they will shoot you. So you'd better fuck off right now."

Dmitri sneered.

"You people are so stupid, but to answer your question, we're here because we were invited. Now enough of this nonsense, where is this woman?"

Dmitri pushed the photographs of Anna so the three men could see them. After examining the photographs the men looked at each other and spoke quietly for a minute and then shook their heads.

"I haven't seen this girl before, and my two friends say they haven't seen her either. Maybe she is in one of the other houses."

Dmitri nodded to Mikhail and Jimmy, and they handcuffed the gangsters' wrists together and then shackled their ankles to the central heating radiator. Jimmy then went round the three men removing their weapons before taping their mouths shut, and disconnecting the telephone. As soon as the men were secured Dmitri prodded them with his AK47.

"You three will remain here while we go and have a look upstairs to see who is at home, and I can assure you that if we find the girl we're looking for, you three will not have time to say your prayers before you die."

As soon as the guards heard these words, they looked at each other and the one who seemed to be the leader managed to pull some of the duct tape off his mouth screamed.

"There is nothing and nobody upstairs. Apart from us this place is empty, so there is no point in going up there."

Jimmy looked at his two friends.

"Look at the sweat on that bastards face. If ever I heard a good reason for searching upstairs, that's it. These bastards are trying hide something from us, so let's go and see if we can find out what it is."

At the top of the stairs Mikhail found the door to one of the rooms locked, so with his Heckler and Koch in his right hand he used his size sixteen boot to unlock it. As soon as the door swung open he dropped to the ground and snaked into the room on his belly. Dmitri, carrying his old old AK 47, covered the room as he followed his friend in, looking for anyone who might have a gun in their hands. Jimmy, the third man to enter the room carried his Heckler and Koch across his chest on its strap leaving his hands free, but he also carried a 9mm semi-automatic pistol in a shoulder holster just in case he needed some back-up. As he stepped into the room he made a detailed visual search but could see nothing that looked dangerous or threatening. The room was stinking from a mixture of drugs, excrement, and urine, and it looked as though someone had recently been sick in a corner. But the room seemed to be empty apart from the old army style metal beds stacked two high around the walls. The only bedding in the room was a pile of cheap, shoddy and dirty blankets heaped up on a grubby mattress on one of the beds. Mikhail rose from the floor and turned to Dmitri, and Jimmy, and in his broken English he growled.

"If we don't find Anna here I'm going to kill that bastard pimp who gave us this bad information, very very slowly!"

At that moment Jimmy, who had been standing motionless suddenly spun round and in two strides was leaning over the bed with the blankets piled on it, quickly he picked up the shoddy blankets and threw them on the floor. For a few seconds there was silence in the room while the three men stared at the small naked female figure curled up in the foetal position on the bed, hardly able to believe their eyes. The woman had been savagely beaten about the body, and the badly bruised face was a mask of blood. Judging by the angle of the left arm, Jimmy could see it had been broken in at least two places. Dmitri reached over and his fingers touched the womans throat. Suddenly he grabbed Jimmy's arm.

"Quickly Jimmy, call for emergency medical help, I've just felt a small irregular pulse, we might be able to save her."

Jimmy raced out of the room and down the stairs to where he had left the telephone, and reconnected it. Then as fast as his fingers could push the buttons he called the emergency ambulance service, gave them the address and explained it might be a drug overdose plus broken bones. Fifteen minutes later the paramedics were gently carrying the badly injured and emaciated woman to their ambulance, and with the sirens screaming they raced off towards the nearest hospital.

The three men checked out the remainder of the house to make sure there were no other women being kept there before walking back into the room where the gangsters were shackled and handcuffed. Dmitri looked at them, and they cringed back away from him.

"You miserable bastards, no wonder you didn't want us to go upstairs. It was you who beat that poor woman senseless and almost killed her. So now I'm going to let my friend practice some of his skills on you just so you know what a good dose of pain feels like, and then I'm going to shoot you."

Dmitri looked over at Jimmy.

"Okay Jimmy, please teach these swine what real pain feels like. You can release them one at a time if you like, or all together, whichever gives you the most pleasure. Oh okay Mikhail, you might as well join in, you look as though you need to stretch your muscles for a few minutes, or if you prefer you can just keep an eye on things in case something goes wrong. In the meantime I'm going to search all the other rooms in this house to make sure we haven't missed anything."

Jimmy glanced at Mikhail, and the two men grinned in anticipation of what was to come, and then released the three gangsters. Twenty minutes later when Dmitri walked back into the room, to find Jimmy and Mikhail with big smiles on their faces cleaning the gangster's blood off themselves. The gangsters were now unconscious and even their own mothers would not have recognised any of them.

"Are they still alive?" Dmitri asked.

"Yes," laughed Jimmy, "we thought we'd better keep them alive so you could speak to them if you wanted to."

"Good, because now we need the addresses of the other houses, so I think we should get Tony the pimp and the first guard up here, and encourage them to tell us what we want to know."

Mikhail nodded and went down stairs to collect the two bad guys. Jimmy in the meantime had found a bucket, filled it with water, and started sluicing down the badly beaten gangsters, but it would take sometime before they recovered consciousness. Mikhail arrived back with the two men in tow, and shoved them into the room. As soon as they saw the condition of the other three gangsters their faces turned white and they moved as far away from Mikhail as they could. But Dmitri was in no mood to play games with these two men, he switched his AK47 to fire single shots and put a bullet into the head of each of the badly beaten men. Then he turned to Tony and the last gangster.

"I will ask you one question, and if I think you are lying to me the next bullets from this gun will blast your kneecaps off, and if you keep on telling me lies I will gut shoot you. The choice is yours. I want to know where the women in this picture is?"

Once more Tony and the gangster had to look at Anna's picture, but this time Tony did no more than glance briefly at the picture, then he shrugged his shoulders.

"I don't know where this person is because I haven't been responsible for her for sometime. The German decided he didn't want her any more and sold her to one of the other gang bosses, a man everyone calls Nino. I don't know where Nino keeps his women but I have heard some gossip that says this one has been ill with the flu or something so she has been in bed with cough medicine and aspirins, but I recently heard that she is now back to normal health again, and should be back at work today or tomorrow. I'm telling you this so you will understand, that I really do not know where she is being kept. But if you want to make sure you could check out the house were my best ladies live because that is where she would be if she still worked for me."

Then he pulled a piece of paper from his pocket and handed it to Dmitri.

"This is the address of the house where they are living. "

Dmitri pushed Tony towards Mikhail and asked him to put the cuffs on him, then he turned and put a bullet into the head of the last gangster.

"If we are lucky," he said to no one in particular, "when these bodies are found, the rest of the gang will rapidly find themselves new occupations."

Then he turned to Jimmy.

"Jimmy, what will your police do when they find all the bodies we've left lying around? Do you think they will suspect that some sort of a gang fight has been going on, or will they search very hard for us?" Dmitri paused for a moment, then continued. "We will take Tony the pimp with us in case we need to ask him some more questions. But before we go to see if we can find Anna, I think we should go and see how that little one is getting on in the hospital, what do think?"

Jimmy smiled and ruffled Dmitri's hair.

"I always knew you were just an old softy but I think it's an excellent idea, and maybe it will still be possible for us to make it to the next address before dawn. I also think we should remove all the money we can find from these miserable bastards so we can give the little one something to keep her going. But as far as the police are concerned, I don't know what they will think, although it wouldn't surprise me if they were very happy to see this lot dead. The only problem is they may very well try to find out who has been involved, and British Police can be very persistent and stubborn. They usually don't give up easily when they are looking for someone."

Dmitri looked serious for a moment.

"What you say makes sense Jimmy, so I will not suggest that we telephone the police to let them know there are some dead bodies laying around, instead we will let them find out for themselves."

Mikhail said something in rapid Russian, and nodded at Dmitri's reply, obviously he also agreed with what had been said and was happy to go to the hospital after he had emptied the crooks pockets of money and collected all the money they had been gambling with. Then Dmitri shrugged.

"I thought for a few seconds that woman we found was Anna, and I have to phone Boris in the next few hours."

Jimmy leaned over and put his hand on Dmitri's shoulder.

"Why don't you just tell him that we haven't found his daughter yet? It's the truth, and right now we don't know that Anna is in any physical danger. It's also possible that we may even have her in this car before you phone Boris."

Dmitri nodded.

"Yes you're right Jimmy, at least it's the truth, and who knows, if his daughter Anna is half as tough as most of the women I have met, she will be able to survive this and kick whatever habit these bastards have hooked her on. But right now the one thing that would probably make us all feel really good would be to go and see how that little one is, and then we will try to find Anna. After we have arranged for the women to be taken to somewhere safe I would love to go and have chat to this big ignorant bastard German, and his goons, who brought her here. I want to meet them so we can give them a taste of their own medicine, before we kill them. What do you think?"

Jimmy nodded.

"I think that's a great idea, and it will give me a chance to use some more of the moves I've only been able to practice on punch bags. But first let's go and talk to the doctors and make sure the girl is going to be okay."

Mikhail gave one of his evil chuckles, which went well with his broken English when he said.

"I also hope these bastards put up some sort of a fight, it will add a nice bit of spice to the proceedings, and I'd be interested to see some more of Jimmy's fancy fighting in action. I think my men would be interested to learn something of this Tai Chi stuff."

Jimmy drove into the hospital car park and parked in a dark corner so they could strip off their black overalls without anyone seeing them. When all their gear had been stored safely and neatly in the boot of the car and Tony the pimp was handcuffed to the steering wheel, they walked into the accident and emergency department. Jimmy walked over to the reception area and asked to see the young woman who had just been brought in. A few minutes went by before a middle aged female doctor with flame red hair came across to them and asked if they were friends of the fair haired woman. Dmitri told her enough of the story to get her sympathy and cooperation, and asked her to try and make sure that the woman was given the very best care possible. He then gave the doctor all the money they had collected from the bad guys explaining that the blood on the money was the result of an accident, but the money belonged to the young woman. As soon as the doctor promised to give her the money, and do her best to ensure that she recovered fully, the three men turned and started to walk away. The doctor was taken by surprise by their response and rushed after them.

"Please stop. Aren't you going to stay and make sure the lady is going to be okay?"

The three men stopped and turned towards the doctor with big smiles on their faces and Dmitri said.

"We're going to find the rest of the men who did this to her to make sure they will never ever be able to do anything similar to anyone else's daughter."

As Dmitri spoke, the doctor glanced up at his face and realised that she was looking into the eyes of a man who is going to kill someone, and enjoy it. It was the first time in her life that the doctor had seen such raw cold emotion in a man's eyes, and the shock caused her to take a step backwards. Immediately Dmitri's face changed and he became his normal charming self, gently taking the doctors hand and raising it to his lips.

"I am absolutely certain the lady will receive the very best care while she is with you, and I thank you for your help. When we have gone will you please contact your most suitable authority to make sure she is going to be properly looked after. We would also be very grateful if you could forget that we have ever been in here to check on her. If the police become involved and start searching for us it will make things very difficult for us and hinder our search for the gangsters who are causing so much pain and suffering to so many women. It could also mean that a lot of these bad men might escape justice and continue to enslave many hundreds or even thousands of good women into drug addiction and prostitution."

The doctor nodded her head in agreement.

"No one will ever find out from me that you have been here, and if someone does tell the police about you, I will give them some descriptions that will confuse them so much they will never find you." The three men grinned at her as they turned and walked out of the door, leaving the doctor looking at the hand that Dmitri had kissed, almost unable to believe the look she had glimpsed in the eyes of the handsome older man, a few moments before. My God she thought I'm very glad that they are not looking for anyone I know, but I hope they catch the men who beat up that woman. Back in the car they released Tony from his handcuffs and pushed him into the back of the car with Mikhail for company. Tony seemed resigned to whatever was going to happen to him and without being prompted started giving Jimmy the directions to the house where he said Anna had been living while she worked for The German.

Chapter 15

A few hours after Jimmy, Dmitri and Mikhail left the hospital, Detective Inspector Peter Jones, was awakened from a deep sleep by the ringing of his bedside telephone, and his wife digging her fingers into his ribs and telling him to "answer the damned thing!"

Grumbling and cursing in his lilting Welsh accent Peter picked up the phone.

"I hope you have a very good reason for waking me at this godforsaken hour!"

"Good morning boss," the Liverpool accent of his assistant John Morton answered. "I'm sorry to bother you but I've just been informed that the local hospital has had a young woman heroin addict brought in, who has been very badly beaten. The three doctors who have worked on her to stabilize her are extremely reluctant to say anything about the situation, but the local police have found out from the Ambulance people, the address where the girl was picked up. They went round to the address expecting to find a squat of some sort and instead they found four men dead from gunshot wounds. A fifth man was found in a different room dead with a broken neck. The local police actually said that three of the four shot men had been beaten with fists and boots so badly that they were close to death before they were executed. So it could be the start of a gang war or maybe something more interesting because it seems that three men called into the hospital to check that the badly beaten teenager was going to be okay. Incidentally the doctors all agree that if the ambulance had not been called when it was, the woman would have certainly died. However there is a problem about the three men alleged to have carried out the killings. The doctors are all giving us very different descriptions of the men, and the senior forensics man thinks the doctors are actually trying to protect them. And before you ask, the woman is heavily sedated and will be unable to speak to anyone for at least the next 12 hours. So what do you think?"

"How the bloody hell do I know what to think," grumbled Peter, "you're the one with all the information, so get down to the hospital and talk to everyone who has been involved with this woman. Then when you've done that, get over to the house where the bodies are, and carefully search the place to try and get an idea of what has been going on there. Oh and don't forget to quiz the forensic people. Also don't forget to call me when you have an address for the house. I'll join you there."

Peter put the phone down then carefully rolled out of bed trying not to disturb his wife and made his way to the bathroom to shave and shower.

As Peter was quietly getting dressed his wife sat up and asked him what had happened, he explained the basics of what he had been told. She thought for a minute and then asked him.

"Do you think these killers are some of the men you have been tracking? The ones involved in the trafficking of women for the sex trade?"

"I really don't know at the moment. But there is something that doesn't feel right about the whole thing. The two main gangs involved in the sex trade are not in competition with each other so why would they be attacking and killing each other? It just doesn't make sense, but it could be the break through we've been hoping for. If this teenager can identify some of the men involved or maybe even the bosses we might have a chance of busting the lot of them. On the other hand if this is a revenge killing by a family whose daughter has been kidnapped we could have a lot more blood and dead bodies before it's finished. Anyway luv I must go and see for myself what's happened. I'll call you later, and I promise to telephone you and let you know what's happening, and what time I'll be home for dinner this evening."

Peter leaned over and kissed his wife on the cheek. "See you later."

His wife blew him a kiss and waved him goodbye before snuggling down under the duvet again and closing her eyes.

Standing on the pavement outside the house where the bodies had been found Peter watched as the five body bags were loaded into an ambulance and driven away, then in deep thought he slowly walked into the house.

"Hi Boss."

Peter heard Johnny Morton and walked over to him. Johnny could see the questioning look in his boss's eyes and said.

"I've spoken to the forensics people, and the local uniformed police who seem to have been very thorough but as usual no one they have spoken to heard anything or suspected anything. So there is nothing new there. But the forensic guys told me that they are fairly sure that one man came in through the back of the house and three other men were apparently invited into the house through the front door because there are no signs of a break-in. Three crooks who live in the house were handcuffed to each other and the central heating radiator on the second floor. A fourth man who had been asleep in his bed had his neck broken by someone who has been well trained and knew exactly what he was doing. Forensics say it was so quick the dead man probably never woke up. The crook who answered the door and one of the men who came through the front door were handcuffed to the bottom of the stairs whilst three visitors searched the house from top to bottom. The search probably produced nothing so the three men released one of the men at the bottom of the stairs and the four men left the house. Oh and by the way, the local police say that this house was used by one of the sex trade gangs to house their women."

John stopped talking and looked at his boss.

"Don't look at me with that smug look on your face," growled Peter, "tell me what it is you have been saving until last."

"You know me too well Boss, but you're right, the forensic guys also told me that before the four men left the house two of them actually freed the three crooks and then proceeded to skilfully and with brutal savagery beat them to a pulp. The beating was so severe that there were not many bones left unbroken in the three crooks and they were close to death. The report says the beating was almost certainly carried out by two men who were extremely proficient in hand to hand combat. One of the forensics team told me that he had never seen a person beaten so badly by hands and feet before, and he was certain that the men who carried out the beating could have easily killed the three crooks if they had wanted to. He also maintained that even if a cricket bat had been used the injuries would not have been worse. What do you make of that?"

Peter, who had been listening carefully to his assistant, looked up at the ceiling and replied.

"I believe we have three men accompanied by a fourth, who gained access into this house and then took the men in the house prisoner. After this they searched the house and found the young woman who had been beaten up. This discovery made the men so angry they decided to teach the crooks a lesson in pain before they killed them. The fact they brought the fourth man with them and then took him away again suggests to me the fourth man has information the three men want. So I'm led to the conclusion that the three men are possibly searching for a woman who has been kidnapped, probably from one of the old Eastern Bloc countries. I'm guessing it's the old Eastern Bloc because this is where a lot of these unfortunate women have been abducted from. It is also obvious to me that these three men will not stop the killing until they find what or who they are looking for, and God help anyone who gets in their way or tries to stop them. John do you think we could get away with doing nothing and just let things take their own course? It would save us and the taxpayer a lot of time and money!"

John burst out laughing.

"Damn me boss, if we did that we would end up being buried under an even bigger mountain of bureaucratic paperwork than usual, but of course you could always ask your wife to come and work as your secretary. At least then you would get a few good cups of tea and coffee. However I truly do not think we could get away with it because I'm sure we haven't seen the last of the killings."

Peter nodded his agreement.

"Okay you Scouse scoundrel let's get back to the office and go through everything we've got. Someone will soon start shouting for a report from us and wanting to know why we haven't already caught these killers, and I don't think they would be very pleased if we told them that we are not planning to catch these people any time soon. But I would love to get the two gang masters into court particularly if we could fit them up for the killing of the four women whose abused bodies were found a couple of weeks ago. Whoever carried out those killings is a sadistic bastard and needs to be behind bars."

Later that same day The German was told about the latest killings of his men and immediately got on the phone to Nino demanding to know why Nino's men had attacked and killed his men. Nino forcefully told The German that neither he nor his men knew anything about these killings, and they had certainly not been involved in killing any of The Germans men. The two men continued to growl and shout at each other for a while but eventually The German realised that Nino was not responsible for the killing of his men. It was at this point that Nino said to The German.

"Listen, if it wasn't me and it wasn't you who ordered the killings, who the bloody hell was it? We've got to find out damned quick because if someone is moving in on our turf we need to join forces and put the bastards out of business before they do any more harm to us. Is it possible the Chinese are behind this? Could they have decided to take over our businesses for themselves! Also the police will already be sniffing around and getting interested in what we're doing, so what do you suggest?"

The German thought for a minute before responding.

"Okay this is what we'll do. First we must warn all our guys that someone has started killing their friends. Then we can send our guys out to talk to all the low lifers that they know to see if anyone has heard anything. At the same time you and I can speak to our police contacts to see if they know anything. As soon as we get some information we should meet up to see if we can make any sense of what has happened. If we find out who is responsible for this we can go and visit them with our best men and terminate the bastards. I for one will enjoy watching them squirm on the meat-hooks in the abattoir while someone cuts off their legs with a chainsaw. But somehow I don't think it's the Chinese they would loose money and the Albanians are too busy doing other stuff to be interested in us."

Nino agreed and cut the connection.

Chapter 16

After packing as many clothes as she could into the plastic bags, Anna crawled painfully onto the bed and tried to relax her stomach to ease the throbbing pain. She lay on the bed hoping she might be able to doze off for a moment while she waited for either the guard or The German to return. But the pain in her stomach and breasts refused to ease and allow her to doze off. The other problem for her was as soon as she closed her eyes the anger that festered inside her quickly filled her mind and slowly turned into an intense red hot rage. She made a determined promise to herself that during the last minutes of his wretched life, The German would be made to suffer every second until he very slowly died in agony. Perhaps, she thought, this would help to bring peace to all the women he has brought so much pain and suffering to, anything less was unthinkable. Then she started to think about Enver Ceka, the man who was the cause of all her pain and suffering. She wanted to pour petrol over him and set him on fire, but then she remembered The German being told by one of his men that the Russian men who were following her had already left him in extreme and agonising pain. She was so engrossed in her thoughts she didn't hear The German come into the room until his harsh voice crashed over her like an ocean wave crashing on a rocky beach, startling her back to reality.

"Get up you lazy cow, get up now and get dressed, I've decided that sexually you're a waste of space and the only thing you're good for is to be a prostitute. At least this way I might make some money from you.

The man who will look after you will be here soon and he will take you to a house where you will stay with some other women."

Ten minutes later Anna was in a car with a man who was dressed in black trousers, black T-shirt, and black jacket with a thick gold chain round his neck. But the thing most noticeable about the man was his face, it was heavily pockmarked. He told her his name was Tony, and he expected her to do whatever he told her, both quickly and willingly. If she didn't, or if she gave any trouble he would get her hooked on heroin or something even worse, after that he was sure she would never give him any trouble again. Anna shivered when she heard him calmly tell her this. Looking at him she realised he meant every word he said to her, and she made a silent promise never to upset this man.

The house that was to be her home for the foreseeable future was a bit scruffy and run down, but at least it was dry and warm. She shared a room with four others, all of whom were addicted to drugs and sometimes woke screaming in the night and were often trying to beg, borrow or steal drugs to feed their addiction. Anna was appalled by the state they had degenerated into, but still felt great sympathy for them. Her normal daily routine consisted of getting up in the morning and getting showered before making up her bed then sitting around reading magazines and books waiting for the phone to ring. It was the third day when during her shower she noticed that she was scratching her leg and realised that she had been bitten many times on her legs by some insect in her bed. When she saw Tony she complained to him saying that no man would want to take her out with her legs all marked with flea bites. After a quick examination Tony swore and shouted for the man who was supposed to keep the house clean. When the man arrived Tony grabbed him by his shirt front and pointed at Anna's legs.

"You dirty lazy old bastard, you see the marks on her legs? They're flea bites, and I remember the last one who slept in that same bed also complained about being bitten. But I guess you didn't bother to do anything about it. Now I'm telling you, get that dirty mattress and all the bedding out of this house and then give the room a thorough cleaning. When the room is cleaned properly, put a new, and I mean a new, mattress on the bed and give her a complete set of new bedding. This is to be finished before I get back here at eight pm. If it isn't done and done to my satisfaction I'll speak with the boss and tell him he is losing a lot of money because you are not doing your job. Do you understand me?"

The man nodded and scurried off to get his cleaning materials. Tony watched him go and then looked at Anna.

"Okay Anna I suggest you get showered again and then put on some clean clothes that haven't been anywhere near the bed. After the old bugger has cleaned the room and removed the mattress and bedding I suggest you wash all your clothes to make sure they are not infested with fleas. I'll talk to the boss and suggest he lets you have the night off to help you get your skin back in order. There is some cream in the first aid kit that is good for flea bites so get that and put plenty of it on the bites. With a bit of luck you might be ready to go back to work tomorrow, and don't forget I'll know if your shirking, and if you are, you know what the punishment will be."

Anna nodded.

"Yes I understand, and thank you for sorting this out for me I really appreciate it."

Tony laughed cynically then spoke over his shoulder as he headed for the door.

"Oh I didn't do it for you, I did it because if you're not working I don't make as much money and I am not going to lose money because that lazy bastard can't do his job. Now I suggest you get yourself cleaned up and sorted out. When that's done you can go down stairs and sit in the back room while your bed is sorted out. I'll be back in an hour and expect to see you showered and dressed."

Two days later Anna was forced to escort an overweight arrogant European business man who suffered from asthma and wanted her to indulge in kinky sex. She managed to avoid his demands by using her hands to make him quickly ejaculate. After that he lost interest in her and fell asleep. It was the start of her life as an escort girl, and because of her good looks she was in demand every night. Then one afternoon a few days later Trevor the guard came looking for her. The German wanted to see her immediately and she knew he wouldn't be happy if she kept him waiting. Anna dressed quickly in casual clothes and went with the guard. When they arrived at the house the guard told her to stay just inside the front door and wait. Then he went off to tell his boss that she was waiting for him. When The German saw her he snarled at her that he had sold her, Anna was shocked but fortunately still managed to hear what he was saying.

> "Your new boss will be arriving soon to have a look at you and see if he still likes what he has bought, so make yourself look as pretty as possible for him. You'll find clean clothes and make-up in one of the drawers of the wardrobe in your old room. So hurry up and shift your lazy arse."

Anna hurried up the stairs to the room where The German had raped her and frantically started searching through the wardrobe, and chest of draws for the best clothes to wear. The German followed her up the stairs to make sure she was doing as she had been told. When he saw that she was complying with his orders he walked out of the room slamming the door behind him.

Oh my God, Anna thought, if he has sold me to someone else it must mean that I will soon have to start having sex with another man and maybe he will force me to take drugs as well. The thoughts shocked her but then she realised there was one good thing about the situation, she at least wouldn't have to let that fat repulsive German bastard use her body again. But what, she wondered, will the new man be like? While these thoughts were flitting furiously through her mind, Anna searched until she found some clothes and shoes that fitted her and looked reasonably good, and then got herself dressed. Further searching produced some pale pink lipstick which she liked and some dark grey eye shadow that she wasn't too sure about. Then finally she brushed her long blond hair into a reasonable style and felt that she was as ready as she could be. She wanted to try and make a good impression on her new owner, and glancing at herself as she passed the long mirror on the wardrobe door. She was amazed to see the same pretty young woman as usual staring back at her from the mirror. Anna didn't know what she'd expected to see, but she felt sure she had changed dramatically in some way during the past few weeks. But no, she still looked the same even though the clothes did not fit her quite as well as her own. Just then came a knock at the door and Trevor, the guard she liked came in. He picked up the plastic shopping bag she had filled with clothes, and put a second plastic bag on the bed for her.

"Please put the rest of your stuff in that bag as quickly as you can and follow me."

Anna nodded and put some boxes of condoms, birth control pills and the make-up that she had found into the second plastic bag together with a couple of warm sweaters and followed the guard down the stairs. At the bottom of the stairs he showed her into what looked like a lounge area with four settees and a number of leather club chairs and coffee tables placed around the room. Sitting at one of the coffee tables was The German and another man she had not seen before. The two men were talking as she walked in but stopped as soon as they saw her, then The German waved her over.

"Come over here and stand in front of your new boss." He commanded.

"When you want to speak to him you will address him as Sir, and only speak when you are spoken to, do you understand?"

Anna promptly answered.

"Yes Sir."

As she spoke Anna glanced briefly at the new man, he was thin faced with beady black eyes and a sharp nose that gave him the appearance of a rodent, a thin black moustache added to the impression. But it was the thin cruel lips covering brown and crooked teeth that gave the man his evil appearance. The skin on the man's almost bald head had a yellowish tinge and there were a few strands of dark coloured greasy hair that was plastered across his skull. Anna thought he looked to be quite small in stature, but at least he was neatly dressed in clean clothes and his hands appeared to be well manicured. The new man nodded his approval at her answer, then turned to The German.

"I've had to pay a very high price for her, but I think she will become very popular with all the businessmen who use my agency, so I'm happy with our deal. The only thing that disappoints me is that she is not a virgin, but I suppose we cannot have everything. Are you sure that she knows what will happen if she causes any trouble?"

The German, with an evil grin on his face,

"you mean like the four women the police found recently."

Nino laughed as if an unspoken joke had passed between them, before continuing.

"Okay my friend, will you have one of your men bring her over to the usual address? Then she will be introduced to the man who will look after her. Sometime later today or tomorrow he will take her shopping to get the sort of clothes and make-up she will need so she can get all the men chasing after her and wanting to spend lots of money on her. By the way my friend is there any chance of a repeat performance of what happened to the four women? I found it so exciting it was almost orgasmic."

The German smirked.

"I also enjoyed the spectacle, especially the whipping. So I'll see if I can find one or two of the women who are no long making me money and we can have fun with them in that special room of yours."

"What a wonderful thought," Nino sighed theatrically. "Please keep me informed."

Anna listened to her new boss speaking and wondered what they meant by having girls in the special room. She also wondered where Nino came from because she wasn't sure about his accent. At first she thought he may be Italian, but after a moment discounted that and decided he could even be from the Ukraine. If she was right and he was Ukrainian, she would have to be very careful how she spoke to him because she had heard her father say that the Ukrainians could be very hard and brutal with their women.

The German grunted, then called to the guard standing in the doorway.

"You there, go and get the car then take this girl round to the house where my friend keeps his new arrivals, okay?"

The man nodded and disappeared, then The German turned and pointed at Anna.

"You, stand there and don't move until that guard comes back, then you go with him, do you understand?"

Anna responded quickly. "Yes sir," and the two men turned away from her. As they were walking towards the door Anna heard The German tell Nino that he enjoyed watching the girls getting punished really hard. But the rest of the conversation was lost to her as they left the room and she was on her own. She decided when she first saw her new manager, that she would try and make him think that she was a timid person who did what she was told. If the new man believed this, he might decide that she wouldn't require drugs to control her. Suddenly it dawned on her that she had been left on her own and immediately her thoughts turned to escape. Would it, she wondered, be possible to escape through the front door and onto the main road? If I could get outside, maybe it would also be possible for me to run as fast as I can until I find some shops or houses where I can appeal for help. Anna walked quietly over to the doorway and cautiously looked out into the main hall. At first glance she thought it was empty and hope surged through her, but just as she was about to make a run for the front door a movement amongst some dark shadows caught her eye, and she froze. It was one of the guards sitting quietly on a chair reading a newspaper in an alcove near the front door, and she knew she wouldn't be able to get past him. The surge of hope died and she quietly went back to the coffee table where she'd been standing, and wondered if she would ever get a real chance to escape.

A short time later the guard called Trevor appeared in the doorway and beckoned to her.

"Come on luv, the car is outside, if you're ready to travel, lets go."

Anna wasn't sure she understood what the man had said because of his accent, but she picked up her plastic bags and followed him out of the house to the car. She was unprepared for the cold wind that suddenly blew around her as she stepped out onto the street and wished she had put her heavy coat on when she left her old house. Soon she started shivering as she waited for the guard to open the car door. The guard looked at her for a moment wondering what she was waiting for, then he realised she didn't know where he wanted her to sit so he opened the rear door for her and helped her into the car. As the car moved off the guard looked at her through the rear view mirror and asked her if she had a coat, Anna shook her head and whispered, "no, not with me."

The guard shrugged his shoulders, then told her to put on the zip fronted jacket that was on the floor between the seats.
"It's okay, it's one of my old jackets. It will be too big for you but it will help to keep you a bit warmer until you can get your own clothes organised."
At first Anna almost cried when she heard the words because someone had actually treated her with kindness, but then, as she smiled gratefully at the man, she realised it was the same man who had helped her when The German had dragged her out of the car when they first arrived at his house.
"Thank you very much," she replied with tears in her eyes, "I appreciate, and happily accept, you're kind gesture. I will return it to you as soon as I can, and one day I hope I will be able to repay your kindness."
The guard smiled and nodded then carried on driving as she pulled on the jacket and zipped it up. He was right, it was old and too big for her but it would help to keep her warm when she got out of the car, and she was thankful for his consideration.

Sitting quietly in the back of the car for the duration of the journey through London, Anna stared out at all the vehicles that seemed to be whizzing around her. She hadn't realised how many people had cars in London, and they all seemed to be out on the road at the same time, but eventually the driver turned into a quiet backstreet and stopped outside a very old and tired looking three storey house with a glossy blue coloured door. As the driver got out he glanced over at her and spoke in his strange accent, which she later found out was called a Yorkshire accent.

"Okay luv, this is your new home, so follow me and I'll see if there is anyone in the house who can show you around and help you to get settled in."

The guard pressed a button on a metal box at the side of the door and spoke briefly into the box, a second later Anna heard a metallic rasping sound and the guard pushed the door open, then gestured for her to go in. As she stepped into the hallway an old man dressed in an old green wool cardigan on top of an off white shirt without a collar and brown corduroy trousers appeared. Walking with a limp towards her and Trevor the guard, the old man started grumbling to the guard in a whining high pitched voice.

"Oh bloody hell, not another one. For Christ's sake there's hardly enough room for the bitches we've got here already. Where the hell am I going to put this one?"

The guard, who had obviously been through this charade before, turned on the old man.

"For fuck sake you gimpy old bastard stop moaning at me, and get yourself organised. This woman is to be treated like a VIP because your boss Nino thinks she is very special, and if I tell him you are not looking after her properly he might decide to break your other leg to teach you a lesson."

The old man glared at the guard.

"I know you, you miserable swine, you really would tell the boss and cause me grief, just for the fun of seeing me get hurt, wouldn't you?"

The guard grinned nastily at the old man and nodded.

"Nothing would give me greater pleasure, you miserable old bastard, now get going and organise a good place for this new girl."

Then he turned to Anna.

"Listen luv, if this old man gives you any trouble, you make sure you tell either Mickey, he's the guy who will look after you, or me about it because if you don't this old bugger will try and make your life as miserable as his own."

Anna had listened to the exchange in amazement. This guard seemed to be trying to help her again by attempting to make sure the old man treated her properly. She smiled gratefully at the guard.

"Thank you very much, you've been very kind to me, and one day I hope I will be able to repay your kindness. Could you please tell me your name?"

"That's okay luv, my name is Trevor, and now I'm working for Nino. Just remember it's better not to get involved too much with the other women because most of them are drug addicts who will make trouble for you if they can. They will do anything if they think they will be given more drugs. So by keeping quiet and doing as you're told, you'll find your life will be as easy as it's possible to be while your here."

The guard then smiled at her and put his hand on her shoulder briefly before leaving her alone with the old man.

As soon as he had gone Anna felt more alone than she had ever felt since her arrival in London. All she wanted to do was crawl into a dark corner and cry her heart out, but the old man didn't give her a chance to feel sorry for herself, instead he shoved her towards the stairs.

"Go on, go on, get up the stairs to the very top, and don't be stopping and looking into any of the other rooms. I've got a good space for you on the top floor, it's not been used before so it's clean and tidy, and all the bedding is new and unused."

Well, Anna thought as she climbed the stairs, at least I wont be getting bitten by a lot of hungry fleas. As she climbed the stairs her eyes took in the rather threadbare red and gold stripped stair carpet and wondered what the rest of the furnishings would be like. At the top of the stairs Anna noticed three doors, each painted a different colours', red, yellow and blue.

"Go into the room with the yellow door, and wait until I get there."

The old man directed, as he puffed up the stairs behind her. Anna was surprised when she opened the door and walked into the room, it was quite large and pleasantly decorated with a bright airy feel to it. While she waited for the old man she took the opportunity to look around the room that was to be her home. The walls were painted pastel pink with a white ceiling and skirting which gave it a distinct feminine feel. There were five beds in the room, one under the window and the others were stacked one on top of the other to make two sets of double bunks that were pushed against one wall. This left quite a reasonable space in the middle of the room. A large floor to ceiling wardrobe with four mirrored doors filled the wall opposite the bunks with a large single wardrobe at the end of the bed by the window, and Anna wondered how five women could fit all their clothes into these wardrobes that altogether were the same size as the one in her bedroom in Russia. The old man came in behind her and pointed to the bed under the window.

"That will be your bed and the sheets and blankets are on the top shelf of the left hand wardrobe. When you get your new clothes you will keep them in that single wardrobe at the end of your bed. It has more space than the others for your dresses and coats, as well as some drawers which should be enough for you to keep your small clothes in. In the future make sure you don't leave stuff on your bed or spread around the room. Any clothes I find outside the wardrobes I will remove from the room, and you will have to pay a fine to get them back, do you understand."

Anna nodded her understanding, and the old man continued.

"These rules are necessary to keep order in the room, and are the same for everyone. Now, in a few minutes a man will arrive to take you shopping for your clothes, he likes to be called Mickey, after some film star that he likes, and he likes to be obeyed quickly. Any of his ladies who don't obey him are bent over in front of everyone in the house and their bare backsides will be thrashed with a stick until the girl apologises and promises to be quicker in future. So you had better make sure you know what size clothes and underwear you need, he doesn't like to be kept waiting."

The slamming of the front door and the sound of heavy footsteps on the stairs announced the arrival of Anna's new manager, Mickey. The old man hobbled away as Anna put her plastic shopping bag under the bed by the window then keeping her eyes on the floor she stood waiting to see what this man Mickey would be like. He walked into the room and stood silently for a minute, then he suddenly barked.

"You there, the blonde scarecrow, look at me."

The shock of the man shouting at her made Anna jump, and instinctively she looked up at him, and for a second the surprise on her face showed as she saw Mickey for the first time. He was only a couple of inches taller than her, but looked as wide as he was tall, with powerful looking arms and legs. Her first thought was that he looked like a frog. His eyes appeared to be bulbous and set in a broad pockmarked face and his wide thick lipped mouth added to the illusion. She struggled hard to keep her face straight and not laugh, but he must have realised what she was thinking because he glared at her.

"I know what you're thinking you little slag, but I'll give you fair warning if I ever catch you laughing at me I'll break all the fingers of your left hand so that you'll suffer all the bloody pain but you'll still be able to lay on your back and earn money. So remember, if you treat me right I'll make your life easy, but treat me any other way and you will regret it for a long time. Now, the rules here are simple, you do everything that I tell you to do, and you do it immediately and without question, do you understand?

"Yes sir, I understand you perfectly, and will try hard not to upset you."

Mickey nodded his approval of her reply.

"That's good. Okay, are those the only clothes you have? Yes I suppose they are. All right leave them under the bed and wait here. I'll go and get the car, so you be ready to go shopping in ten minutes. The boss says you are to be dressed properly because he expects you to make him a lot of money, which means I have to take you to the good places. But don't try anything foolish while we are out, like running away because if you do I'll catch you, and then me, all the guards, and the old man, will all have our fun with you, and we will not treat you gently. Then the boss will take you away to the special room where your screams for mercy will not be heard and I guarantee you will never return here."

Anna's face went white with the appalling thoughts of what he was threatening her with and she shook her head. Mickey grunted as he noted her reaction to his threat and knew she wouldn't give him any trouble while they were out, so he left her and went to get the car.

The shopping trip went by in a whirl for Anna. Mickey took her into some very famous London stores to buy dresses, underwear, make-up, shoes and toiletries, so when they arrived back at the house she was loaded down with bags full of quality well fitted clothes. But she could hardly remember anything about the trip. She had tried hard to take in the fact that she was shopping in some of the stores that she had always dreamed of visiting. But Mickey was rushing her as much as he could, and she was trying hard to concentrate on making sure everything matched and fitted properly that she could only remember the insides of the fitting rooms. Later, while Anna was putting away all her new clothes a young woman walked into the room and slumped onto the bottom bunk nearest to Anna's bed, and sighed deeply before looking at Anna.

"Hello," she said, "my name is Anzhela, but everyone calls me Angel. Where did you live before they kidnapped you?"

Anna smiled.

"Hello Angel, my name is Anna, and my home is in Ekaterinberg in Russia. Where do you come from and how long have you been here?"

"Hi Anna it is nice to meet you, but I would rather be meeting you in Russia under more pleasant circumstances. I've been here for about six months, and they've been the worst six months of my life so far. Being a sexual plaything for strange men is not what I had planned for my life, but at the moment there isn't much choice. My home is a small place called Faleshty in Moldavia, and I am here because I believed a smooth talking bastard who told me he could get me a wonderful job as a secretary in London. What about you?"

"I was emailing with a man in Albania who turned up in Ekaterinberg one day and invited me out to dinner. I met him in a nice restaurant and I was enjoying the evening until I went to the toilet. When I got back to the table I had a drink of wine and the next thing I knew I was in Tirana being sold to a German man. The German brought me to his house in London where he raped and abused me, then forced me to have sex with lots of other men before selling me to the man who owns this house. But enough of me. What is it like working here?"

Angel gave a grunt of derision.

"What we do here isn't really what would normally be regarded as work. What do you know about sex?"

Anna was surprised at the question, but shook her head.

"I know almost nothing at all. So far I've just laid on my back and let them get on with it. The German was the first man to touch me, and since then I've been forced to let about forty men, or more, have sex with me, but so far they have all been fairly normal and gentle."

Angel smiled sympathetically.

"Well, one piece of advice I can give you is get plenty of alcohol down your throat when you go out to meet a man because it will help you to get through all the things they want to do to your body. But the best advice I can give you is whatever you do never kiss them, and always, always make them use a condom."

Suddenly the bedroom door was thrown open and Mickey looked in.

"Okay you two, get yourselves dressed and made up to look your best, I have two wealthy businessmen who want to take you out tonight for dinner before they take you back to their hotel for a few hours of fun. I will drive you to the hotel and introduce you to the men, after that I will be in the background keeping an eye on you to make sure you don't start talking about things you shouldn't be talking about. I'll be ready to go in an hour and a half, so you had better be ready."

The door closed with a bang as Mickey disappeared down the stairs.

While they were getting themselves ready to go out Anna asked Angel what the situation about drugs was, and were the women forced to take them. Angel laughed.

"Mickey doesn't force us to take any drugs unless we give him a hard time by refusing to go with the men, so he has a steady supply of free drugs which he can sell on the street. It's a good deal for him because he makes a lot of money, and as long as we don't give him any trouble he and the boss are happy."

Anna smiled.

"I'm very happy about that because I don't want to take the drugs if I can avoid it. I think I will just have to learn to smile at the men when I meet them, and keep my real thoughts to myself."

Angel laughed.

"That's a very sensible attitude, and I think you and I will be good friends. Oh, and one very important thing that you must always remember. Whatever you do, do not ask any of your clients for help to escape from this life. If you do they will probably report it to Mickey who will then take you away to a special quiet place and at least a dozen filthy old men will beat you, rape you, and sodomise you repeatedly. After the men have finished with you, Mickey will pump you full of Heroin every day for a week until you are heavily addicted. A few of the women have tried to escape from this life, but everyone of them was caught and suffered this punishment, and all of them now wished they had not tried to escape. I've heard that the alternative to this is what happened about a month ago to four of them tried to get help from their clients, the minders found out and told Nino and The German. The four were taken away and according to a recent newspaper story they were found with their heads, hands and feet cut off. The newspaper also said that parts of the girls bodies had been stripped of flesh to remove tattoos, and they had been badly tortured. So it is possible that these girls will never be identified and their families will never know what happened to them."

Anna listened in horror to the punishment for trying to escape, and decided that no matter what happened she must never try to escape unless she was certain they would not catch her. Thanking Angel for her advice she started to get herself dressed in some of her new clothes. They were more or less ready when Mickey opened the door to their room and ordered them to get downstairs and into the car.

Chapter 17

Dawn was breaking and the details of the houses and streets were becoming quite visible as Tony the pimp directed Jimmy towards a house that was in better condition than the last house they had raided. Although the area was not as run down as some of the nearby streets, it was still a little seedy. Tony saw the three men looking around gauging the value of the properties and said.

"These are the best places to house the women because around here no one cares what anyone else is doing so even if they hear a woman screaming no one interferes or phones the police. If we put them in houses in better areas, someone will call the police and tell them what is going on, and if we put them in worse areas, people think we are trying to make a squat or something and tell the police about us. So now you know why we choose this sort of area to house the women."

Dmitri looked at him in surprise, but nodded his understanding of the simple logic and asked.

"Who made the decision to buy houses in these sorts of areas?"

"The German, he was the first gang boss, and everyone else followed his lead." was the grunted answer. Suddenly Tony shouted in panic.

"Oh shit! Quickly stop the car and pull in here."

Jimmy's reactions were fast and he smoothly pulled the car into a parking space behind a large panel van, at the same time Dmitri turned to Tony.

"What the hell is the matter with you? What have you seen that caused you to panic like that?"

Tony shook his head.

"I'd forgotten that the men who guard the girls change over at dawn every day, and I've just seen four of the night guards coming out of the house, so the day guards must have just come on. This means they will be alert and ready to take action if there is any trouble, so maybe it would be better to come back tonight around one or two o'clock in the morning when they are tired and not so alert."

Jimmy looked over at Dmitri and Mikhail.

"He could be right. If we go in now they will all have their weapons on them so we could end up with a big shoot out, and there is no telling if any of the girls will get caught up in it. The goons may have already been told that we are on the hunt, so maybe a visit here during the early hours of the morning would be best. What do you two think?

Both of the Russians nodded their agreement with Jimmy's suggestion, but Mikhail wanted to know what they were going to do with Tony, and Dmitri smiled.

"We'll take him to the hotel and book him in with us. Then we can shackle him to the bed with the handcuffs and he can sleep for most of the day. But apart from that the only problem with leaving our visit until tonight is that the bodies we have left around will probably be found today so it's almost a certainty that all the goons will be on high alert and looking for trouble."

Jimmy smiled at his two friends.

"Judging by the look of expectancy on Mikhail's face I think he would be happy to go in and face the lot of them right now. However if we leave it until the early hours of the morning, we will have the advantage of our friend Tony here, who should be able to get the door opened for us."

Mikhail looked sad but nodded his agreement, and Dmitri looked at Tony.

"Well Tony, will you behave yourself and help us gain access to that house over there? If you do help us we will make sure you can go free once we have freed the girl we are looking for."

Tony was quiet for a moment as he thought over what had been said, then he decided.

"Yes, I will help you because I know if I don't one of you will make sure I don't survive until dawn, but remember if she has been taken to The German's house, I cannot help you because I don't even know where he lives. It is also possible that she may have been taken to Nino's house, so she can entertain some of his friends, and before you ask, no I don't know where he lives either. I don't get to speak to the bosses, it's always one of the boss's bodyguards who gives me my orders. All sorts of things might have happened, but I wont find out what's going on until I can speak to one of the bodyguards. I'm just a small cog in a very big business and the bosses tell me nothing so I owe them nothing. I just work for wages and make my extra money by selling a few drugs and skimming a small percentage off the money the women make. I don't owe loyalty or anything else, to anyone and I intend to survive and enjoy my life until I am an old man. So you will get no trouble from me at any time, as long as you don't try to get me killed.

The three friends nodded their understanding, and Dmitri told him they wouldn't deliberately put him into a dangerous situation, but they would not be able to guarantee him a long and healthy life. Jimmy put the car into gear and eased out of the parking place, and the passengers crouched down on the floor so no one in the house could see them as they drove past en-route back to their hotel.

Back in their hotel Jimmy suggested that they cut the cards to see who shared their room with Tony, and then hopefully they would get some sleep. Mikhail, with a flourish, produced a pack of playing cards and shuffled them like a professional dealer then placed the pack in the middle of the table. Dmitri turned up a Queen of Hearts, Jimmy a Jack of Spades, and Mikhail, after drawing an eight of Clubs, scowled at his two friends then picked up the pack of cards and handed them to Dmitri.

"These are more friendly towards you than they are to me so you'd better keep the pack, and maybe they will win some money for you one day."

Mikhail gestured to Tony.

"Come on little man, you can have the window side of the bed, and I will handcuff one of your hands to the bed so we can both get some sleep."

Jimmy and Dmitri headed off to their rooms smiling, while Mikhail, still scowling pushed the pimp off to their shared room.

It was two pm before the four men surfaced, and then only because their stomachs were growling with hunger so after showers and shaves they met in the hotel bar for a beer and something to eat. The bar menu had a Shepherds Pie special on which intrigued Mikhail. He wanted to know if it had originally contained a dead shepherd, a comment which made the barman smile, although he had probably heard the old joke many times before. The difference this time was that Mikhail seemed to be asking the question because he was honestly unsure of the answer.

"There are," he told them, "places in the wilds of Siberia, when it's freezing and food is short, where they make a similar dish but they actually make it with body parts from people who had died."

Hearing this Jimmy thought he should explain to Mikhail exactly what Shepherds Pie really was. But as Jimmy finished the explanation Mikhail shook his head and could no longer contain his laughter because he thought Jimmy had believed the story about the Russian version of Shepherds Pie. Then he settled for a large gammon steak with four eggs, mushrooms, French fries and beans for his breakfast, and was suitably impressed with his portion when it arrived. Jimmy took one look at the huge portion and slapped his friend on the shoulder and told him that after that terrible joke about the shepherds pie he hoped the gammon was like leather. In response Mikhail grinned and cut himself a large piece of gammon and chewed on it with a look of rapture on his face. After the meal the four men left the bar and found themselves a quiet corner table in the lounge well away from the other customers so they could discuss the coming action without being overheard. Even Tony, much to everyone's surprise, seemed keen to join in, and when asked if he could draw a detailed plan of the house where they thought the women were being held, he asked for a pencil and paper. When he had finished sketching the inside of the house, Jimmy noticed that there was a skylight in the roof that seemed large enough for a man to get through and suggested it might be a good entrance. But the pimp shook his head and told them that it was over a bedroom that could contain a group of maybe five or six women, and if someone dropped into their bedroom they would all start screaming. Dmitri grinned and commented that even a fit man would soon be exhausted if he was attacked by half a dozen horny women, so it wasn't a really good idea. Mikhail, with a solemn look on his face, nodded, but then muttered quietly,

"Yes, but what an incredible way to go, so if you need a volunteer I'm your man."

Tony heard the comment and started to laugh, but quickly stopped when Mikhail glared at him, but then all four men burst out laughing.

"Okay," said Dmitri, "the best plan for tonight is for us to gain entrance to the house the same way as last time. Jimmy takes the rear, and Mikhail and I, with you Tony, will go through the front door. Now Tony how does Jimmy get to the back door of this house?"

"It's the same as the last house. There is a lane that runs behind the houses, and the house that you will need is number thirty-three. There is a seven foot wall with a wooden door in the middle that might be unlocked, but if it isn't, it could be very difficult to open because it has a heavy bolt at the top and bottom. But the wall is easy to climb because there are some broken bricks that can be used as foot holds. However the back door into the house is always kept locked, but the lock is a cheap one that shouldn't be too difficult to open."

"Okay," said Jimmy, "give me four minutes start and I'll be inside waiting for you guys to talk your way in. But now I suggest we should take a time-out and relax for a few hours followed by a light meal and then some action, but first I think a drink would be a good idea." Dmitri called over a passing waiter and ordered a large whisky each for Jimmy and the pimp, and a large vodka for Mikhail and himself.

It was midnight when the three men and Tony the pimp met in the foyer of the hotel ready for a night of action. Jimmy drove carefully to the house where the new girls were being held, keeping to the speed limit so they didn't arouse any police interest. Soon they were parked a hundred yards from their target. The entrance to the lane that ran between the back of the houses was only a few yards from where they were parked. Jimmy took his kit out of the car and was soon dressed in his black overalls with his guns and ammunition stored in their holsters and pockets. Reaching over he patted the two Russians on the shoulder and gave them a thumbs up before disappearing into the darkness. Dmitri checked the time and as soon as the four minutes that Jimmy required were up, he gave the order and the three men walked to the house and knocked on the blue painted door. A shutter in the door opened and two dark eyes looked out and sized up the pimp who was stood there. A short muttered conversation took place between the man on the door and the pimp, but eventually the shutter closed and the Russians could hear the bolts being withdrawn. Fortunately the Russians made no attempt to rush the door because the door only opened a couple of inches on three strong looking chains. The doorkeeper looked out again, and after carefully checking that he could only see the pimp he closed the door again and took off the chains before finally opening the door to let Tony in. Mikhail was first through the door and he chopped the doorman in the throat to stop him calling out a warning, and Dmitri caught him before he could collapse on the floor and make more noise. Mikhail then handcuffed Tony and the doorman to a central heating radiator at the bottom of the stairs and told Tony that if he kept very quiet they would release him in a few minutes.

Jimmy appeared out of the darkness carrying an unconscious man over his shoulder and quietly told Dmitri this was the only goon in the back of the house so the downstairs rooms were now clear. Then he shackled the unconscious man to the same radiator as Tony and the doorman. With the downstairs area cleared Mikhail led the way up the stairs to the first landing. The three rooms that led off from this landing all seemed quiet and there were no lights showing. Dmitri indicated that they should each take a room and see if anyone was in there. Mikhail and Jimmy nodded agreement and the three men went to their respective doors. Quietly each man turned the handle before slowly pushing the door open enough to enable a quick glance into the room. There was one gangster asleep in each room and a few seconds later they had been rendered unconscious and handcuffed. Once more the three men gathered on the stairs and made their way slowly to the top floor where they found four closed doors. Once again Dmitri indicated which doors they should open. Two were empty and in the other Mikhail found four women who seemed to be sound asleep, so they turned their attention to the fourth door. Jimmy quietly opened it and glanced quickly inside. It was empty. Standing on the landing it was quietly agreed they should wake the girls and see if any of them knew where Anna had been taken. Waking the girls was easier said than done, it seemed that two of them were suffering from the after effects of whatever drugs they had taken, and were in a deep sleep, but the other two seemed to be more or less sober and stable. One of the women who woke quickly looked familiar to Jimmy and it was a while before he realised that it was the woman he'd seen in the club on the night they had taken Tony the pimp prisoner. Jimmy sat on the edge of her bed and looked into the eyes of the frightened woman before handing her the picture of Anna.

"Hello, I'm Jimmy. Don't be afraid we're here to set you free not to hurt you, but I need to ask you a very important question and I need a truthful answer. I think you know who this girl is and I need to know where she is living."

The girl stared at the picture for a moment then looked up at Jimmy.

"Hi, Jimmy I'm Debora. Yes, I know this girl, but earlier today our boss sent for her and one of the bodyguards took her away. I think the boss wanted her and some of the other girls to entertain his friends but I have no idea where he lives. However I think one of the men who guard this house would know where they have taken Anna, or at least how to find out where they have taken her. I'm sorry I can't be more helpful, but they never tell us girls anything."

Jimmy smiled at her.

"Thanks Debora, you've been very helpful and the information you've given me will help us find Anna and take her home. Now, if you girls would like to go back to your homes and families, I will call some people and make arrangements for you to be looked after by the authorities. They will make sure you are all treated well and returned to you parents. So please speak to your friends here and ask them what they want to do while my friends and I go and talk to the guards."

Debora nodded and turned to the others who had started to wake up. The three men left the women to discuss their unexpected situation while they went to talk to the guards. The goons were trying to look aggressive and unconcerned when Jimmy and the two Russians walked into the room. But when Dmitri stood in front of them and jacked a bullet into the breech of his handgun, they began to look frightened.

"Okay," said Dmitri, "I am going to ask you some questions. If you answer me correctly I will let you live, but if you don't I will shoot your kneecaps off. Then about ten minutes before you die from the loss of blood I will put a bullet into your belly about two inches below your navel which will ensure that you will die in extreme agony. Now who knows were this girl has been taken?"

After Dmitri had shown the goons the picture of Anna one of them started to try and say he didn't know anything about the girl but before he could get the words out one of the other goons snarled at him to shut his mouth if he wanted to stay alive. For a minute there was a shocked silence, but then the goon who had told the other man to keep his mouth shut, looked up at Dmitri and spoke.

"The bitch you are looking for has been living here for a while, but earlier today she was taken to the bosses house. Nino the boss is throwing a party for some of his friends, and very often his parties go on for days. We are not important members of the gang so we have never been told where the boss lives. The only other thing I can tell you that might be useful, is about a group of Albanian gangsters who do a lot of deals with Nino and The German. I'm sure they will know where the bosses both live, and they are meeting in a little Turkish restaurant at ten o'clock tomorrow night. If you ask them nicely they may tell you what you want to know."

Dmitri looked long and hard at the man before turning to Mikhail.

"He has confirmed what the girl told us. Will you make sure they are securely cuffed together so they can't leave the party too early. I think we need to talk to the women upstairs and see what they want to do."

Mikhail bent over the prisoners checking the cuffs were all tight, then gave Dmitri the okay gesture of finger and thumb circled, and the three friends made their way up the stairs. When they arrived in the bedroom all the girls were fully awake and a little frightened by the turn of events. Debora, told him they were worried about being sent back to their families because of what had happened to them. But Dmitri and Jimmy assured them in English and Russian that their families and friends would all be very happy to see them again. After some discussion between the women they decided that if they could get some help to break their addiction to the drugs before being sent home they would agree to go with them. Jimmy phoned a 24 hour telephone number he had memorised for just such an event and explained that he knew four women who had been forced into drug addiction and prostitution, but who now had the chance to break away from the gang that kept them drugged. The only thing they needed was help with their addiction and some counselling to help them come to terms with what they had been forced to do. They would also need help from the authorities to get them back to their families. The pleasant male voice at the other end of the phone gave Jimmy an address in London where the women should go and they would get all the help they needed.

Jimmy asked the man to contact the safe house and let them know there would be four women arriving in the next hour. The friendly voice assured him that they would be made very welcome and treated with sympathy and respect. Then Jimmy phoned for a taxi and was told the taxi would be with them in 15 minutes. As soon as the girls heard the news they rushed about packing everything into their cases to make sure they were ready to go when the taxi arrived. Dmitri gave each girl a hundred pounds to cover their initial expenses which surprised them, and added to the excited chatter as they finished their packing. In the end Jimmy had to shepherd them into the taxi before giving the driver the address and a big tip to make sure that he actually saw the ladies go inside the house they were going to, and not just leave them on the street.

With the women off their hands the three friends then discussed their next move. Jimmy suggested they go back to their hotel so he could phone his friends Danny and Lenny and put them in the picture. Then they could rest up and relax before they went looking for this Turkish restaurant where the Albanian gangsters were meeting. Mikhail nodded his agreement and suggested they would have to be on top form when they entered the restaurant because there would probably be at least a dozen gangsters there. Gangster's who would not take kindly to being questioned, even if they were asked in a very nice manner to tell them where Anna was being held. Mikhail's remark raised a laugh from the other three, but there was a general agreement between the men. Then Mikhail wanted to know what should be done with the guards that were presently all handcuffed in a bedroom. He was worried that if they left them alive they would very quickly tell every gang member that there were three gunmen searching for Anna, who are very happy to kill anyone who gets in their way. This would almost certainly sign the death warrant for her because once the gang bosses knew, they would kill Anna to stop her speaking out against them. They would also tell everyone that Tony was operating with them which would probably result in Tony being shot. Dmitri agreed, and although he was unhappy with any unnecessary killing he felt it was essential they kept their mission secret for as long as possible from the gangsters who were holding Anna. Jimmy suggested a single head shot would be the best way to dispense with the five handcuffed men. Five minutes later the job was done and Mikhail was fitting all the handcuffs back into his pockets as the three friends, and Tony the pimp, walked out of the house and climbed into their car.

During the drive back to the hotel Dmitri again assured Tony they would release him unharmed after they had found the girl alive, and then he could do whatever he wanted, but in the meantime he had to stay with them in case they needed his help to get into more houses. Tony nodded then surprised everyone by laughing.

"I'm very happy to stay with you guys, because you're the people with the biggest guns, so it's probably safer being with you than the other guys, and besides I enjoy sleeping with Mikhail!"

When they heard the pimps remark, Mikhail's mouth fell open, and Jimmy and Dmitri looked at each other in surprise, then Jimmy started to laugh and suddenly the four men all burst into peals of laughter. Then Dmitri's face took on a serious look.

"I suggest we all get whatever food and sleep we require and meet up again this evening to make sure we know what we are going to do when we find this Turkish restaurant. I also think it would be a good idea if our friend Tony here was left at the hotel tonight. If any of the Albanians recognise him it could make life difficult for him. One thing is for sure, I don't think the Albanians will be so easy to take down as the dregs of humanity we've dealt with so far, and once we've dealt with them we'll need to sort out this drinking den we've been told about. However, this could well turn out to be a job that would suit the physical talents of Lenny and his pal Danny rather than our killing techniques."

Turning to Jimmy, he asked if it would be possible for his two friends to join them for a night or two of activity. Jimmy nodded his agreement.

"If we didn't invite them down to join us, I'm sure they wouldn't speak to me for a month or more, so when we get to the hotel I'll phone Lenny and get him out of his bed so he can hear the good news. They should be able to join us for a couple of days, which hopefully will fit in well with our plans."

Chapter 18

Detective Inspector Peter Jones slammed the phone back onto its cradle with great force, his face bright red with anger. Detective Superintendent Banner, who was the cause of his anger, had just called him asking for information relating to an old case. Peter told him that he couldn't remember the case in question and didn't have that information handy, but Banner would find it in the archives. To which Banner had replied that he, unlike Peter Jones, was very busy and didn't have time to go pissing about in the archives, and couldn't Peter get his fat arse off his seat and search for them. Peter had told Banner in no uncertain terms that he was not fat, he was either a rotund or a portly gentleman. And as Banner didn't have the brains to read simple English he had better send one of his junior constables. What a way to start a bloody day he thought as he tried to calm himself. Peter was still angry at Banner's remarks when his office door opened and his assistant Detective Sergeant Johnny Morton walked in, at the same time Peter's phone started ringing. Waving Johnny to a seat he picked up the phone and after listening in silence for a minute he replaced the phone carefully back down on its cradle. Briefly the anger he felt showed on his chubby face as he looked at his assistant.

"Do you think we could arrange for this damned Hit Squad to knock off a few of our bloody political masters as well as all the sex trade gangsters? No, no, please forget I said that. I have no wish to be forced into early retirement just yet. But I have to admit the thought of a change at the top has a very attractive ring to it."

With a shake of his head to clear his thoughts Peter smiled at his assistant.

"Now then John please tell me you have something interesting for me and not just more of this damned bureaucratic trash," as he waved his hand over the piles of paper on his desk.

John Morton chuckled.

"My God boss you've certainly got it bad this morning. What have the old farts on the top floor been doing to you? But before you answer that, it would be a good idea if you listen to the latest information on the activities of the people we now call the Hit Squad. I've just received a call from our forensic friends to say that the Hit Squad has been busy again, and this time they have executed five more small time gang members. The bullets found in the bodies are the same, and the shell cases found at the scene are the same as those from the first house they hit. So there is no doubt it's the same people, and they don't seem to be too bothered about us finding out about them. Although at this moment in time we have no idea who these people are or even where they come from, or why they are on the rampage. It is also true that ballistics show the bullets come from guns that are unknown to us or the Europeans. Forensics also say they are sure it was the same four men who got into the house, but only three of them were responsible for the killings. They know this because the fourth man had been handcuffed from about the time they entered until just before they left the house. However forensics also said that the Hit Squad released four women who had been kept in the house. According to the local police they have located them at a hostel for females with addictions. It seems a man who spoke with a slight northern accent rang their contact number and told them to expect four women who needed help with their drug addiction and also help to get back to their families. The hostel where they had been taken was located by a local detective who realised the women may have been sent to a rehab house. He phoned around until he found the right place and then went round to speak to the girls. Unfortunately it seems the girls don't speak very good English so he couldn't get anything positive from them, and even the descriptions of the three men varied so much that they were virtually useless. That's the news in a nutshell boss so what do you think?"

Peter shook his head slowly and sighed deeply.

"Bloody hell John we definitely didn't need another five bodies. At this rate I'll be writing reports about this until I retire. Have you been over to talk to these women who were released? Also have you any information about the four murdered girls?"

John shook his head.

"I'm glad you mentioned more bodies boss, and yes I've got another report from forensics that tells us the four female bodies that were found recently were not English. The report speculates that based on DNA two of them could have come from Albania and the other two possibly from southern Russia which suggests to me that they could have been part of the sex trade run by the two bastards we've been investigating. So if the Hit Squad kills all of those parasites I for one will buy them a pint and give them a medal. But in answer to your first question, no I haven't spoken to the girls in rehab. yet."

Peter nodded.

"I agree with you about the Hit Squad John, but we mustn't let anyone else know how we feel. Now, will you go over and talk to the women as soon as you can, and please treat them very gently. They have been through more trauma in a short space of time than most people go through in their whole lives. They will probably be terrified of anyone in authority, and the thought of going home to their families who could be Muslim, probably frightens the hell out of them. It's quite possible that their families may refuse to accept them because of the sexual aspect of what they've been forced to do. The girl's honour is of major importance to some of these people and consequently they may find it impossible to see past their religion and their traditions. If the girls refuse to be repatriated you will have to set the wheels in motion to let them stay in this country for a while until they get over their trauma. Try to make sure they get all the help they need and with a bit of luck they may come to trust you enough to help us put the gang bosses behind bars. But whatever you do, don't say anything about us prosecuting the Hit Squad. These girls probably see the men who released them as heroes who have done more to help them than anyone else, so they will not give us any information that might harm them. By the way, are the local police checking with immigration to see if a small group of maybe two or three people has recently arrived in the UK from Russia or one of the old Eastern Bloc countries?"

John shook his head again and replied.

"I don't know about that boss, but I'll have a word with them and suggest they chase up the Immigration people to see if anyone has arrived here. Then I'll go and talk to the girls."

Peter smiled at his assistant.

"Okay you little scouse sod, what are you hanging around in my office for when you have so much leg work to do?"

But John was already waving as he went out the door.

Chapter 19

While Mickey was driving them to the hotel, Anna and Angel sat in the back of the car quietly describing their lives before they were kidnapped, telling each other about their parents and friends. As the time passed Anna became more and more nervous about what she was about to do. Even though this was not her first time to be a prostitute she still felt very nervous, maybe it was because it was her first time on what she thought of a double date. In the past when she had been with a man on her own, her mind had switched off and she had no real memory of anything that happened. But this time it seemed very different for some reason and she knew she would remember everything. Her nervousness showed as she bombarded Angel with questions about what she should do or not do, and how to act when she was in the company of these two men. Angel tried her best to answer all her new friend's questions in a way that would help to calm her a little, but nothing she said seemed to help and in the end Angel gripped her friend's shoulders and shook her.

"Anna," she whispered in an urgent tone, "stop this now. We are only going to meet a couple of ordinary everyday normal men. Most of the men we will meet are married with families, and they would be terrified if their wives knew they were with us, so they always use condoms to avoid any risk of catching a disease. And, because they are married, they are afraid of becoming involved with the law which means they never hit us or do really bad things to us!"

Mickey turned from his driving and in a harsh voice told the girls not to make so much noise because it was distracting him from his driving.

Slowly Anna got a grip of her emotions, and straightened her back. With a small smile she looked her friend in the eye and whispered.

"I'm sorry about that Angel, I promise I won't let it happen again. At least we do not have to walk the streets picking up anyone who is drunk and fancies our bodies."

The girls then tried hard to make their conversation as light hearted as possible, even managing to giggle a few times as they talked about old boyfriends. As Mickey pulled up outside the hotel he could hear the giggles and was pleasantly surprised, obviously Angel had managed to calm the new girl, and it sounded to him as though they may become good friends. If they did become friends it would make his life so much easier because individually they would be less likely to cause him problems in case they made trouble for their friend. As he climbed out of the car he raised his voice.

"Come on you two, get your sexy arses into gear and get out here. There are two wealthy men waiting to meet you so they can spend lots of money on you."

The car door opened and both girls stepped out onto the pavement then twirled around in front of Mickey to get his reaction to their new clothes. Although he had become hardened to the wiles of all the good looking women who had passed through his hands, he was silenced by the scene in front of his eyes. They were certainly two very good looking women, but it was their elegance that really stunned him, there was certainly nothing cheap about them. Suddenly the thought came to him that these two girls were beautiful, and for a moment he wished he could have met either of them under different circumstances. Then he shook his head and turned to wave to the two well dressed men who at that moment had walked out of the hotel. Mickey opened the rear car door so the two men and the girls could get in and make themselves comfortable. As the men were getting into the car, the taller of the two turned to Mickey and asked him to take them to a very well known restaurant called the Ivy that was usually frequented by well known media and other wealthy people, where a table had been booked for them. The two men gazed at the women obviously hardly able to believe how lucky they were to be with them, and introduced themselves as Steven and Brian. Angel carried on the conversation for a while to allow Anna to get used to what was being talked about, but Anna soon relaxed and joined in, and before long they were all chatting away like old friends.

By the time the car arrived at the restaurant Anna could hardly believe that she was actually enjoying herself talking with the two men and her friend. I bet, she thought with a smile, we all sound like old friends who have been dating for many months. Brian, the taller of the two men spotted her smiling and looked at her with a question in his eyes. Anna saw the query and laughed.

"I was just thinking that a stranger listening to us all chatting away would think that we have been friends or something for a long time, and I'm very happy that we all seem to hit it off so well. What do you think?"

Brian's eyes twinkled as he smiled.

"Great minds think alike," he said, but before he could continue Anna responded with the old quote.

"Yes, but fools seldom differ."

Hearing her response he burst out laughing.

"For someone whom I'm informed, has only recently started to speak English regularly, you are obviously a well read and very well educated lady, and it is my great pleasure to be spending some happy time with you."

As they got out of the car Brian stood next to Anna while Steven took Angel's arm and led the way into the restaurant. A waiter appeared and took their coats, then another waiter led them to their table and made sure they were all seated comfortably. The scene reminded Anna of the last time she had dined out at a good restaurant. I only hope, she thought, that I don't live to regret this night as much as the last time I dined out. Then she smiled at Brian and asked him what he recommended as the main course.

"I rather like the thoughts of tucking into the stuffed mushrooms followed by the fish," he said.

"That sounds good to me also, so I think I'll have the same, and could you please pour me a glass of that white wine, my throat feels quite dry."

Brian smiled at her and poured the drink before signalling for the waiter.

Anna glanced across at Angel and smiled because Angel was deep in conversation with Steven and looked as if she was enjoying herself.

Two hours later, after an excellent meal, they were all enjoying their coffee and brandy, and although the conversations were still interesting, they were slowly starting to dry up, so Steven asked the waiter for the bill. They had reached the point were the conversations were becoming more personal and neither of the men wanted to discuss their private lives. In fact both men, after enjoying the wine and food, were starting to feel much more interested in getting the girls back to their hotel rooms and into bed.

"Okay ladies," said Brian, "if you are ready, shall we ask your driver to take us back to the hotel?"

Both girls nodded their agreement and asked the waiter for their coats. Mickey had the car ready for them as they came through the door. Once in the car the men put their arms around the girls so they could pull them close. At first Anna was a little reluctant but a quick glance at Angel indicated that this was considered normal because Angel had put her arm around Steven's stomach and snuggled up to him. So Anna leaned against Brian and rested her head on his shoulder, and smiled to herself because Brian appeared so happy and relaxed that if he'd been a cat she would have heard him purring. Suddenly the cold curling tentacles of fear stirred deep in her belly. What, she thought, is going to happen when we are in his hotel room? Is he going to be gentle and loving, or is he going to be rough and take me by force? If he is loving and gentle I will acquiesce and let him have his way with me, but if he is rough I'll wait until he hurts me enough to leave a bruise then I'll fight back, and we will see how he likes to be hit and hurt. With these thoughts she reluctantly dragged her mind out of the warm snug little place where it had been hiding. It was now time for her to get back to reality and start planning her responses to the various moves that Brian might make when they were alone together. As Angel had told her, if she knew what was likely to happen it wouldn't make her feel so vulnerable. After arriving in the hotel foyer the men were about to go and get the keys for their rooms when Angel suggested that as the bar was still open it would be nice to have a nightcap together. Anna clapped her hands delightedly and looked at Brian.

"Oh yes that sounds wonderful, can we do that, please?"
Both men nodded a little reluctantly and led the girls into the bar area where they found an empty table in a quiet corner and ordered brandy for the girls and whisky for themselves. The conversation around the table was rather desultory but the girls managed to hold out for a further three more drinks before agreeing that it was, at last, time for bed. The short distance to the bedrooms was completed in silence, and Anna soon found herself alone with Brian in his bedroom. He stood there just looking at her for a while admiring her beauty and elegance before opening his arms to her. Slowly she walked into his arms and put her arms around his neck as he gently but passionately kissed her. Anna soon felt as though her legs were melting, and was surprised when she suddenly realised that most of her clothes were lying on the floor where Brian had dropped them. She was even more surprised when he picked her up in his arms and carried her to the bed where he laid her down and covered her with the lightweight duvet. It was at this point that Anna suddenly realised how aroused she was. She wanted to make love to this man and she wanted him to make passionate love to her immediately, so she held her arms out to him as an invitation. Brian obviously did not need a second invitation and was quickly holding her naked body against him, but somehow he managed to keep complete control of himself and his body. He started by kissing her in the same gentle but passionate way that he had before, and it wasn't long

before Anna had almost lost complete control of her body to the pleasure that she was receiving from his tongue and fingers. If only she could have lost her virginity to this man, she thought, but maybe this was fate showing her that making love could be wonderful. Then the word condom flashed across her mind.

"Please Brian," she whispered to him, "please don't forget to use a condom. If you don't have any, there are some in my handbag."

He looked down at her with a smile and nodded before reaching out and after a few seconds searching he found the group of small packets.

The next morning Anna opened her eyes to find that Brian was already up and in the shower, getting ready for a day at the office. She stretched luxuriously and felt wonderfully content as memories of their love making came back to her. Immediately she started to feel aroused and ready to re-live it all over again.

"Brian," she called, "what time do you have to go to work?"

The bathroom door opened and his smiling face appeared around the corner.

"Am I to understand," he asked, "that you are in need of further physical comfort?"

She laughed and nodded vigorously.

"Yes please. So come here and make love to me, I need you inside me now."

Fifteen minutes later they were so involved with each other they didn't hear the phone ringing, or the knock on the door, but then the phone rang again and Brian reached out for it and listened to whoever was on the other end.

"That was Steven to say that we only have half an hour to get some breakfast before the car arrives to take us to the office,. So my sweet Anna, I'm afraid I have to get ready. But I would be very grateful if you could ring room service and ask them to send up scrambled eggs, toast, and coffee for me, and whatever you would like for yourself, while I finish off my shower."

"Okay," she said with a disappointed look on her face, and picked up the phone.

Anna managed to get showered and dressed whilst Brian grabbed a quick bite of breakfast before they met up with Steven and Angel in the hotel foyer, just in time to see the company car pull up outside the hotel, and with a wave the two men went out to the car and were driven away. Anna and Angel made themselves comfortable in the hotel lounge and waited for Mickey to come for them.

"How was your first night as an escort on a double date?" Asked Angel.

"He is such a lovely man, and so gentle but with lots of passion," replied Anna with a shy smile, "I really enjoyed myself and would be happy to have sex with him at any time. But how was your night?"

Angel laughed and winked at her friend.

"They are all the same to me, but at least he didn't want to do anything kinky or perverted, so I'm grateful for small mercies, and he only managed to do it once which meant I managed to get a good nights sleep. But Anna, you are treating this like a night out with your boyfriend which is great. But you must remember that the next man you are with will probably make you feel like a slut, and a whore, and you could loose your self respect. When that happens you will probably start to think about taking the drugs to try and make you feel better about yourself. But if you do that you will have lost everything, so please don't let this happen."

Anna nodded her understanding of what Angel was telling her.

"Yes I understand what you mean and I promise to try and avoid falling into that trap, and if it does seem to be happening to me will you please help me?"

Angel gently squeezed her friends arm.

At that moment Mickey arrived and was happy to see Anna and Angel smiling at him.

"You girls must have been bloody good last night because those two guys have already phoned the office and arranged for you to join them

again tonight. They want to take you for a night out to one of the best nightclubs in town. The boss is very happy with you both and plans to keep you just for the big spenders, and he's given you both the rest of the day off. So get yourselves in the car and we'll get back to the house."
While he was driving Mickey spent the time thinking over what he had been told earlier that morning when one of the The German's bodyguards telephoned him. At first he could hardly believe what had been said, but common sense told him it must be true. At least ten members of the gang, who like him looked after the women, had been executed by some unknown gunmen. The bodyguard had told him that nobody knew why this had happened or who had carried out the killings, so it was essential that everyone started asking around to try and find some answers. To Mickey the answer seemed obvious, someone was searching for one of the kidnapped girls, and he wondered why his boss hadn't figured it out. But it wasn't up to him to tell his boss how to sort this problem out or get involved with the sick bastards at the top. When he'd read the story about the four murdered and tortured girls in the newspaper Mickey had been stunned because it was so obscene. Then he remembered some gossip he had heard which indicated that The German and Nino had been involved with the murders and Mickey didn't doubt it. He knew for sure that both men were sadistic bullying bastards who enjoyed mentally and physically torturing the girls. But then another worrying thought hit him, what if these killers were looking for one of his girls? If they were it was highly likely that the killers would put a bullet in him when they came to rescue the girl. Mickey was much more interested in staying alive than trying to find out who had been killing the gang members. He wanted to carry on with his easy life looking after the girls and earning extra money from the drugs, he certainly didn't want to get involved with any killers. As long as he was safe and healthy he was happy. But what could he do about it? He shook his head, nothing he could think of made any sense to him so he decided he had to keep his wits about him and watch out for any strange things going on. Some hours after arriving back at the house, Mickey was in his room and once again taxing his brains to find the best way to keep

his skin from getting bullet holes in it when the phone rang. It was the same bodyguard who had phoned him and told him about the killings, this time the news was even worse. The bodyguard told him about an explosion in a Turkish restaurant that had killed all the Albanian gang who had been eating there. Mickey promised the bodyguard that he would ask around to see if he could find out who was responsible for the killing. But after putting the phone down he began to wonder if it would be safer if he went on holiday to somewhere far away. The problem with this plan was his boss would immediately think he was involved with the killings and have him hunted down and killed. Mickey began to feel sorry for himself because whatever he did he could end up dead.

For Anna and Angel this was to be just one of many visits they made to this particular club in the company of different men. It was a place they enjoyed and they looked forward to it. Angel had first heard about the club from one of the other girls shortly after she arrived in the house and told Anna that it was supposed to be where a lot of celebrities went to let their hair down. So it was possible they would see some well known actors and singers. Anna was quite excited about going to the club and possibly seeing some of the celebrities she had heard about. For the rest of the day the two girls spent their time washing their clothes and cleaning their room before relaxing and dozing in preparation for another night out. While laying on their beds they discussed the men they would be going out with, and once more Angel sounded a note of caution to Anna. She tried to impress upon her that not all men were as nice as the two they were going out with, and because of this Anna should keep her emotions and feelings under very strict control.

Chapter 20

The day after the explosion that devastated the Turkish restaurant, the local newspapers and TV reported that the explosion had been caused by a faulty gas heater. But Liverpool born Detective Sergeant Johnny Morton knew better because he had read the forensics report, and was looking forward to getting his teeth into the investigation. In his mid-thirties and still single Johnny was an impressive looking man, a little over six feet tall with an athletic, well muscled, build that he maintained with regular workouts. He enjoyed his work as a detective, pitting his wits against some of London's cleverest criminals was a bit like playing his favourite game, chess. And the report he carried in his hand indicated he would need to be at his best if he and his boss were to resolve this case satisfactorily. The initial forensic report made very interesting reading, indicating that the explosion had been caused by some sort of plastic explosive. They would know exactly what sort after they had completed their tests. This, he thought, was not the normal method used by local criminals to knock each other off, so maybe something much bigger was afoot. Knocking on the door of what was laughingly called his boss's office he walked in waving the report. The room was around ten feet wide by fourteen feet long with a large window at one end covered by bright yellow curtains which his boss's wife had made, and the door at the other. It contained three filing cabinets and a medium sized oak desk and three plastic chairs. From behind the desk Detective Inspector Peter Jones looked up at his assistant with a pained expression on his face.

"What have you got there John? Something interesting I hope because I'm bloody sick of all this damned paperwork. I'll even enjoy listening to your Liverpudlian accent if you've got something interesting to tell me."

After living in London for the past twelve years John's accent was no longer strong enough to be really noticeable unless he'd drunk too much red wine. So he ignored the remark, but noted that his bosses lilting Welsh accent had developed a distinctly sour note and decided against making a comical response. Instead he handed the folder over.

"You should read this very carefully because it throws a totally new light on what happened at that Turkish restaurant. For instance the explosion was caused by some sort of plastic explosive, and we now know that at least four of the bodies died from gun shot wounds before the explosion. It also appears that some if not all of the bodies were part of that Albanian gang of people traffickers we have been trying to nail down for the past eight or nine months."

"Well that's a good result, it will save us a lot of work and at least we will not have to try and deport the buggers. So tell me what conclusions have you already come to?" Peter urged.

"After reading the report I came firstly to the conclusion that there are some new players in the mix and these new players have decided to get rid of the opposition. If this is the case it would seem that some unknown person has hired himself, or herself, a hit squad to carry out the work. The chances are this hit squad have been brought in from abroad. None of our home grown killers would have carried out anything like this, or in this manner. But then it occurred to me that this explosion and the shootings may be connected with all the other shootings that have happened over the past few days. We will know for certain after forensics have matched up the bullets and shell casings. So after giving the matter some further thought the question I asked myself was, what scenario could cause a man, or men, to suddenly start killing off the criminals involved with importing women for the sex trade, and the people traffickers? Unfortunately I don't have an answer to that yet."

Peter Jones sat back in his chair with a far away look in his eyes as he considered everything his assistant had said. After a minute or two he leaned forward.

"I've also been giving some serious thought to these shootings and it occurred to me that if you were a father whose daughter had been kidnapped by the Albanians or someone who worked for them what would you do? Under normal circumstances you would put it in the hands of the police. However, what would you do if the police in your country were not always as efficient as they are supposed to be in the UK? Added to that, what would you do if you knew of, or were friends with, some ex-military special forces men?"

Looking at John Morton's eyes Peter saw the light of understanding switch on and nodded.

"Yes John, that's exactly what I would do as well. Now John also consider this, most of these girls come from the old Eastern Bloc so it is reasonable to think that the men who are giving our criminals a headache are probably ex-Spetznas or whatever they call the Russian special forces. However these Russians would almost certainly find it difficult to carry out these hits without the help of someone who lives in this country and knows his way around. I suspect this person could also be ex-military. So John can you please have another word with Immigration and find out if we've had a group of two or three men from Russia or one of the old Eastern Bloc countries landing in this country during the past two weeks. If such a group has entered the country find out where they are staying while they are here, and then let me know so we can go and call on them. This is very important so you can be a bit heavy handed with them if you feel it will speed things up."

John grinned at his boss's reasoning.

"Sounds good to me boss. Immigration has not come back to me or the local police yet about possible suspects coming into the country, but I'll chase them up again before I get on with everything else, and I'll keep you informed of any progress. But please remember to read that forensics report. Now I'll let you get back to those exciting reports you're doing for the top brass, I know how much you enjoy doing them."

Peter snorted and growled.

"Go on you little Scouse sod, bugger off and get some work done instead of bothering me."

Peter smiled as his assistant waved and left the office. At fifty five years old Peter tended to think of John Morton as the son he and his wife Myrtle had longed for but never had. The two men got along very well even though they were both highly competitive, and thoroughly enjoyed their battle of wits on the chess board. Their frequent verbal battles were legendary and much enjoyed by any of the police force who happened to be around at the time. The subject of these battles was invariably their differing views about a case they were working on. But the results were always the same, the two men agreeing on the motive for the crime and then taking the perpetrator into custody. They had worked together for more than five years and John Morton had quickly learned that his boss's appearance was a wonderful camouflage for his quick brain and bulldog like persistence. If ever a man looked less like a policeman it was Peter Jones. In fact John tended to think of him as someone who looked a little like Friar Tuck from the Robin Hood stories because he was five foot eight inches tall and rather rotund. His face was plump with rosy red cheeks and piercing bright blue eyes, and what was left of his hair was a band of wispy curly white hair that surrounded the bald patch on the top of his head. However Peter quite liked his appearance because it gave the criminals the feeling that they were dealing with someone who was a bit of a soft touch. This gave him a big advantage during interrogations because it made it easier for him to trap the bad guys into admitting their guilt.

Opening up the forensics report Peter immersed himself in the gory details. The doctors and scientists had almost found enough body parts to make up the bodies of twelve men which probably meant that the gangsters were either celebrating something or planning something. The fact that maybe half of them had been shot prior to the explosion told Peter that a hit squad had entered the restaurant to obtain information. At a guess he thought the squad must consist of at least three men, fewer would not be enough to overpower the Albanian gang of killers, and more than six would probably require two vehicles for transport which would make the squad more obvious. In view of the shootings and the explosion it seemed obvious to him that this Hit Squad were quite prepared to use whatever means necessary to get the information they wanted. Peter was sure there must have been at least three people responsible for the shootings because the Albanians would have been armed and not easy to take by surprise. Then a thought crossed his mind that really surprised him and it took him a moment to realise why he was surprised. Forensics had not found a single weapon or mobile phone amongst the wreckage. The only possible answer was that the Hit Squad had removed them all before the explosion. This scenario fitted quite well with the other shootings that had occurred and the more he thought about it the more he became convinced that the killings would continue until such times as the Hit Squad, whoever they were, found what they were looking for. Peter smiled to himself and relaxed back in his chair and let his thoughts wash over him. Maybe he should just let the Hit Squad kill off all the gangsters. It would certainly save the police, and the public purse a lot of time and money, and it would also save some space in the gaols. There were certainly plenty of other crimes that needed to be resolved, and he was fairly sure the general public wouldn't worry too much about these sex trade gangsters being killed off. But then he looked glumly at all the bureaucratic paperwork and wondered what the Politically Correct lobby would say if they knew what he was thinking. The sight of all the paperwork that he still had to sort out, brought him back to reality and he thought, I'll never have time to catch damned criminals with all this paperwork to do, even if they let me hire a secretary.

Chapter 21

Anna and Angel were exhausted after spending most of the night on the dance floor and were happy to have spent the time with Brian and Steven. But by two o'clock in the morning they were all ready for sleep and Brian suggested that it was time for them to go back to the hotel. Brian and Anna enjoyed another passionate night while Angel was happy to get a good eight hours sleep. The next morning the two men dragged themselves off to work and the two girls got into the back of the car and fell asleep while Mickey drove them to the house. As they got out of the car Mickey told them that they had been chosen to attend Nino's house party. So once again they had to be dressed and ready to party at 7pm. The girls went to their room, rolled onto their beds and slept for a good six or seven hours before waking and getting showered ready to face the day. Angel asked Mikey if he would order a large pizza for them because they were very hungry. He retorted that their problem was too much sex and not enough sleep, but he picked up the phone and placed the order for them. Later as the two girls sat on their beds devouring the pizza Anna asked her friend what the party at Nino's house would be like for them. Angel snorted in disgust.

"For the men it's a chance to drink more free alcohol than they can really hold and brag to each other about how strong and fearless they are. Or maybe how good they are at out-smarting the police. For you and I and all the other girls who will be there we will be given something like a mini-skirted Roman toga to wear without knickers or bra. Then we will have to mingle with the guests and let them stick their hands up our skirts and feel our bottoms and breasts without complaining. Any girl who complains will immediately be injected with heroin or something similar, and by the way the only girls who ever get invited to these parties are girls who are not addicted to drugs. The bosses do this because they know these are the girls who will try hard to please so they don't become addicted."

Then Angel's eyes twinkled and a wicked smile curled her lips.

"However there is a way that I've found which stops most of these dirty bastards from putting their hands up my skirt, but it is a secret that I have managed to keep to myself. It is very simple really and I will tell you, but you must promise to keep it secret."

Anna laughed.

"Oh yes I promise to keep your secret, please tell me what it is."

"Well, as I said, it is very simple you just rub butter all over your vagina and bottom. When the men put their hands up your skirt they feel this sticky slippery stuff and immediately pull their hands out because they think it is another man's sperm. Most of them think another man's sperm is a disgusting thing for them to touch, and because they are drunk they never notice the smell. So you see Anna once they think you have already had sex with someone a lot of the men will not want to have sex with you and leave you alone. The only thing you have to do with the men who still want to have sex with you is stay out of their way and maybe put some tomato sauce on your vagina. The men will think you are having your period. Or you can keep mixing with the guys that are not interested. Occasionally you can go right through the night and not have sex with any of them, but you have to be a good actress to do that."

Anna's happy smile had disappeared and been replaced by a look of disgust.

"Do you mean that while we are at the house any of the men there can just demand to have sex with us whenever they feel like?"

Angel nodded.

"Yes, that's exactly what I mean. It's just like an old Roman orgy, but because Nino likes teenage boys, most of his friends also have similar tastes. Nino sometimes arranges for five or six teenage boys to be brought in from Thailand, but maybe tonight there will not be any boys. Then the problem is when Nino's friends get drunk they think it would be a great experience for them to treat any of us like boys. You'll soon know when they are starting to feel like this because they will ask you to get dressed up in grey shorts, a white shirt and to wear a school cap and hide your hair under it."

Anna slumped back on her bed.

"Oh my god, I can't believe I might have to go through that anal sex thing again. That fat ugly German bastard forced me to go through it a few times and I couldn't believe how painful it was, and he only had a small dick. What the hell would it be like with someone who's dick is six inches or even more! I have a feeling that tonight they will have to inject me with heroin or something to make me do that again, at least with the heroin I'll be totally relaxed so maybe it wont hurt so much."

Angel however, instead of agreeing with Anna about her vision of what might happen, started to laugh.

"Anna you worry too much. Some of the women think that anal sex is wonderful and are very happy to have sex that way. But let me tell you about a very easy way to avoid the anal sex situation you're so worried about. What you do is push a couple of pieces of dark chocolate up your bum so that when it melts it looks as if you have shit yourself. Then when the bum boys see that they will leave you alone. They only like to play with your bum when you've had an enema and cleaned yourself out. They do not like to shove their dicks into a bum that is covered in shite."

At first Anna didn't look too sure about Angel's method of avoiding anal sex, but then she started to laugh.

"Oh Angel what a crude pair of women we have become. If only my friend Katya could hear us talking like this she would be very surprised, but I suspect she would also find it very funny. When I eventually meet up with her again I'm going to take great delight in telling her about some of the things you and I have been talking about. You know I think the three of us would have a wonderful time together, and I pray the day we all get together will be very soon."

Angel smiled but her eyes had a misty look.

"I think that would be wonderful Anna and I look forward to meeting your friend Katya, I'm sure we would all become very good friends. You are very lucky to have such a loving family. My family is also a loving one but unfortunately when they find out that I have been a prostitute and not a secretary my father will say that I have dishonoured the family. Then I will no longer be welcome in the family home. If and when this happens I don't know what I will do. As a Muslim woman my education has been very limited so I'm not really equipped to do any jobs except perhaps for domestic work. So if I am ever released from the clutches of these gangsters I think I'll stay here in London and work for myself as a call girl and try and save up a lot of money. Then if I am lucky I could maybe go home dressed as a respectable secretary and my family will welcome me home. So who knows what the future holds for me."

Anna reached over and hugged her friend.

"If we ever escape from these people, you must come home and live with my family. My father would be very happy to have such a lovely lady staying with us, and he can soon arrange for you to learn all you need to know about how to be a very good secretary. Please say that you will think about this, rather than planning on staying in London and being a call-girl."

Angel looked at her friend with tears in her eyes.

"I'd be very happy to stay with you and your family Anna, and meet your friend Katya. Oh it sounds almost too good to be true. Please promise me that if we escape from this place you will not forget me because since we met, your friendship has kept me sane."

Mickey's voice broke into their quiet and a little tearful conversation telling them to get some sleep instead of chattering about all the things they wanted to do in the future. This stopped the girls in their tracks and they wondered how he could have known what they were talking about, but they soon realised that he had just been guessing about the subject of their conversation. Then they smiled at each other and lay back on their beds to try and sleep for a few hours, but for a while Anna could only worry about what she might encounter during the coming party.

A few miles from where the two girls were trying to sleep, Nino and The German were in a worried discussion. They couldn't believe that no one within their organisations had been able to discover anything about the men who were responsible for the killing of their men.

"Who the hell is behind these shootings," Nino groaned, "if I could get my hands on them I'd soon make them sorry they ever bothered us." The German who for a few days had thought about nothing else, didn't answer because he had remembered the message he had received when he had picked up Anna the blonde girl from the Barn in the Albanian hills. The message that told him there were four Russians chasing him to rescue the young woman, and these men had already killed and tortured Turkish Ali and all his bodyguards before setting fire to Turkish Ali's house. It had suddenly all become very clear to The German when he remembered the message. But this knowledge frightened him because he knew how brutal and efficient the Russians could be when they were tracking someone. It was at this point that he came to a decision and told his friend

"Nino, my friend, I think it could be the Russians who are looking for one of the girls that Turkish Ali's men kidnapped. I've been been told that Turkish Ali and his men were tortured and killed by these Russians, so it's possible that Ali may have told them that it was me who bought the girl. If this is the case I suggest that we put all our guards on duty for the party tonight. Then if the Russians do decide to pay us a visit we will have maximum fire power available."

"Bloody hell," screamed Nino, "why didn't you fuckin' tell me about this before? Who is the female they are searching for, do you know?" The German nodded.

"Yes I'm sorry Nino I should have told you about this before, but I never thought all this killing would happen. I think I know who they are searching for, it's the blonde beauty that you bought from me recently. Her name is Anna, and her family obviously have very good contacts with some top political and military men. Right now I would guess they are planning to hit you and me to find out where she is being held, but I cannot believe they are clever enough to have figured out where we live or the fact that we are having a party tonight. Although I do think we should have all the men on duty tonight."

Nino was shivering with suppressed rage but the rage was a façade to hide the fact that fear was like a serpent writhing in his belly.

"Okay I'll call all my men in for the party, and I suggest you do the same. One good thing about this is the girl will be attending to the guests tonight so with all the men on duty I don't think even the Russians would take a chance and try to get in. I'll have Trevor my top man stick with Anna all night and if anyone tries to take her I'll instruct him to kill her if he can't stop her being taken. Then at least there will be no one to give any evidence or information to the police."

"That sounds like a good plan," replied The German. "I'll get onto my men in a minute and make sure they are all at your place tonight. Also I'm inclined to agree with you that even if the Russians are planning to pay us a visit tonight the sight of all our men around the place will put them off. Then we have to decide what to do about the girl. I think the best idea would be to sell her onto someone in France or Germany, or maybe even the Italians, they like blonde women there. Then we can put the word out on the street that she has been sold on. Maybe then the Russians will find out and go looking somewhere else for her. What do you think of that?"

Nino nodded eagerly.

"Yes, yes. That sounds like a good plan and I agree with you. Right my friend, now that we have got that problem sorted out, I have lots of work to do so I'll leave you and look forward to seeing you tonight at my place."

The German put his hand on Nino's shoulder in a friendly manner.

"Don't worry about a thing, I'm sure that everything will turn out well, and your party will be a great success. So go and get yourself organised and I'll see you later."

The two men parted company and although they both seemed confident and relaxed, they were both very worried about the possibility of the Russians breaking up Nino's party. In particular The German felt sure that if the Russians did find Anna and she told them that he had raped and abused her, they would make sure his last moments of life would be moments of agonising pain. With a shudder he tried to put these thoughts from his mind, but no matter how hard he tried his mind kept coming back to the Russians. Then he wondered if he should take a holiday for a couple of weeks and let nature take its course. When he came back he could soon get the business running again, and maybe he could take over Nino's business as well. Now that was an interesting thought.

Chapter 22

The day before Nino's party, Jimmy received a phonecall from Lenny and Danny to say they would be arriving in London in the afternoon and looking forward to some excitement. Jimmy suggested to Dmitri and Mikhail that they take the opportunity to let Tony show them around some of the tourist attractions while he waited for his two friends. The two Russians thought it was a great idea and they were soon walking out of the hotel with their cameras at the ready and Tony in tow. Danny and Lenny arrived at the hotel in their hire car and were soon sat in a quiet corner of the hotel bar with Jimmy discussing all aspects of the search for Anna, and the trail of bodies they had left behind. When he had finished painting the verbal picture, his two friends sat back in their chairs with big smiles on their faces.

"It sounds to me," said Lenny, "especially after that Turkish restaurant explosion, that you guys have deliberately kept all the fun to yourselves and only invited us down to help mop up the odd bits and pieces that will be left over at the end. But because we like you, we'll let you off this time as long as you don't do it again."

Jimmy laughed.

"I think you two should get along really well with Mikhail, he's as bloodthirsty as you guys. Which reminds me Mikhail and Dmitri are out sight seeing with Tony the pimp, but they should be back fairly soon. In the meantime I think it would be a good idea for you two to get some rest so you will be on top form and ready for what could become a right rumpus. We're going to a drinking den where some of the gang bosses' bodyguards go for their relaxation, and hopefully we will find out where their bosses live. Once we have the addresses we are planning on going to pay these people a visit and ask them nicely where they have hidden Anna. If they give us truthful answers we shall quickly put them out of their misery, but if they don't we shall encourage them to change their collective mind. However it's highly likely that all these guys will be carrying weapons of some description, so we can expect some sort of resistance. But most, although not all, of these people, are just second rate small time crooks who think that carrying a gun makes them a big man."

"Sounds good to us," said Lenny after glancing over at Danny, "but we're not carrying at the moment. Is that a problem?"

Jimmy shook his head.

"No, it's not a problem. I made sure we acquired a Glock handgun for each of you with a choice of holster. They're hidden in the hire car at the moment so we can all tool up before we go into the lion's den tonight."

Lenny looked doubtful for a moment as he considered a new thought that occurred to him before replying.

"I'm not sure that would be a good idea. If Danny and I go in to the bar tooled up and one of the bad guys spots it, it could end up with a bloody shoot-up and someone could easily get hurt. We don't care if its them, but it would really piss us off if it was one of us. So we'll go in as a couple of security guys who work for Ricki Brownlow in Manchester and we've come down to see if we can find a couple of good paying jobs in London. I know Ricki very well, and we have been friends for a number of years, so I'll ask him to give us a good report if anyone rings and asks about us. If we tell the bad guys we've heard on the grapevine that they all have good jobs working for a top man I'm sure one of them at least will not be able to stop himself from boasting a little bit. So we may find out what we need to know without any trouble."

"Ha," Jimmy snorted obviously not impressed with the idea. "If you believe that you must also believe in bloody fairies, but I suppose it's worth a try, and if it doesn't work we can always revert back to some heavy persuasion."

Their discussion continued for a while before they headed off to their rooms so that Danny and Lenny could unpack their cases and relax for a couple of hours.

At 7pm the five men and Tony the pimp assembled in the pleasant pale green, light pink and gold trimmed dining room, settling themselves around a quiet table set with crisp white linen and sparkling silverware. It was a corner table set back from the other tables and ideal for discussing their plan for tackling the drinking den without being overheard. By the time they had finished eating it was agreed that Danny and Lenny would go in first and try their friendly chatty approach while the other four would stay in their car. Then if that didn't work they could try something a bit different. But, as Dmitri reminded them, the bad guys probably already knew there were some very nasty people who have been going around killing off other members of their gang. So they will definitely be on the lookout for any strangers showing too much interest in them. Jimmy looked around the table at his friends and commented.

"Okay I think we know what needs to be done, but we have to remember that we need to keep at least one or two bad guys alive so we can find out the security codes to get into the houses of the gang bosses. Other than that I think we should get ourselves organised and ready to go at 10pm."

Then Dmitri stood up and paid the bill while everyone else headed for their rooms to get ready for the action.

The two cars followed the directions they had been given to the drinking den and it wasn't long before Lenny, who knew London very well, had figured out exactly where they were. He also recognised some of the street names and realised they were in an area not far from Soho. An area that had a reputation for being a bit on the wild side. The sort of area the more innocent visitors to the city could find plenty of hostess bars where under dressed women were happy to help unwitting businessmen spend their money. After parking the cars about 100 yards from the drinking den Lenny and Danny made their way to the front entrance. Slowly Danny opened the door and with Lenny behind him, made his way up a flight of bare wooden stairs that creaked and groaned very loudly. Then with a slight stagger and a foolish grin on his face Danny entered the bar room and looked around to make sure he knew where everything was positioned before walking over to the bar. Lenny following him into the bar also paused for a moment to orientate himself. With the low pink lighting the room looked quite nice and the bar appeared to be well stocked and laid out. The tables and chairs looked neat without being to close too each other, and each table was covered with a red and white chequered table cloth which gave the place a nice atmosphere. This place, Lenny thought, would look bloody awful in the cold light of day. In the daylight it would be possible to clearly see the poorly upholstered chairs, and cheap tables with beer mats stuck under the legs so they didn't rock and spill the drinks onto the threadbare carpet. Daylight would also show that the bar was chipped and scratched and cheap looking, and the well stocked bar could be seen to be well stocked by a lot of mostly empty bottles. But at night with the very low soft pink lighting the place could have been the best club in town. There were only three or four people sitting around drinking so navigating their way to the bar in the near darkness without colliding with a table was managed without accident. One thing that really surprised them was the lack of women sitting around waiting to scrounge drinks from an unwary customer. But they assumed the women would all be in one of the back rooms with the bad guys having a good time, waiting for the barman to call them when someone came into the bar. It was certainly different to the type of drinking places Lenny and Danny normally used, and after paying four times the normal price for a bottle of cold beer, they could understand why there were not too many customers. There was no apparent sign of the men they were looking for, but they guessed the bad guys would be relaxing in one of the back rooms with some of the women. These weren't the type of men who socialized with the ordinary punters at the bar, they preferred to mix with their own kind. Danny and Lenny walked to the darkest end of the bar and called the little bald headed barman over, and after ordering a couple of beers asked him where everyone was. The barman laughed revealing a mouth full of bad teeth and leaned over the bar so he could quietly tell them that all the men were in the back-room checking out a couple of new women. Danny and Lenny laughed in a friendly way with the barman giving the impression that they wished the boys well. Then they introduced themselves and started telling jokes. It wasn't long before the little barman was laughing so much the tears were running down his face and he was gasping for breath. Danny and Lenny were concerned that the little barman might have a heart attack or something so they stopped telling jokes and waited to see what would happen. Slowly the barman got his breath back and wiped the tears from his face.

"For God's sake, please stop with the jokes or I'll never make it to closing time. I haven't laughed so much for years. But I'm glad you're here and because I like you, you two buggers are welcome in here any time. Honestly you're a bleedin' sight funnier than any of those bloody 'willy woofters' on the TV. Here you go, have a couple more beers on the house."

The barman handed over two bottles of cold beer, and then spotted someone he recognised and called the man over.

"Hey Geordie, come over and meet a couple of nice guys.

The man who came towards them looked as though he spent a lot of time every day working out with the weights. Standing at an inch or two under six feet he looked as though even his muscles had muscles, and Lenny wondered to himself if the man could do anything except flex his huge muscles. The man even had tattoos on his shaven head and down his neck which helped to make him look quite fearsome, but Lenny knew that he or Danny could take him out without breaking into a sweat. It never ceased to amaze him that guys like Geordie hadn't realised that big muscles developed solely by using weights did not react quickly enough to beat someone who had trained and worked out correctly.

"Hey Geordie, I'd like you to meet two of the funniest guys I've heard for years,"

and he introduce Danny and Lenny. The newcomer looked at them over carefully and suspiciously before asking the barman for a beer. After taking a mouthful of his beer he turned to Lenny and Danny.

"What brought you two in here then?"

He asked, his voice full of suspicion and antagonism.

Danny gave him a disarming smile.

"We're down here from Manchester trying to find some contacts in the security business. We'd like to move down here where the pay and perks are better. Do you know anyone in the security business?"

The man called Geordie scowled at the two friends, and Lenny could almost see the man's brain working out what to say next.

"I might know someone but I don't know if he's interested in taking on more staff. I'll tell him you're here, he may come out and see you but then again he may not. Who did you say you worked for in Manchester?"

"I didn't say," said Danny, "but if it would help, we work for Ricki Brownlow. If you want I can give you his phone number so you can check us out."

Lenny nodded enthusiastically and said.

"Hey mate if you know someone and can put in a good word for us, that would be great, and we'd be really grateful for your help."

Geordie nodded and walked off towards a door that led to the back-rooms. As soon as he was out of hearing range the barman leaned over the bar.

"Take no notice of that fuckin' bad tempered bastard's attitude. For some reason all the men in that gang are walking around with long faces but no-one is saying anything to me about it. I think he'll tell Trevor, who's the senior one, about you because I heard a couple of them talking last night and it seems they are looking for some new guys. Anyway have another beer or two and by that time you'll know if there's a possible job or not."

Lenny and Danny lifted their beers and toasted the barman, then Lenny wandered off to find the toilet. When he found the place was empty he quickly called Jimmy on his mobile phone to tell him there was a good chance they might find all the information they wanted quite soon, then broke the connection. Back at the bar he and Danny were into their third beers when a man came through the door that led to the back room and walked over to them. This man looked very different to Geordie, he was taller with the build of a long distance runner. Immediately Lenny knew this was a man to watch out for, he looked very capable and had almost certainly been a military man for a number of years. He was neatly dressed, clean shaven and surprisingly seemed quite sober. His strong Yorkshire accent seemed warm and friendly and gave the impression that he was someone who would be easily approachable.

"Are you the two guys looking for a job?"

Danny and Lenny nodded in response to his question and introduced themselves. Then Danny gave him the story about coming down from Manchester and looking for a job that had better wages and perks. The man smiled and introduced himself as Trevor.

"My boss recently told me that he was looking for some extra staff. But before we discuss it lets go and sit over in the corner so we can't be overheard by some of the gossips that get in this bar."

The three men took their beers over to the table indicated and made themselves comfortable.

"Geordie told me that you were working for Ricki Brownlow in Manchester. As it happens I know Ricki quite well and phoned him to check you out. Ricki said you are a couple of really good lads to have around when things get rough, and you are not adverse to using any weapons that came to hand. With this in mind, and if you're really serious about looking for a job in London, I'll have a word with my boss in the morning. I think he will be interested, so if you come to the address I've written on this paper, tomorrow night he will see you.

When you get to the big wrought iron gate just announce yourselves on the entry phone and someone will let you in and meet you at the front door of the house and take you to see the boss. After that it's up to you. Is that okay with you?"

As he finished speaking he handed Danny a piece of paper with an address on it. Danny and Lenny grinned at each other and shook Trevor's hand enthusiastically, and promised to be there on time. Then Lenny said.

"I hope you don't mind me asking, but what is your boss's name?"

"Sorry I forgot to tell you. Everyone just calls him Nino. Now unless you have some more questions I'd like to get back amongst the animals before they start trying to kill each other."

Danny and Lenny laughed and thanked Trevor again for his help. Trevor stood up and returned to the back room while Danny and Lenny finished off their beers. Casually they left their empty glasses on the bar and after waving to the barman they walked out. Back on the street they strolled slowly back to their car, keeping a careful eye out behind them to make sure they were not followed, but there was no one taking any interest in them. Back at their car, Danny climbed into the driver's seat while Lenny walked over to where Jimmy was parked.

"Let's go and find somewhere we can talk and plan without anyone overhearing us. There's a supermarket car park about half a mile from here which should be empty at this time of night."

Jimmy smiled.

"I take it your little escapade has unearthed a gold mine, and yes the car park is fine, so let's go. I can't wait to hear the results of your scheme."

Lenny trotted back to Danny and jumped in beside him suggesting that they drove carefully to the car park so that Jimmy could follow them easily. Once they were there they parked in the darkest part and Lenny related everything that had taken place in the bar, and then showed them the address they had been given. It was agreed that they should go and have a look at the place to see what it was like and check out what security arrangements were in place.

The house was set back from the main road behind a wall that appeared to be about seven feet tall with an electrically operated iron gate wide enough to allow a large car to enter. On top of the wall there were large pieces of glass set into concrete and above that were two layers of razor wire, and the wire looked as if it was alarmed. Jimmy and Dmitri walked over to the wall and Jimmy climbed onto Dmitri's shoulders so he could see into the grounds. It looked as though the main deterrent to anyone entering the grounds other than through the main gate were a number of high intensity lights mounted in the numerous bushes and trees. Some of these lights were set at ground level and all were operated by fairly standard looking motion sensors. The drive from the main gate to the house was lined by three foot high bushes and around 50 yards long. It also appeared as if the tennis court to the right of the house had been turned into a car park for the guests. The main door to the house appeared to be substantial, similar to an old medieval castle door complete with big iron studs and to add to this visual effect most of the front of the building was covered with ivy. All the windows at the front of the house were leaded in a diamond pattern which made Jimmy smile. This meant that the windows had probably been replaced sometime in the last couple of years because this was when that style of double glazed window had been very popular. It almost certainly meant that all the windows were double glazed. Jimmy had seen enough and jumped down to the ground and brushed off any dirt left on Dmitri's shoulders.

"I've seen enough," Jimmy whispered, "to suggest that it might be difficult to get into the place without making a noise. Let's go and bring the others up to date."

As soon as Jimmy had finished speaking Danny laughed and nudged Lenny.

"Lets go and have a quick look at those windows. It might be easier than you think."

In less than five minutes the two men were back, and Danny had a big smile on his face.

"What you don't know," he said, "is that I once worked for a double glazing company making those types of windows so I know how to take them apart quickly and quietly. But not only that, I can also leave the frames in place and just remove the glass so any alarm wiring will not be touched, and I can soon teach you guys how to do this. So my friends the only thing you have to do is learn quickly about double glazing, and cope with the motion sensors on the lights, and a strip of duct tape or a can of black spray paint should do that job very effectively."

Dmitri looked thoughtful for a moment before looking at his friends.

"Are these motion sensors the type that use a programmable wide spread infra-red beam? If they are, they will be set up to only react to a mass of at least 100 lbs moving at between two and four miles per hour. They set them up like this so that the animals don't keep setting them off. Therefore if we approach the sensors slowly from behind or slightly to the side we should be able to stick three or four layers of duct tape on them quite easily."

There were nods of agreement from the group and slowly the tension dropped away from the five men, and even Tony the pimp was relieved as they realised the end of their search for Anna could soon be over and he would be released. Half an hour later they were back at their hotel getting themselves ready for a welcome eight hours sleep.

Chapter 23

Since arriving back at his office from his lunch break D.I. Peter Jones had been reluctantly working his way through the latest government information pack. As he reached the end of the pack there was a knock on his door and his assistant John Morton walked in. John took one look at his boss's face and said.

"I can see you're busy so I'll come back tomorrow morning when you've cooled off," and rapidly turned to make his escape.

"Don't you dare leave this office you little scouse sod." Said Peter. "I'm in desperate need of sensible adult conversation, so you will have to do for the time being. Now what have you got for me?"

John smiled and shook his head slowly as he sat down in the chair facing his boss.

"I don't know why you let the old farts upstairs get to you, you know they don't really know what's going on at ground level. However, I thought this might make you feel good. I've just received a note from the forensic people to say they are certain that the four women who were murdered had been brought into the country illegally and were therefore part of Nino and the Germans sex trade business. So it's highly likely those women were tortured and murdered either by the two bosses or by someone else on their orders. Also the immigration people called me this morning to say that two weeks before the first shootings, there were perhaps 100 people who had arrived from the old eastern bloc. Amongst these people there were two groups of fifteen who were part of some organised tours and most of the rest seemed to be individuals travelling on their own. However when I refined this information I found that during the week before the shootings there were only 30 individuals who flew into the UK, and amongst these people were two people who travelled together. Both of these people are business men from Ekaterinburg in Russia. I got in touch with a friend of mine in the Foreign Office and asked if he could find out anything on the background of these two men. The information he sent to me is fascinating and inclines me to think we may have found two reasonable suspects for the Hit Squad. They are a Mr. Dmitri Novikov and a Mr. Mikhail Bukolov, both are ex-members of the Russian Spetznas and are both regarded as heroes for their actions in Afghanistan."

Then he handed over a folder and suggested that his boss take some time to read it. As Peter opened the folder, John stretched out his legs, leaned back in his chair and closed his eyes. Peter glanced at his assistant and smiled to himself before turning his attention to the typewritten sheets in front of him. The information confirmed what John had said. Adding that both men had served with distinction and Mr. Dmitri Novikov had been wounded while saving Mr. Mikhail Bukolov under heavy enemy fire. At the end of the notes John had pencilled in a postscript to say that he had contacted the hotel where the men were supposed to be staying, but they had never checked in. When he had finished reading Peter looked over at his assistant and straight away John opened his eyes and grinned.

"Well," John asked, "what do you think?"

"I think we need to get photographs of these two gentlemen, but I'm sure that if we asked the soviet authorities for them, the gentlemen in question would be immediately informed of our interest in them. This would probably mean that they would quickly finish what they set out to do and disappear back to Ekaterinburg. Of course this would be the end of the problem for us because I can't imagine that anyone will bother trying to obtain an extradition order. Neither the public or the politicians will be interested in causing problems because a few low life criminals have been forced to 'pop their clogs' and enter the afterlife. In fact I could imagine that certain groups within the general public would probably prefer to give the Hit Squad a medal. Anyway John, if you were searching for a woman who had been abducted and forced into prostitution where would you start looking?"

"Well I guess I'd try and find out who had bought the woman, then pay him a visit and make him tell me where the woman was being held. But having said that, I suppose if I was a Russian it would not be easy to find out which gang boss now owned the girl."

Peter nodded. "You're right John, and it is this fact that makes me think the two Russians have an English accomplice. But knowing this doesn't help us very much. However, we now know that both of the major gang bosses who are involved with prostitution and drugs have had men killed by our friends the Hit Squad. Which I think means that they now know who has the woman they are looking for, and even now are probably preparing to go and call upon this damned gangster. The only thing I'm a little unhappy about is that we will not be able to bring one or both of the gang bosses to trial after the Hit Squad has finished its business. But on the other hand it will be doing us a favour by saving us an awful lot of leg work. Let me make a suggestion John, then give it some thought and see what you think. If we were to follow normal procedure we would contact the authorities in Ekaterinburg and ask for photos of these two men. So I think we should do this as soon as possible."

John Morton burst out laughing.

"Bloody hell boss you are a sneaky fellow. You want these guys to get away with it don't you?"

"Well I'm always happy to help anyone who helps us to reduce the number of evil people. After all it makes our life a lot easier."

"Okay boss I'll put in an urgent official request to the Ekaterinburg police through the Russian embassy for recent pictures of Mr. Dmitri Novikov and Mr Mikhail Bukolov. Then we can sit back and see what happens. Oh and by the way, a chap I know rang me this morning to say that our two gangsters are having a party at one of their houses tomorrow night."

Peter smiled.

"Well that is very interesting, and I think I can tell you what will happen. Right now we have at least three men who have at last found out who is holding the woman they are looking for. So in all probability they will pay a visit tonight or more likely tomorrow night to whichever of the two gang bosses has the girl. If she isn't at the house they will question everyone until they know where she is. Then everyone at the gang bosses house will be shot. They will then collect the girl from wherever she is being held and be on the next flight back to Russia and our problem will disappear. It will disappear quite simply because the political situation between ourselves and Russia is a little delicate at the moment. The politicians will not want to rock the boat by saying that we believe, but cannot prove, that two of their military heroes have been killing off our criminals and we want to extradite them. The Russians will tell us politely to get involved with sex and travel, or in other words to fuck off, and that will be the end of that. The old farts upstairs will do anything rather than upset the politicians because it might mean they will not be in the New Year's honours list. So I'm fairly sure we'll not hear anything else about it. Of course if we really wanted to find these three men we could put the houses of both gang bosses under surveillance. Then when all the killing is finished we can pick up the three men and the woman and charge them with all sorts of criminal charges. But of course we don't officially know where these three men are and we don't officially know why they are killing off the criminals. Nor for that matter do we officially know were the gangsters live. Maybe it would be better if we don't think about carrying out surveillance on the gang bosses for another three days or so. I know this is a bit naughty and if we are found out it could mean me taking early retirement, but I think it would be worth it. What do you think John?"

John started laughing and it was half a minute before he stopped and wiped his eyes.

"Boss you're a very devious man, but I think it might be better if we go over to Nino's house and see if we can catch the Hit Squad before they go into the house. Then we can warn them off. The only problem is we don't have nearly enough evidence to arrest the gang bosses and make the charges stick. Which means if we can't make the charges stick we could both find ourselves without a job. Therefore I think we have to approach this gangster party that is taking place tomorrow night very cautiously or the repercussions could be bad for us. I think we both need to give it some serious thought tonight and hope one of us can think up a plan for tomorrow night. Anyway boss it's time for me to go home and do some serious thinking. Goodnight."

It was lunch time the following day before Peter and John managed to meet again in Peter's office. Peter had been called into a meeting with the top brass to explain what was happening with the shootings case. Fortunately he had managed to stop the brass interfering by telling them that he was quite sure there would be a good result during the next two or three days. The top brass were not too happy with Peter's explanation, but as soon as he had mentioned that it might involve at least two all night surveillance jobs the resistance disappeared and he managed to escape from the meeting. The brass knew if they sanctioned the all night surveillance teams the overtime bill would be huge, and that would result in the politicians poking their noses into police business. However if two nights surveillance produced a positive result everybody would be happy so it would be worth the cost. Back in his office Peter had just settled himself in his chair when John Morton knocked on his door and walked in with a big smile on his face. Peter glowered at his assistant and growled.

"What the hell is making you look so happy, you little scouse sod?"

John tried to look surprised and shocked, but couldn't stop himself smiling.

"Hi and good day to you boss. I feel very happy because last night I had a really good idea and no matter how I try to tear it down I couldn't because all the bases are covered. Even after a good sleep I still can't see anything wrong with this idea, so I'm quite a happy man."

"Oh for gods sake John, will you stop waffling and bloody tell me what this wonderful idea is."

John shrugged his shoulders.

"Those old farts upstairs really gave you a hard time this morning didn't they. But I think I can make you feel better. I have found out from some people I know that the bosses of the two gangs, The German and Nino, will definitely be holding their party at Nino's house tonight. As usual for them there will be maybe thirty or more of their friends with maybe twenty or thirty young women attending to their needs. They will also have around thirty of their goons at the house, all armed and ready for trouble. Under these circumstances what do you think our Hit Squad would do if we stopped them just before they went into Nino's house and introduced ourselves?"

By way of an answer Peter just shook his head. So John continued.

"Well at first they might want to kill us, but hopefully when we explain that we need their help to get confessions from Nino and The German they will agree to our plan. We'll have to fit them up with a recording device or a voice transmitter so that we can record everything. Then we can tell the Hit Squad that if they get full confessions of all the gangsters dirty deeds for us, we will turn a blind eye to them leaving the country. Once we have the confessions and statements from all the girls and maybe some of the guards, and the information from forensics we can arrest the two evil buggers. With all this evidence we'll get a good conviction that will send the pair of them down for maybe twenty or thirty years. After that you and I will be hailed as heroes for catching the bad guys. Everyone will be so happy that we caught these criminals and broke up their gangs they wont even notice that the Hit Squad has disappeared into thin air, and no one will be interested in what happened to them anyway. What do you think of that for a plan boss?"

Peter spluttered behind his hand as he tried to stop himself laughing.

"How can you call me devious after coming up with that plan. John you are such a devious little scouse sod, but as a plan it does sound very attractive. Do you think we could get away with it, and do you think we could get the Hit Squad to get the confessions for us?"

John's face had a serious expression on it when he replied.

"Oh yes. These guys may be very hard men but I believe they are also intelligent and they know what makes the world go round. I think they will be very happy if we tell them that we'll look the other way so they can quietly disappear, if they get the confessions for us. Of course we'll have to insist they don't kill anyone this time, but we don't mind if they break a few bones to get the confessions. I'm sure they'll go for it. The only thing we have to do after that is keep our mouths shut about our part in this plan."

Peter sat back in his seat, with a big smile on his face and his eyes twinkling.

"Damn me John, the more I think about it the more I love it. But can you find out from one of your contacts which house the Hit Squad will go for?"

"Yes I've already asked, and been told it's fairly common knowledge there is a party at Nino's tonight and it's highly likely The German will be there as well. However The German and Nino have been very clever at hiding their addresses by moving every-time their address became known to the police. So someone on the inside is keeping them informed. The last time Nino moved was about twelve months ago, about the same time that I went to visit some old friends of mine. My friends and I went to the local pub for a pint and got chatting with a fellow who was moaning about the amount of work being done by his new neighbour. It seems the neighbour was having a large conservatory built to house a hot tub that could hold maybe ten or fifteen people. I asked the man the name of his neighbour, he didn't know but he described Nino very well. So I know where Nino lives, but the information must never be put in a report, unless we want to see him move again.

Now then. I'm sure the Hit Squad will have found out, one way or another, where the party is being held and be planning to become welcome or maybe unwelcome guests. So with a bit of luck we will get both Nino and The German at the same time."

"Oh joy," whispered Peter, "the thought of catching both of these evil sadistic bastards at the same time is so luxuriously exciting it's almost orgasmic. I haven't felt this good since I was on the beat trying to run fast enough to catch the bad guys. But enough of this reminiscing. Right John lets take the rest of the afternoon off and get ourselves organised for what could be a very long cold night. But before you ask, no we will not need to draw guns or any other similar weapons. The only things we will need is our good old fashioned truncheons, and a very persuasive way with the Hit Squad. Then with a squad of maybe forty big burly uniformed policemen, all armed with truncheons, we should be able to quieten the bad guys without too much trouble. Especially after the Hit Squad has frightened them into submission. Now off you go John, I'll meet you back here at seven pm then we'll go and have some fun. Don't worry about getting the uniforms organised, I'll arrange that with the old farts upstairs. It's about time they did something to earn their wages."

Chapter 24

The group of men known by the police as the Hit Squad were sat around a dining table in their hotel enjoying an early dinner. As usual Lenny and Danny were entertaining the rest of the group with their jokes and over the top stories although behind all the laughter there was a sense of tension. They all knew that the night could end up in a furious shoot-out and anyone of them could be seriously injured or killed in the fight, but even the threat of death or injury couldn't dampen their enthusiasm. Half way through the main course Dmitri held up his hand up to stop the general chatter around the table.

"I'm sorry to tell you that we could have quite a serious problem. As you know I speak to Boris and my daughter Katya every evening to let them know what is happening, but tonight it was Boris who had the important news. Boris is very friendly with a highly placed policeman in Ekaterinburg. This policeman phoned Boris earlier and told him they have received an urgent request from the British Police for photographs of Mr. Dmitri Novikov and Mr. Mikhail Bukolov. Boris has asked his friend to try and delay sending the photographs for 48 hours to give us enough time to get out of the UK. Obviously some clever British policeman has figured out what is going on and somehow realised that Mikhail and I could be involved with the shootings. Which means we have to find Anna in the next 48 hours and get her out of the country. So my friends let's hope that the gods will smile on us for the next two days. Now let's raise raise our glasses and wish each other good health, and damnation to our enemies."

The glasses clinked together then the serious faces started laughing again as Lenny told a very dirty Blonde joke that caused loud raucous laughter from his friends and rather disapproving looks from some of the other diners. As soon as Lenny and Danny realised they were annoying a few pretentious diners they increased their efforts to make their friends laugh even louder. But as soon as the meal finished Lenny looked at Danny and nodded.

"It's time for us to make a move mate," and both men stood up. "Okay," said Jimmy, "Let's meet in the bar in thirty minutes and finalise our plan for tonight. We don't want any cock-ups, they could be painful. I also suggest that we let Tony the pimp go free because we will either free Anna tonight or we will all end up dead and if the unthinkable happens who will free the poor bugger? But don't forget to warn him to keep his mouth shut and to stay out of sight for the next three days."

There nods of agreement from the men around the table as they made their way to their rooms to get ready.

At 9.30pm the five men known as the Hit Squad climbed into their cars and set off for the gangsters house with Lenny in the lead because he knew the address. The men were all silent, deep in their own thoughts, playing out the various scenarios in their minds trying to spot any danger points. They had discussed the plan to gain entrance to the house, which was probably the easiest part of the whole thing. But there were a lot of things that could go wrong once they were inside so they had decided to play it as it came to them. It was a dangerous situation but at least they would have surprise on their side. At the same time as the Hit Squad drove away from their hotel Peter Jones and John Morton drove away from the police HQ en route to Nino's house followed by five mini-buses with ten uniformed policemen in each bus. Both John and Peter were silently praying that they could convince the Hit Squad to accept their plan to get the confessions from the two gangsters. Peter had come up with a slight addition to John's original idea, he had typed up a statement saying that the confessions were given freely, so all that was needed was for the gangsters to sign on the dotted line. That, plus all the statements, recordings and forensic evidence, coupled with the small amount of evidence from the four murdered girls would send the two sadistic perverts to jail for life.

Peter and John arrived outside Nino's house and had twenty men surrounding the house with the remaining thirty ready to support any action that took place. John and his boss were standing the shadows not far from the house when they saw two cars pull up. Five men got out and started walking purposefully towards to main gate. Peter instinctively knew these were the men he was waiting for and walked towards them closely followed by John. When the two groups were within three yards of each other John smiled and said, "good evening gentlemen would I be correct in thinking that you are Mr. Novikov and Mr. Bukolov, and company? If you are, would it be possible for us to speak with you for a few minutes?"

The Hit Squad looked suspiciously at the two men in front of them for a few seconds that seemed like a lifetime to Peter and John, but then the older man in the group stepped forward and introduced himself as Dmitri Novikov before asking how they could help. Peter introduced himself and John and identified themselves as policemen.

"We are here to ask you for your help. We think we know why you are here and why there have been some shootings, but we are not interested in that. However we are interested in putting the two gang bosses and their goons behind bars so they will not be organising the abduction of any more women from the old Eastern Bloc. Now as you intend to go and join the party I would like to request that you obtain confessions both signed and verbal from these two evil men so we can start legal proceedings against them. I have some tape recorders for the audio confessions but most of all I would love to hear their confession with particular reference to four women who were very sadistically tortured and murdered. Unfortunately apart from some DNA traces and some other forensic evidence we have nothing to prove The German and Nino carried out these killings. But I know in my heart they did it. I also have to ask you to to please refrain from any more killings. We don't care if you break a few bones and frighten the crap out of these bastards to get the confessions because these can be put down to them avoiding arrest, but killings cause a lot of interest from my Senior Officers and we don't want this. If this can be done, none of you will have been seen and as soon as we have the confessions, you can leave and go wherever you want. Do we have a deal?"

Suddenly the tense dangerous atmosphere that surrounded the group of men changed. Dmitri laughed and held out his hand.

"It is a pleasure to do business with you Mr. Jones, are all British Policemen like you? Maybe you should put in for a transfer to the Ekaterinburg Police Department and teach them how to be real policemen. But how do you two unarmed men plan to take all the armed men in this house, prisoner?

Peter and John smiled at the men in front of them and happily shook hands with them all.

"It is my pleasure to do business with you gentleman," said Peter, "but I'm not too sure that my wife would be happy to leave her family behind and move to Russia, even though it is a very interesting thought. However in answer to your question about our ability to arrest these evil men. We have 50 large policemen armed with their truncheons looking forward to getting into the house and banging a few heads. So after you gentlemen have had your way with the occupants of this house, I'm sure that my men will not have too many problems. By the way, it would be good if there are a few gunshots fired through the windows because then we can legally respond to the situation and arrest everyone. Myself or John will find you and lead you all out of the house during all the pandemonium so you will have no problems leaving the premises and going about your lawful business. As soon as the uniformed policemen move in will you make sure that your weapons are not visible or you may be mistaken for gangsters.

Everyone nodded their agreement, and Lenny stepped forward.

"Inspector, my friend and I have an appointment at 10.30pm with a man called Nino to discuss possible employment as part of his goon squad, and I think we will be happy to obtain his confession. When we go through the front gate we will jam the lock, and five minutes later the rest of you should go in and blank as many of the remaining flood lights in the garden as possible. This should help your uniforms to enter the grounds and surround the house without being easily spotted. Then as soon as we blast a few shots through the windows your men can enter the house with due caution. We'll try and disarm all the gangsters but it's always possible we might miss one or two so please tell your men to be very careful."

Peter looked at the men in front of him and smiled.

"Thank you for your help gentlemen, I sincerely hope that none of you gets hurt in forthcoming action. Also I think I can safely say that if certain residents of Ekaterinburg, at sometime in the future, wish to return to the UK on holiday they will be welcome, and I hope they will contact me. I'm sure my wife will be very happy to lay on one of her extra special dinners for the occasion. But now I must go and brief the uniforms on what is expected of them tonight."

John and Peter waved goodbye to the five men and walked away.

"Well that was certainly a very welcome surprise," said Lenny, "but at least we now know there won't be anything nasty coming out of the woodwork to bite our arses when this is all finished."

"Yes, but I was looking forward to shooting the German bastard and hearing him scream," growled Mikhail.

"I know my old friend," said Dmitri as he slapped Mikhail on the back, "but at least this way we get to go home without any black marks against us, and we even have an invitation to return in the future."

Lenny shuffled his feet and looked at Danny.

"Well mate I think the time for talking is over and it's now time to get this show on the road. Are you ready?"

"I sure am, so lets get at it."

But before the two men could move away Dmitri asked them if they had their weapons secreted about them and was happy when they both nodded.

"Okay, off you go and take damned good care of yourselves. If it becomes necessary to shoot someone to save yourselves then do it, we can argue about it later with the two policemen."

The two men walked casually to the door at the side of the large double gates where Lenny pressed the button on the intercom box and introduced himself and Danny, and explained that they had a meeting with Mr. Nino to discuss a possible job offer. They were told to push the door open and walk along the path to the front door of the house where they should knock and wait. Lenny slowly pushed the door open giving Danny a chance to quickly wedge a piece of cardboard into the lock to stop it working. The two men walked casually along the path, out of sight of the house, looking for the sensors that switched the lights on. Every time they saw one within five yards either side of the path they placed a piece of duct tape over the sensor making sure that it wouldn't switch the light on if anyone walked in front of it.

The two men reached the front door of the house without incident and using a large brass knocker in the shape of a lions head they announced their arrival. Two or three minutes passed before the big heavy door swung open and a squat heavyset figure waved them in. The heavyset man then patted them down in an amateurish way to check if they were armed before indicating that they should follow him. He led them down a large hallway then up two flights of thickly carpeted stairs where he knocked on a door and showed them into a large elegant room then turned and left. At the end of the room sideways on to a large curtained window was a beautiful rosewood desk that Danny figured must have cost at least a thousand pounds. Sat behind the desk was a small man dressed in a light blue polo neck sweater and tan slacks with his hair combed over the bald area and slicked down. Lenny's first impression of the man's appearance was he looked like a rodent. His nose seemed quite long and his forehead and chin sloped backwards giving his face a sharp pointed look, but his black eyes were totally focused on the two men and they both noticed that Nino never blinked.

Danny stepped forward.

"Good evening Mr. Nino I'm Danny and this is my friend Lenny. We've been told that you may have a couple of vacancies on your team and we would like to apply for the jobs."

At this point Lenny heard a sound behind him and spun round in a defensive stance but relaxed when he realised it was Trevor the man who had arranged for the interview. Trevor laughed.

"What do you think Boss? I told you these two looked as if they could take good care of themselves as well as any problems that you might want sorted out."

A grimace that might have been a smile flitted across Nino's face.

"Yes I think these two will fit in very well. Arrange with the accountants to put them on our books at the normal rates plus expenses."

Then he turned back to the two men.

"Go with Trevor, he will give you your orders in the future, and explain to you the way we do things in this organisation."

Then he waved the three men away.

As soon as the three men were outside Nino's office with the door closed Lenny turned to Trevor.

"Thanks for the introduction Trev, and for putting in a good word for us, we really appreciate it and I'm fairly sure that we will be able to do you a good turn in the near future."

"No thanks needed guys, I'm just happy to have a couple of normal people on the team, the rest of them are psychos with a combined IQ of around ten, you know the sort, big muscles and nothing between the ears. There is only me who is ex military the others are all living in fantasy land. They think because they have a gun in their hands they are king of the world. Of course it doesn't help that they all like to snort cocaine or get loaded with heroin and I'm surprised that they haven't shot each other while they have been high. The only good thing about it is they do exactly as they are told which means I don't get involved in any of the sadistic stuff or the killings. Anyway, follow me and I'll show you around."

As they walked towards the stairs Danny asked where the rest of the men were, and Trevor laughed.

"I've ordered them to stay on the ground floor and make sure that none of the guests hurt the girls in anyway. The girls have to go back to work tomorrow and they wont be able to make money if they have black eyes or broken bones. At least if they're downstairs they wont be able to bother the boss, if they do it's me that gets the bollocking."

As they approached the top of the stairs Lenny caught Trevor by the elbow.

"Listen Trev I have something that I think I should tell you. Is there a quiet room around here where we can't be overheard?"

Trevor immediately turned with his hand on the butt of his pistol and looked at Danny and Lenny with suspicious eyes.

"What's all this about? If it's so important why didn't you say something in the bosses office?"

Lenny smiled his innocent smile and held his hands palm out up to his shoulders.

"I'm sorry mate I didn't mean to alarm you it's just that we heard a rumour that you have lost some men in a shooting and we wanted to talk to you about it. That's all."

Trevor immediately relaxed.

"Oh well that's okay then. There is another office just over there that is never used, come on we can chat in there."

Trevor led the way into the room unaware that behind him Danny and Lenny had drawn their concealed handguns and while Lenny closed the door Danny pressed the barrel of his pistol against Trevor's neck.

"Trevor," said Danny quietly, "please keep your hands well away from your weapons. You're too good to be mixed up with this bunch of sadistic bastards and it would grieve me to have to kill you, but I will if I have to. Now put your hands behind you."

Trevor did as he was told and Lenny fitted the handcuffs.

"What the bloody hell is going on lads?" Trevor asked as Lenny led him to a chair and told him to sit down. Lenny patted him on the shoulder. "We're sorry about this Trev, but I'm afraid Nino and The German have upset some very serious people, and we are going to make sure that they get lifted by the fuzz and put in gaol for the rest of their lives for all the murders they have committed. However Danny and I have a good gut feeling about you and feel it wouldn't be right if you were slung in the slammer just because you work for Nino. So we are going to give you a chance to get out of this unmarked. What do you say?"

Trevor's face softened and he grinned ruefully and shook his head.

"I knew there was something different about you two. But your not the fuzz are you?"

Danny and Lenny laughed.

"No we are definitely not the fuzz, if they knew anything about us they would be asking us a lot of embarrassing questions. So Trev this is the plan. We will leave you here and ask you to be very quiet whilst we go and encourage Nino to confess to the murder of four women whose mutilated bodies were discovered recently. The poor girls were hideously tortured until they died from loss of blood so we want to see him inside or dead. When we have the confessions from Nino and The German, the fuzz are going to raid this place and arrest everyone in the building, but we have a deal with them. We give them the confessions and they look the other way while we leave. So unless you have great loyalty to Nino or The German you can leave with us, a free man. However we would like you to tell the fuzz about what went on here, and anything that helps incriminate the two bosses will be very gratefully accepted. What do you think of the plan so far?"

"If it was anybody else I'd say you haven't got a hope in hell of getting away with it. But you two crafty bastards could just pull this off. So I'm with you and I'll be happy to chat with the fuzz about anything they want. Just leave me here in these cuffs in case something goes wrong, then at least I've got a good excuse for not being involved with the shoot out if it happens."

Danny chuckled and patted Trevor on the head. "Good thinking Batman, and I promise we wont forget about you and leave you here."

While Danny had been chatting with Trevor, Lenny had gone to the window to check on the progress of the police and their three friends.

"Everything seems to be going according to the plan," he said, "the fuzz appear to have the place surrounded, and most of the garden lights are off so I imagine that our friends are now in the building. It's time for us to go and get our confessions."

Closing the door on the handcuffed Trevor the two men had only taken a few steps along the landing towards Nino's office when one of the goons appeared at the top of the stairs. He stared at Danny and Lenny suspiciously.

"What are you two doing up here?" he demanded.

Lenny laughed in his most friendly manner.

"We've just been talking to Mr. Nino and he has offered us a job and we start work tonight with you lot. Have you seen Trevor around? We have to check with him and find out what he wants us to do."

The man relaxed and almost became friendly.

"Hi guys, I've not seen Trevor. I thought he might be up here using the small office again, so I'd better check it out while I'm here."

"Oh great," said Danny, "if you don't mind we'll string along with you because we don't know our way around this house yet."

The three men walked towards the room where Trevor was hidden. As the goon opened the door Danny cracked him over the head hard with the barrel of his pistol. The man collapsed but Lenny caught him under the shoulders before he could hit the floor and dragged him into the room. Trevor chuckled as Lennny came into the office dragging an unconscious body behind him while Danny checked to make sure no one had heard the slight disturbance.

"I hope you're not going to fill this little office up with knocked out and handcuffed bodies. Most of these guys are a bit shy about personal hygiene so the room will soon stink as though a wet mangy dog with the shits has been in here. But if that is your plan please let me sit near the partially open window otherwise I might end up puking all over the place."

Lenny grinned and sniffed theatrically.

"Phew I think your right it's started already so I'd better open the window now. How's the cuffs? They're not too tight are they? It could be a long night."

"Your a cheeky git," retorted Trevor, "but I like you. And yes the cuffs are fine thanks."

Danny snorted.

"Will you two stop flapping your gums like two old women, and you little man," he pointed at Lenny, "get your arse into gear we've got a lot to do. It's time we started collecting confessions."

"See what happens when people love you," said Lenny, "they get very possessive."

Then he quickly ducked to avoid a swipe from Danny's large hand.

"Come on then mate," said Lenny with a grin at his friend, "let's go and do the stuff that you really enjoy, like bashing people."

With Danny leading the way they walked along the landing towards the room that Nino used as his office. Knocking a respectful tap tap on the door they waited for thirty seconds for Nino to invite them in and then walked into the room. Nino looked up at them.

"What the hell do you two want this time?" He snarled slapping his hands on the desk top, "can't you see I'm bloody busy."

"I'm sorry to bother you Mr. Nino," said Lenny stepping up to the edge of Nino's desk, "but we have some important questions to ask you."

While he was speaking, Danny moved out of Nino's line of sight behind Lenny and drew his pistol. Then as Lenny finished speaking Danny walked around the desk and shoved the barrel of his pistol very hard into Nino's ear.

"I would like to cut your tongue out you dirty miserable little toe rag," Danny growled, "but if I do that you wont be able to answer our questions so instead I'm going to break all the bones in your left hand."

Nino's jaw dropped as he gaped at Danny. It was as if Danny had grown horns and a tail, but as Nino tried to get out of the chair the butt of Danny's pistol crashed down on Nino's hand. As he started to scream Lenny clamped his hand over Nino's mouth to stifle the scream.

"He sounds just like a little girl whose had her arse slapped," laughed Danny.

Lenny nodded his agreement and slapped Nino's face hard to help him focus. Nino whimpered like a child, an impression that was enhanced by the tears running down his face.

"What do you want from me?" He croaked, "I'll tell you anything you want to know as long as you don't hurt me any more."

Lenny set up the miniature tape recorder and nodded at Danny who gripped Nino's wrist and once again lifted his gun.

"Tell me what you and The German did to the four girls before you killed them, and do it now or I'll smash the rest of the bones in your hand."

"No," Nino screamed, "please don't hurt me any more, I'll tell you what happened. It was The German who tortured and killed the four girls, I was only there as an observer and couldn't do anything to stop him."

Once Nino started talking he told them that the special room was built under the factory he owned, the same factory where he and The German planned to keep all the Chinese girls they had bought. Then he gave them all the sadistic and depraved details of what he maintained The German had done to the girls before they died. Throughout the confession Nino constantly claiming that he had not been involved. It took around half an hour to get all the details on tape then Danny made Nino sign a document to say that he had given his confession freely and of his own free will. The handcuffs were put on the whimpering man and he was dragged off by the scruff of his neck to the small office where he dumped him on the floor.

Back in the main office Danny looked across at Lenny who was sat in the big leather chair behind the desk.

"Okay genius how do we get The German away from his goons and up here?"

"Oh that's the easy bit, we just phone him and ask him to come up, or maybe better still we ask Trevor to go down and tell The German that Nino wants to see him urgently in his office. What do you think of that?"

"Bloody hell mate, you come up with the craziest schemes sometimes, but I guess it's one way of finding out if Trevor is the decent fella we think he is. Okay I'll go and get him."

A few minutes later Trevor and Danny walked back into the office and Lenny explained what they wanted him to do.

"Okay," said Trevor, "give me five minutes and I'll get him here for you, and if he brings one of his bodyguards, I'll deal with him. Can I borrow a pair of your handcuffs?"

Danny and Lenny looked at each other grinning, then Danny asked him.

"Okay, but first before you go what do you know about Russia?"

"That's a strange question, but actually quite a bit," Trevor replied. "I was in signals when I was in the military and volunteered for an intensive course in the Russian language so that I could translate Russian newspapers and any Russian signals that we picked up. But I haven't spoken the language since I left the army. Why do you want to know?"

"Because we are looking for a pretty blonde Russian girl who was kidnapped by some Albanians and sold to The German who then sold her onto Nino. Her name is Anna. I don't suppose you know her do you?"

Trevor laughed out loud.

"I'll say I know her, she is the gorgeous blond. I'm supposed to be looking after her tonight to make sure she doesn't get a chance to escape and no one gives her a hard time."

Lenny delightedly slapped him on the back.

"That's bloody fantastic mate. Listen as soon as you get The German up here to us will you go back down and find Anna then bring her back up here as well. Then you can make sure she stays safe in comfort."

"That," said Trevor, "will be my pleasure. She is a lovely woman who I have a great respect for. But first where are the handcuffs?"

Danny handed a pair over.

"I'm glad we were right about you Trev it will certainly make this job a whole lot easier."

It was actually closer to seven or eight minutes after Trevor left the office that The German barged his way into Nino's office looking red faced and angry at being called away from one of the girls he had been pawing, but his face changed colour when he found himself looking down the barrel of the pistol in Danny's hand. Then he heard the door close and the bolts lock into place behind him. This was when he felt the cold hand of fear close around his intestines, but he masked it well and with a show of bravado he looked at Danny with disdain. But it didn't make any difference to Danny or to the outcome. Lenny threw him into the leather chair and held The German's left hand on top of the desk so Danny could smash the bones in the hand to a pulp. Then he threatened to drive a letter opener through the other hand and pin it to the desktop. It was enough to make The German beg for mercy. He gave them all the details of his business and intended future business with the Chinese, complete with names etc. Then they had to listen once again to all the sickeningly horrendous details of what The German said Nino had done to the four girls. When it was over and The German had signed the document to say that he had given the confession of his own free will, Danny handcuffed him and dragged him along to the small office while Lenny put the tapes and signed confession papers inside a padded bag. When Danny came back into the office Lenny dug him in the ribs and asked him if he was ready to start world war three. Danny nodded and fired three shots through the window on the opposite wall.

"That should put the cat amongst the pigeons," he said. "Do you think we should go and join in? Or maybe we should just sit here and wait for our pals to do all the hard work downstairs. What do you think?"

"Well," said Lenny, "we could sit and wait, but I don't see why we should let those three reprobates and all those uniforms have all the fun. So come on let's go and knock some heads together. Trev would you go down and get Anna and keep her safe up here in the big office and when we've sorted out the goons downstairs we'll come back here for you. Then we can all walk out of here together so that the fuzz think you're one of the good guys. Okay?"

"That's sounds like a bloody good plan to me Lenny, so lets get at it."

Chapter 25

Five minutes after Danny and Lenny had walked through the gate and into the grounds of Nino's house, Jimmy, Dmitri and Mikhail made themselves ready for the next stage of their plan. The wrought iron gate in the wall that Danny had jammed opened easily and the three men slipped through and spread out into the gardens to block off as many sensors as they could find until the garden remained in darkness. Then made their way round to the back of the house and found the rear entrance. It seemed like a substantial door, but Jimmy soon had the lock undone and the heavy door swung open silently. Moving like black wraiths the three men moved quickly into the house. With the back door once again closed and locked Dmitri found a light switch and bathed the room in a sharp fluorescent glare. They were in a large well appointed kitchen. A quick discussion brought agreement from the three men that they would stay in sight of each other until they knew where Danny and Lenny were. Jimmy agreed he would start finding the goons and bringing them to the kitchen on the pretext that there was a fire that needed dealing with. Dmitri slowly opened the door that led out of the kitchen to the rest of the house and glanced out. The hallway was well lit and they could hear music and the sound of many people talking, but the hallway itself was empty. Jimmy walked along the hallway and opened the first door he came to. The noise of a good party in full swing was very loud so he calmly walked in and looked around for the goons. After a quick glance around he realised the goons were easy to spot because they were the guys with the sullen faces and wearing jackets to cover the shoulder holsters and guns they carried. Three of the goons were standing together trying to look tough so Jimmy walked over to them and asked if they would give him a hand to put out a fire that had just started in the kitchen. They just nodded and started walking towards the kitchen. As they stepped into the kitchen Dmitri and Mikhail swiftly put them to sleep before taping their mouths shut and handcuffing one man's wrist to the next man's ankle and so on. Sometime later all the goons that Jimmy could find on the ground floor were out cold in the kitchen. In the hallway outside the kitchen Jimmy told the two Russians.

"I think the only people left down here are the party guests, so I guess we had better start moving up the stairs and leave this area clear for our policeman friends."

No sooner had he said this than they heard shots being fired through the windows upstairs. The three men looked at each other for a split second then raced for the stairs.

"I hope our two friendly policemen find us quickly," said Jimmy as they ran up the stairs, "because very soon this place will be full of uniformed police looking to beat the crap out of anyone who resists arrest."

Trevor meanwhile had found Anna and Angel standing in a corner trying to blend into the background and hoping that none of the drunken party goers would notice them. He walked over and stood close to them then after glancing round to make sure no one could hear him he said quietly.

"Come on with me please Anna, I have some friends of yours upstairs who have been looking for you and as soon as they have dealt with the goons we'll all get out of here."

Anna's mouth fell open and her face went pale with the shock until Angel shook her arm hard and told her to get her act together and not let anyone know that her friends had arrived to rescue her. Anna quickly recovered and gripped Angels hand. Turning to Trevor she whispered to him that she would not go anywhere unless Angel was allowed to come with her. This turn of events took Trevor by surprise but then he reasoned that if he wanted to get Anna out of the room quietly he would also have to take Angel as well.

"Okay," he told the two girls, "just keep your heads down and don't look too happy about this. Now come on and follow me."

The three of them left the lounge and casually climbed the stairs to the large office. Once inside the office with the door closed the two girls sat on the desk excitedly chattering and hugging each other in delight as the realisation that they had been rescued sank in. Trevor stood away from the door with his gun out to make sure that no one was going to come in and spoil the party. A few minutes later Dmitri, Mikhail and Jimmy burst through the door and spotted Anna. Dmitri swept her up in big hug and kissed her on both cheeks then he turned and saw Trevor. Immediately the atmosphere became electric as the three men stopped and turned towards him.

"Who the bloody hell are you," growled Jimmy, hand on gun.

But Anna cried out.

"Don't you dare hurt him he is my friend."

Then before anyone could say anything else Danny and Lenny walked into the room and immediately realised what had happened..

"It's okay fellas," said Lenny, "Trevor is a friend of ours. He is our inside man if you like, and has been a great help to our cause, in fact without him it would have taken us a lot longer to get the confessions and find the girls."

The atmosphere immediately turned friendly and Trevor put his gun away.

"Jesus I'm bloody glad you two arrived when you did, and thank you Anna I have a feeling you just saved my life."

Anna laughed delightedly and introduced Angel to everyone as her friend who was coming home with them to Russia before smiling at Trevor and saying.

"If you remember I did tell you that one day I would be able to repay your kindness?"

"Yes you did," said Trevor, "but I never thought it would be at such a defining moment."

Dmitri took the opportunity to introduce all the men to Anna and Angel. When Angel heard Mikhail's name she looked up at him with a shy smile.

"What a big good looking man you are Mikhail, I think any girl would feel very safe with you to look after her."

Mikhail's face broke into a big beaming smile and at the same time he blushed. He had never had a lovely woman speak to him in such a friendly way before and for once in his life he didn't know what to do or say. Then Dmitri, who had never seen his friend blush before, laughed and nudged his arm.

"I think this lady has taken a fancy to you, old friend, so you had better take good care of her and make sure she gets safely home with us. I have a spare passport that she can use and I'm sure Boris can soon arrange all the necessary paperwork for her."

Then he turned and smiled at Trevor.

"What about you Trevor? I would be very happy to arrange for you to travel to Russia where you can stay with us. It will keep you out of police hands until they forget about you, and I'm sure Mikhail could find a job for you in the organisation. At a rough guess I think Boris could get a visa and all the paperwork sorted out with our London Embassy within a few days so you should be able to travel in a week or two. What do you think?"

Trevor glanced at Anna who nodded and gave him an encouraging smile.

"Thanks Dmitri I think it would be lovely to spend sometime in Russia with all of you, so I happily accept your offer."

Jimmy, who had been waiting to break into the conversation called out.

"Okay everyone listen up. The boys in blue are going to be taking this place apart in a few minutes so we have got to get ourselves ready for them. If our two friendly policemen don't find us first we will have to smile nicely at the uniforms and hope our friends turn up quickly, but please do not say anything to anyone while the uniforms can hear us. By the way Lenny did you manage to get the confessions, and where are the two bastards who caused all this trouble?"

"Yes the confessions are on tape together with quite a lot of other information, but we had to break a few small bones to make them talk. Nino and The German are together with a few of their goons in a small office a few yards from here and they are all handcuffed together. Would you like to see them? I think we have a few minutes to spare before the uniforms arrive up here."

Both girls immediately jumped to their feet and made for the door saying, "we want to see them," so Lenny led the way. The two girls stormed into the small office and made their way to where Nino and The German were sitting on the floor and stood in front of them. Anna looked around the small office, her eyes searching for something, and then she spotted what she was looking for, a letter opener and a bottle of ink. She casually walked over to the desk and picked them up. The opener was in the shape of an old fashioned two handed sword about seven or eight inches long with a half an inch wide blade. She tested the point, it was quite sharp and then ran her finger along the blade. It wasn't really sharp but it would do for what she had in mind. Slowly she walked back to stand in front of The German with the letter opener held carefully in her hand so he could see it. His face went white as he realised she was going to do something very bad to him, and he started to try and wriggle backwards away from her. Anna knelt beside him and asked Angel to hold his head very steady. Then after telling him to keep very still she slowly and carefully used the letter opener to carve the words 'QUEER' across his forehead. When she was satisfied with her handiwork she opened the bottle of dark blue ink and dribbled it across the open wounds and proceeded to rub it deep into the cuts, making sure that when the cuts healed the word would still be clearly visible. Sitting back on her haunches she admired her work then looked at Angel and smiled.

"What do you think Angel, is it enough?"

"No I wish I had a knife so I could cut his testicles off. But when he is in prison I'm sure that he will get his fat arse gang-banged quite frequently."

Anna laughed but her laughter sounded a little hysterical then she slammed the letter opener straight down into the German's groin area. For a moment she looked down at her handiwork shaking her head. Because of the thick material and zip at the front of the trousers she hadn't done any damage to the man she hated. So she stabbed him again but this time she drove the blade in from the side so it avoided the zip and thick material. She felt the blade rip into the German's body as she forced it into him until it would go no further. Looking into his face she watched as his eyes rolled back in his head and felt his body go limp. Dmitri and the rest of the group made no attempt to intervene, they just let her take her revenge. Suddenly, before anyone could stop her Angel knelt down beside Nino and screamed at him, "this is for all the bad things you have done. You are slimy little rat faced bastard." Her extended fingers with their long sharp nails jabbed into Nino's eyes and deep into the eye sockets until she felt his eyeballs collapse. Nino couldn't scream properly because the gag prevented most of the sound, but there was no mistaking the trauma he was going through. His body twitched and jerked spasmodically before going rigid until he fell unconsciousness and his body went limp. After wiping her fingers on his shirt she stood up and allowed the anger and hatred to leave her face before turning to look at Mikhail who was shaking his head in admiration.

"Mr. Big Man I'm sorry you had to see that because I'm not really a callous person but after all the bad things this bastard has done to me and thousands of other women, and young men, he deserved it. Now he wont be able to take advantage of anyone ever again."

In response Mikhail walked over to her put his arm around her shoulder and smiled as he said.

"Don't be sorry Angel, I'm very impressed because you did it exactly right. I couldn't have done it better myself, and as you said, he deserved it. But you can be sure that I will never allow anyone else to hurt you in any way. However, if you are nasty to me I might just put you over my knee and smack your bottom."

Angel laughed as she looked up at him and reached out to take his hand.

"That sounds like it could be a lot of fun for both of us."

The sound of feet pounding up the stairs focused the attention of everyone. Jimmy opened the door and walked to the top of the stairs in time to see the two friendly policemen approaching.

"Gentlemen I never thought I'd be so glad to see a couple of policemen approaching me in a business like manner, but you are very welcome here."

"We're damned glad to see you as well," said Peter, "but the uniforms are a bit pissed off because there is no one around for them to beat up. Have you got the confessions for me?"

"Yes indeed," he said as he handed over the packet, "and I think they have confessed to everything they ever did wrong since they were at school," said Lenny with a laugh, "but they may need an ambulance because some of the girls managed to get at them."

"If they're not likely to die, they can wait for a while, or at least until we make sure we have all the bad guys rounded up. But enough of this pleasant stuff. I imagine that you would all like to get back to your hotel and get a good nights sleep before leaving on a flight back to Russia tomorrow. So my assistant John here will lead you out of the house and back to your cars just to make sure the uniforms don't get you mixed up with the bad guys."

Dmitri walked over to the policeman and held his hand out.

"My grateful thanks to you Peter, and to you John, for all your help and consideration, it has been a very interesting experience. But please remember that there will always be a welcome in my home in Ekaterinburg for both of you and your families. If you do decide to come and visit us, I'm sure that Anna's father Boris would be happy to arrange the visas for you."

Peter's face beamed.

"Thank you Dmitri, I think my wife and I will take you up on that offer maybe next summer. Now then all of you take good care of yourselves and please do not get into trouble with the law."

With thanks and good wishes ringing around John led them, without incident, back to their cars where he shook hands with them all before waving and walking quickly back into the house.

Back at the hotel Dmitri booked rooms for Trevor, Anna and Angel. Then he arranged with the receptionist for a lady to come in at 1000 the next morning and measure them so she could buy clothes for them to travel in. Then they went off to bed while the men got a bottle of whisky from the bar and sat around chatting and drinking for an hour while the adrenalin washed out of their system and they were able to relax properly. After Anna and Angel had gone to bed Dmitri asked Trevor for his passport then went to his room to phone Boris and tell him the good news and to ask him to arrange a visa and the paperwork for Trevor. Boris was so happy to hear his daughter was alive and in good health that he could hardly speak because he was both laughing and crying with happiness, but he assured Dmitri he would quickly arrange things for Trevor.

The next day while Anna and angel were organising their clothing, Jimmy, Lenny and Danny made their arrangements to travel back on the lunch time train to the normality of their lives in Stockport. As they were finishing off their packing Dmitri spoke to Danny and Lenny and told them that if they wanted to come to visit Russia they would be very welcome and all they had to do was to send their passport details over to him. Boris and he would make all the arrangements and the flights. Then they shook hands and wished each other well. Then Dmitri knocked on Jimmy's door and walked in. Before Jimmy could say anything Dmitri grabbed him in a bear hug and kissed him on both cheeks.

> "You are a good man Jimmy it has been a great pleasure spending time with you, and I can see why Katya really likes you. I don't think I mentioned to you before but I have a large printing plant in Ekaterinburg producing quality books and magazines. I also have a large empty factory that I would like to turn into a newspaper printing plant. However I know nothing about newspaper printing or

journalism or any of the other things that are needed to run a successful newspaper. I know you work for a newspaper so if you would consider coming over to stay with Katya and me for a few months it would give you a chance to look around and then we could discuss the newspaper business. What do you think about that for a plan?"

Jimmy laughed. "Dmitri I think you must have gone to a very good charm school because you've convinced me that I should come over and visit you very soon. But of course the most convincing thing about the plan, for me, is the chance to see Katya. However setting up a newspaper is very thought provoking because it gives the publisher a lot of political power if he wants it."

"Yes my friend, this I know," laughed Dmitri, "and I'm intrigued by the possibilities. But first would you email your passport details to Katya together with the dates you would like to come over and she will ask Boris to arrange all the details. But now it is time for us all to get some sleep so we can all be ready to travel tomorrow."

Five minutes after Anna and Angel and their six rescuers had left Nino's house Peter Jones had arranged for enough suitable transport to take forty guests, thirty five goons and their two bosses to the police station and put into the holding cells. The police had found thirty of the goons already handcuffed when they had stormed into the house. They were a bit put out by this because they were looking forward to a good punch up. But then ten large policemen found five goons in a second floor bedroom playing cards and drinking whisky. Much to the satisfaction of the policemen the goons put up a fight which allowed the police beat the crap out of them. These five would also be charged with attempted grievous bodily harm for attacking the policemen whilst trying to escape. The guests had all been interrogated and while they were waiting for the transport Peter and John listened to some of the taped confessions. But even though they were hardened to the bad things that men could do to each other the descriptions of the torture carried out on the four girls horrified them. After listening for a few minutes Peter switched off the tape player.

"I'm sorry John," he said, "I can't listen to any more of that. It's making me feel sick, and I could end up having nightmares."

"I know exactly how you feel boss. But at least we know that these two bastards will go down for life, and the goons will all get three to five years for carrying weapons and being involved in the gang's activities. And who knows what the so called guests will get. So all in all it's a bloody good result, thanks to our friends."

"That's true," agreed Peter, "but lets hope we never have to call upon their services again, I don't think we'd get away with it next time. Now lets get the rest of the women and the goons who are guarding the houses rounded up before some other smart-arse bastard comes along and takes over the business."

John grinned at his boss.

"Yep, but at least it gives us a job for life which is more than a lot of people can say."

The noise of the prisoners being moved out of the house and into the waiting transport interrupted their conversation, and they slowly made their way to the front door to wait for their driver. During their wait, both of the men were having similar thoughts, this was the perfect end to this whole dirty business.

.oOo.

Lightning Source UK Ltd.
Milton Keynes UK
UKOW02f1119150814

236986UK00004B/47/P